SORROW'S TURN

SORROW'S TURN

DANIELLE DEVOR

CITY OWL
PRESS

SORROW'S TURN
The Marker Chronicles: Book Three

CITY OWL PRESS
www.cityowlpress.com

Cover Design by MiblArt

Edited by Tina Moss

For information on subsidiary rights, please contact the publisher at info@cityowlpress.com.

Paperback Edition ISBN: 978-1-944728-11-3
Digital Edition ISBN: 978-1-386-16597-2

Printed in the United States of America

CITY OWL PRESS
Escape Your World • Get Lost in Ours

ALSO BY DANIELLE DEVOR

The Marker Chronicles

Sorrow's Point

Sorrow's Edge

Sorrow's Turn

Sorrow's Lie

Sorrow's Fall

Tail of the Devil

The Devil's Liege

Constructing Marcus

Dancing with a Dead Horse

Strange Darkness

Anthologies

The Dark Dozen

Love Potion #9

PRAISE FOR DANIELLE DEVOR

Named Examiner's Women in Horror:
93 Horror Authors You Need to Read Right Now

"Defrocked priest Jimmy Holiday's narrative voice is a strong blend of insightful, self-deprecating, and sincere." — *Publisher's Weekly*

"These very diverse characters take the reader by the hand and lead them through the intrigues of the plot with humor, anger, faith, love, and wonder… *Sorrow's Turn by* Danielle DeVor is well worth the read and will be thoroughly enjoyed by those who love this genre." — *Readers Favorite*

"Move over, Stephen King. Danielle DeVor is on her way!" — *Katie O'Sullivan, author of Descent*

"*The Marker Chronicles* was a thoroughly enjoyable read. Three books in one meant not having to scrabble around for the next book, and with a story as riveting as this one, that is a big plus. A real mixture of horror, fantasy, the paranormal, and a bit of romance and humor thrown in for good measure made this series well worth the read. Ms. DeVor has mastered this genre straightaway with a thrilling, edge-of-the-seat plot that is packed with surprising twists and turns – believe me, nothing is ever what it seems!" — *Readers Favorite*

"*Sorrow's Point* was probably one of the most terrifying books I've ever read. The book is a page-turner, but definitely not for the faint of heart. There were a few chilling scenes that will leave me with nightmares for weeks." — *Heather Wood, Book Chatter*

"DeVor weaves a clever plot and brings the reader a huge mixture of emotions such as fear, anxiety, wonderment and complete shock." — *Lilian Roberts, author of Arielle Immortal Awakening*

"*Sorrow's Point* is a great horror story read. For me, this harkens back to the books of my youth, where the mystery and the horror were the main characters." — *Rebecca Trogner, author of The Last Keeper's Daughter*

"*Sorrow's Point* by Danielle DeVor is a new take on *The Exorcist* and for me a much better read. The author has invoked pure spine-tingling flesh-crawling terror from every chilling page." — *Simon Okill, author of Murder Most Deadly*

"The thing I love most about Danielle DeVor's work is that she never takes the easy road. Her imagination seems boundless. Sure, there's horror, demons, ghosts, and a myriad of other spooky goings-on. But I've noticed that she likes to mess with her characters. A lot. And the reader is better for it. And speaking of roads, the entourage is now headed for Tombstone, Arizona, in *Sorrow's Edge*, where more ungodly things are brewing. Good luck, Jimmy!" — *Steven Ramirez, author of The Girl in the Mirror*

"Once again DeVor hits a home run with a novel that will capture your attention and steal your time. *Sorrow's Turn*, like the other two books in the series forces your attention away from the real world and directs it into DeVor's universe where exorcists fight the unseen world. DeVor's talent for storytelling comes alive on the printed page. Sorrow's Turn has a quick pace and DeVor's writing makes the novel an easy read that you can lose yourself in." — *Louann Carroll, author of Innocent Blood*

Jimmy Holiday, reluctant exorcist, is finally getting the help he needs from the higher-ups. The Order of Markers is sending him to the Vatican's exorcism school. Now, he'll receive the training he should have gotten at the beginning. One problem, someone wants to sabotage him.

When his time at the school is cut short, Jimmy receives an interesting new case. It is the assignment that no one wants—a corpse has come back to life. And it isn't a zombie.

For Tabitha Barber—
Thanks for letting me torture your alter ego.

ONE

EVERY LITTLE THING SHE DOES IS MAGIC

IF EVER I thought stuff couldn't get any weirder in my life, boy was I wrong. Getting out of Arizona was—well, interesting to say the least. No way could we take Lucy on a plane—not without documentation or permission from her parents, which wasn't going to happen. Poor kid had it rough learning how to walk on real feet again. Then there was the airplane itself. She'd been through enough having been possessed, separated from her body, and ultimately left with me to take care of her. Now this.

How did you call up someone to ask if you could take their daughter's spirit that had just developed its own body on an airplane while they still had her real body in Virginia? It was enough to make my brain bleed.

And of course, I didn't have their new phone number, but that was beside the point.

Like I said, things had gotten a whole heap weirder.

"Are you going to help me or not?" Tabby stood behind the car, fiddling with the suitcase.

I was in trouble again. It was starting to become a trend. One of these days she would clobber me. I could see it coming. I got out of the car, took the monstrous suitcase from her, and loaded it into the trunk.

"Car rental place said we can have the car, but there's a fee," I said, closing the back hatch.

Of course there would be. It wasn't like some big organization was going to be nice or anything. Hell, I had trouble with people in general. Why would a corporation be any different?

"How much?"

I shrugged. "I didn't ask."

Thwap. My head rocked forward.

"Did you hit me?" I stared at her. Maybe being psychic was another added bonus to this marker thing. Nah, if that were the case, I wouldn't have screwed up in Arizona.

Tabby stood with her hands on her hips. Her red hair framed her face like she was some sort of pissed-off goddess. Her eyes darkened, and I was reminded of that guy on TV who kept hitting his workers on the back of the head.

"Yes, I did," she said. "Just because you love that magic black card, it doesn't mean you don't have to worry about it."

I rubbed my head. Damn, she hit hard. "If this was my sort of normal I'd be worried. But how else are we getting this menagerie home?"

"Good point."

I was glad she saw it that way because there wasn't another option. It wasn't like I had some amazing powers like flight or anything.

"Was that the last of it?" I asked. The trunk was almost full. I could maybe fit a small stuffed animal in there, but that was questionable.

"Yep."

"Okay. Let's blow this popsicle stand." I jumped behind the driver's seat and glanced in the rearview mirror. Lucy was strapped in the car seat Tabby had bought at Wally World after the fleshing rod had done its business. Doc sat next to her, showing her card tricks. I was glad for Doc. Who knew having the sentient ghost of Doc Holliday hanging around would be so useful? His relation to me was beside the point. No way was I going to complain about his help with Lucy.

I glanced at Tabby. "Ready?"

"As I'll ever be."

It took roughly three days, fourteen hours, and seventeen minutes to get back home. I knew because I counted every single minute. I probably should have let Tabby drive, but I needed something to hold, and the steering wheel served as a great source to out my frustration. My brain wouldn't stop coming up with various worst-case scenarios.

Every so often, Tabby would ask if I wanted her to drive. I refused. It was a shitty enough trip as it was. No sense in making it worse for her. I might as well keep my asshole behavior in check.

Plus, I had to get used to a child's bladder. Lucy—now that she was whole—had normal bodily functions again. Yet another thing I hadn't counted on. The next time I saw the Devil I was going to hit him with that rod. Well, not really, but it was nice to dream about.

Still, it was nice to be home. The old house with its white siding and black shutters never looked so good. It might be old, but it was mine. As soon as I stepped foot from the car, the smell of the Virginia air hit me and I smiled.

"What?" Tabby peered at me while she brushed her long hair away from her face.

"Glad to be home."

She shook her head. "We'd better get on it."

I blinked. "Get on what?"

"Get the car unpacked?"

Lucy gaped at her with wide eyes. Doc was watching the sky.

"I don't want to start anything, but I'm too tired. Let's unpack tomorrow."

Tabby glared for a minute, and then slumped her shoulders. "Okay. We can wait until tomorrow."

I hugged her. Nothing in there that couldn't wait. At least as far as I was concerned.

"Shouldn't you get your holy iPad?" Tabby asked as she unbuckled Lucy from her car seat.

Even Lucy seemed tired. Her long blond hair appeared stringy and lifeless.

"Someone probably wants to talk to you," Lucy said.

I peered at her through the car window. The kid saw right through me. "Okay. Fine."

I closed the door of the car, handed Tabby the house keys, and pulled all the crap from the trunk. I guessed it wasn't in the cards to wait until tomorrow after all. Fine. But I wasn't unpacking all the shit right that instant either.

Tabby chuckled and opened the door to the house.

As soon as I got all the crap inside, I noticed Lucy perched in her usual spot in front of the TV. Doc hovered next to her. It was kind of nice having Lucy solid. She could turn on her own TV whenever she felt like it. Eventually, I was going to have to come up with something else to entertain her. And more importantly, some sort of schooling for her.

"If you want a chair, feel free to grab one," I said to Doc. Just because he was a ghost didn't mean he shouldn't make himself comfortable. I knew he was being polite since this was the first time he'd been in my home, but I didn't want him to feel like a guest.

Doc nodded in his way. "Mighty obliged."

"I'd like you to feel at home." Since he was going to be staying with us for the unforeseeable future, he should act like family.

Isaac let out a loud meow as I put his pet carrier down and freed him from it. He sauntered over to the couch, hopped up, and promptly went to sleep.

"Yes, Your Highness." I bowed in his direction. "I swear, in my next life, I want to be a cat."

Lucy laughed.

"Jesus, Jimmy. That's just what we need," Tabby said.

I snorted. Part of me thought it would have been great to have her wait on me hand and foot, but the lack of sex would suck. I didn't even want to think about her threatening to neuter me.

"You hungry? I'm going to throw something together," Tabby said from the kitchen.

"Good luck."

I couldn't lie and say I wasn't happy to be in my own bed. Lucy stayed downstairs like she had before. Oddly, even though she seemed to have normal metabolic processes, she still didn't appear to be able to sleep. How this worked? I didn't know. It made me uneasy. A kid needed to sleep, and if her body didn't change to adjust, I didn't even want to think about the health problems. I needed to figure out a way to spread the worry a bit; otherwise, I was going to get high blood pressure.

"What has you so," Tabby said as she turned to me, "odd?"

I rolled over in the bed. "I'm worried about Lucy. Nothing about this seems right."

She nodded. "Did you check your email?"

"No."

Tabby rolled her eyes at me. "Didn't Lucy say that you should?"

I could have kicked myself. If I didn't get my shit together, everything was going to end up completely craptastic. "I'll be back."

I headed downstairs. Lucy was watching some documentary on the effects of uric acid on the brains of chickens. I raised an eyebrow at Doc. He shrugged. At least she was getting an education about something.

"Everything okay down here?" I asked.

Lucy glanced up from the TV. "Uh-huh."

I snatched the iPad off the table where someone had put it. I hadn't even unpacked it before I went to bed. I jogged back upstairs. Might as well leave Lucy to her chickens.

"Everything okay?" Tabby asked once I got back into bed.

"So far." I fired up the tablet. Sure enough, there was an email waiting for me. I took a deep breath and tapped it.

Mr. Holiday,

It is my pleasure to inform you that you have been accepted into the next class of Exorcism at the Vatican— Exorcismo E Preghieri Di Liberazione. We will be sending you your requirements shortly.

Fr. Martin

"Fuck me." Granted I'd been whining about wanting help, but this wasn't exactly what I had expected. Looked like the church did want me in some capacity after all.

"What?" Tabby asked.

"They are sending me to school to become an exorcist."

Tabby guffawed. Literally, guffawed. In fact she laughed so hard she fell out of bed. No joke.

"What's so funny?" I asked. Granted, I already was an exorcist, but it wasn't like I knew what the hell I was doing.

"Do you even speak Italian?"

"Well, no." Damn. She was right. The school for exorcism was at the Vatican. I was so screwed.

"Oh, God. This is going to be interesting."

I glared at her. "Okay. Yeah. But this does nothing to help with Lucy, now does it?"

I didn't mean to be a bastard, but Lucy was a hell of a lot more important than making fun of me going to exorcism school. We needed information to help the kid. The sooner the better.

Tabby got quiet. "No, it doesn't. Question is—do you want to let them know about her?"

I thought about it for a minute. I'd been Lucy's protector for so long now it would feel wrong to hand her over to someone else. And not to be mean, but she was likely to end up as some Vatican experiment. I wouldn't put anything past any of them. The Order of Markers was connected to the Vatican—not run by them. I had to be damn careful. Periodically, I found myself looking in corners of the rooms for micro-cameras or something, but I never found any. Still, since the Order had broken into my house before (when they set up the holy iPad), I knew they were watching. The question always was...how much?

"No, we aren't telling them about her." It was better that way. Maybe. If they had footage of her entering the house, they would think Lucy was a relative.

"All right then, what are we going to do?" Tabby asked.

I sighed. Sometimes, I wished she wouldn't expect me to have all the answers. I needed more of a give-and-take. "Get some sleep."

The next morning I got up to nothing. There was no sound. No weird events. It almost had me worried. Kind of sad I was getting so used to the unusual that when something normal happened it felt suspect.

I got up out of bed, went downstairs and found Tabby, Doc, and Lucy sitting on the sofa. They all looked like their pet rocks had died.

"What's up?" I asked.

"Something's wrong," Lucy said. She glanced at the floor. The TV wasn't even on. Bad sign where Lucy was concerned.

Nothing like those two words to scare the shit out of me.

"Wrong how?" I asked. It could be anything: a new demon, bad luck about to befall me. I began to sweat.

"I don't feel very good," she said.

Her skin had a sort of waxy appearance to it. Okay. I could work with sick. Lots of over-the-counter remedies to try. I waved at Tabby.

"Is she running a fever?" I asked.

Tabby shook her head. Doc's lips pursed together. If she was normal-sick, Doc wouldn't be acting so strangely.

"Make it stop," Lucy said suddenly. She held her head with both hands.

I patted her arm. "If I can, honey, I will."

"Any ideas, Doc?" Tabby asked.

He huffed. "All I know is that this ain't natural. And when something ain't natural, lots of bad can happen."

I ground my teeth together. It wasn't like we could take Lucy to a doctor. It was not what any of us needed right now. Not to mention the kid was in pain and I didn't know how to fix it. "We'd better look into what a fleshing rod actually does."

"Guess so," Tabby replied.

TWO

TIME IS ON MY SIDE

NOW, the problem was—where the hell to get information about the damn thing. No way was I going to get another Ouija board after what happened the last time. No way in Hell. It wasn't like I could call up the Devil and ask him questions. I did not want to go down that road. Part of me did think it would be kind of cool if I could send him an email, but I didn't even want to think about the possibility of demonic computer viruses.

I also didn't want to have to explain to my neighbors the bands of birds acting weird when I destroyed it, either. No sense in imagining the same thing wouldn't happen here that happened in Arizona. There wasn't any reason at all that brand of weird wouldn't stir up again. Thank God I didn't live in a development. Somehow, I don't think me and an HOA would get along well.

I booted up my big computer, finished all the updates I missed, and started reading. Sadly, typing "fleshing rod" into a search engine only brought up a bunch of pictures of giant penises. That was something I could have gone without seeing. I was going to need to buy stock in brain bleach.

I was up a shit creek without a paddle. There were only so many options open for me now. And I was left with a pretty damn unsavory one—trying to find a person who was a true practitioner of the so-called Dark Arts. Where I would find that? Who knew.

"Here," I heard Tabby say.

I glanced up. She was holding a steaming mug toward me.

"I'm sunk," I said. She might as well know.

"Sunk how?"

"You don't even want to see what I've been looking at." In fact, if I had to look at it again I was going to need a stiff drink. Stiff. Heh.

She laughed. "Anything useful?"

"Not a thing. That's why I'm stuck." The information I needed was probably hidden in some ancient tome somewhere.

She sat down at the table beside me and threw her hair over her shoulder. "Want to talk about it?"

"Not yet." I didn't want to unload all of my fears onto her. It wasn't necessary. Especially since I didn't exactly know what I was talking about yet. My brain was latching onto random shit to worry about.

"Well, we still need to go to the store, or do you want me to do it?"

I shook my head. I wasn't accomplishing anything anyway. I might as well get off my ass and do something. "No, I'll go. Keep an eye on Lucy. Maybe I'll come up with an awesome idea."

"It would be different if she'd just gotten sick or something."

I nodded. If it wasn't for Doc's reaction, I would be thinking it was the flu or something. But his comments about the unnatural made me definitely feel it was not an illness. And, well, Lucy wasn't actually supposed to have a body to begin with. She already had one. "Tell me about it. Not with the way Doc is acting; that isn't it at all."

"I know."

I grabbed my car keys from the dining room table. "We need to return that rental car."

Tabby sighed. "Okay. I'll follow you—keep Lucy in the car

with me. We can get rid of that thing and then you can drop us back by the house."

"That works." Plus that way someone living had their eyes on Lucy. I wasn't too sure what else we could do. Maybe she'd get over whatever this was.

It didn't take long to drop off the car. Luckily, there wasn't any damage to it. They still stuck me with the drop off fee, but I'd been expecting that. Now we could go about our business and not have to deal with anything left over from Arizona. At least, anything physical anyway. The rest of it was a work in progress.

Lucy still looked horrible. Her skin appeared waxy, like it was fake, and she seemed to get paler by the minute. And she wasn't talking. At all. I think that bothered me most. Hell, it wasn't even demonic Lucy. This was something new. Usually, she would at least chuckle at stuff Tabby and I said, but there was nothing. The silence seemed so wrong.

I dropped the horde back at the house. I paused before turning off the car. Then, I glanced over at Tabby. "I'll be back as soon as I can."

"Okay. Be careful," Tabby replied.

I nodded. "I will."

I got out of the car, walked up to the house, opened the front door, and waited for Tabby to unbuckle Lucy from the car seat and carry her to the house. I opened the front door for her and waited until she and Lucy were safely inside. Then, I closed the door. As soon as I knew everything was okay, I left.

The irony did not escape me that even though I was at a complete and utter loss, I ended up doing something with food. I was starting to think that Tor's food obsession had somehow rubbed off on me. Lucy's mother had a real obsession with food. I'm sure a shrink would have a field day with that. Of course, the dude probably wouldn't believe in exorcism either and that's where the real trouble would begin.

I pulled into the parking lot of the mega-mart. As usual there was nowhere to park except Timbuktu. At least it wasn't hot like it had been in Arizona. Spring was still nippy here back East. I had to appreciate the little things. If I didn't, I would start to get cynical and that wasn't going to help a damn.

I wandered the aisles without paying too much attention. Stuff landed in the cart almost by osmosis. Needless to say, I was preoccupied by the Lucy problem. Spirits didn't get sick, did they? Not like that. I mean, Lucy had faded when she expended a lot of energy before, and it was the same way with Doc. But they never seemed to feel ill or in pain. That damn rod had caused us a nest of problems.

And since Lucy already had a body, a real one, my mind could only rest on one thing. Her spirit was rejecting this body. It was not conscious. If it were, Lucy would stop it because it was hurting her. This was completely out of her control.

I didn't even know what that meant for her. As far as I knew, her real form was still on a machine in Virginia. The Order had directed me to cease trying to contact them. But the Order wasn't aware of this latest development. At least, I didn't think they were. Something told me that Lucy would already be with them if that were the case. Their all-seeing eye had limitations.

All of this stuff with spirits and rules was making my head spin. I took my haul out to the car and headed back home. Maybe Tabby would have another idea, but I figured that my suspicion was right. Doc had alluded to this very idea. And if my hunch was correct there was no telling what it meant for Lucy.

When I got home, Lucy was laid out on the couch—breathing heavily. Tabby seemed scared to death with her eyes wide and her hair all messed up. Strands were falling out of her ponytail and whorled around her head like a red cloud.

"I take it she got worse?" I asked. At that moment, I felt

completely helpless. I wanted to jump in and save the day, but I knew nothing to fix this.

Tabby nodded. "Doc left to see if he could figure out something."

I dumped the bags onto the floor and pulled her into my arms. "This sucks."

"What if the Devil won?" she asked. Her head angled toward me, her eyes brimming with tears.

It wasn't supposed to happen like this. The Devil didn't win. That was the whole point of everything. I sighed. This was not something I wanted to mull over. "I don't think that's it. If he had, he'd come and take her and let old Asmodeus have his way. There's something else afoot here."

She sighed and leaned her head against my chest. "Could the higher power be calling her home?"

I shook my head. "Keep in mind it was that damn rod that gave her another body in the first place. I think she's rejecting it."

Tabby leaned back. "Like some organ transplant?"

"Something like that."

"What can we do?" Tabby stepped back from me and wiped her hand through her hair.

"Nothing. I don't think anyone has made anti-rejection medicine for this." I wished God would tell me what to do, but, as usual, I was left on my own. Shit.

"What about her real body?" Tabby asked.

I sighed. Sometimes, it was helpful to bounce ideas off her, but now it wasn't helping. Her fears put a voice to my own, and I just wanted to bury my head in the covers upstairs. "Alive as far as I know. I think someone would tell us, don't you?"

She nodded. "I hope they would. So what do we do?"

I began picking up bags off the floor. "Make her as comfortable as possible."

I wished I had some light bulb moment, but I had nothing.

This was one of those times when I wished that Tabby's witchery worked like it did on TV, but this was reality.

Tabby sighed. "I don't know if I can do this."

I didn't know if I could either, but I couldn't tell her that. I needed to buck up and get my shit together. It was time I stopped thinking about myself and my reaction to crap alone. "If you want to, go upstairs until it's over. I'll understand."

Tabby closed her eyes for a minute. "No, I can't do that to her. It wouldn't be right."

"I'll put this stuff away, then." I was at a loss as to what else I could do.

"All right."

I brought Tabby in a soda and sat down on the floor beside her. Every so often, she would stroke Lucy's head. Isaac perched on the back of the sofa, watching intently. The expression on his face was a mix of anger and sadness. I knew exactly how he felt.

Lucy's breathing was getting more and more labored, and her skin didn't look quite real anymore. It was starting to take on a plastic quality that reminded me of the creatures in that bad vampire movie based on Matheson's *I Am Legend*. I wondered how many times this kid was going to have to experience death. Once had been bad enough.

Suddenly, there was a bang. I jerked up. Doc was standing next to me. He watched Lucy and shook his head.

"Might be better if you didn't see this," he said.

I felt like my stomach had fallen down and bounced off my asshole. It wasn't fucking fair. I glanced up at him. "That bad?"

His eyes went dark and sad. He nodded.

That decided it. I turned my attention to Tabby and tapped her on the shoulder. I wanted to remember Lucy as herself, not as whatever she was going to become in the next few minutes. "Doc is going to care for her now. We need to go."

Tabby's eyes flashed. "Go where?"

For once, I wished she wouldn't question me. And if Doc felt we shouldn't witness it, it was pretty damn bad. I didn't want her to have this pain. She needed to learn to trust me once in a while. "Just leave the room. Doc said we'd better not see what's coming."

"How dare you," she said in a hushed voice. "I am not going to leave this little girl." Her eyes were on fire, and if her powers worked that way, I would be about to find myself melted into a pile of red goo. There was that red-headed temper I knew and loved. But this was not the time for it.

I sighed.

Doc cleared his throat. "Ma'am. Some stuff is better left unseen. I am the doctor, after all."

She peered at him for a minute, her bravado gone. Then, she stood up. "You really think this is for the best?"

Doc nodded. "Yup."

Tabby took a shaky breath and grabbed me by the hand. "Come on, Jimmy."

I hopped off the floor and guided her upstairs to our bedroom. At least we knew Lucy was in good hands. If there was anyone who would want to make her hurt less, it would be Doc. Heck, if he knew of some way to make this painless, he would do it. She was basically his grandchild, after all.

Once we got upstairs, I closed the door to the bedroom behind us and sat her down on the bed. She shook all over.

"None of this should be happening. If it wasn't for that stupid stick," she said. She moved her head.

I glanced over at where she was looking. The fleshing rod was still sticking out of her backpack. I had my doubts that the Devil meant for this to happen, but considering who he was, there was no way to know for sure. Still, though, if he meant for it to happen, that would have been against the agreement he had with the big guy upstairs. Or maybe not. Hell, this was confusing.

"Well," I said. "He did say to be careful with it." I wasn't trying to take up for him, but, obviously, putting it in a backpack was not careful enough.

Tabby glared at me. "I'd rather get rid of the fucking thing."

I sat on the bed beside her. I wasn't ready to let it go yet. There was some motive the Devil hadn't revealed as to why he'd given it to her. I wanted to find out the purpose. "I don't think that would be a good idea. It was given to you for a reason. Best not to mess with that."

"Well, we'd better figure out a fucking case for that thing. I don't want any more mistakes." She hunched over and hugged her knees to her chest.

"Me either." She was right. There needed to be something to protect people from the effects of it. Otherwise, we may have more mistakes than just what happened with Lucy. And if it kept happening, stuff could get a whole lot worse.

Suddenly, there was an odd howling sound from downstairs.

Tabby let go of her knees and jumped off the bed. I grabbed hold of her arm before she could get very far.

"If Doc wanted us to come down there, he would call for us," I said.

She glared at me and snatched her arm out of my hand. "I still don't have to like it."

"No, you don't."

It felt like hours. Tabby and I sat on the bed, gaping at the wall. TV would have reminded us too much of Lucy, and we weren't doing all that great a job of talking to each other, so staring at the wall it was. At least then we weren't fighting. I didn't bother looking at the clock. It would have made me more uneasy. Better

I didn't know how much time had passed. It would only make my frustration and fear worse.

Finally, after what seemed like a very long time, Doc popped in.

"You all can come downstairs now. But just to warn ya, there's some weird afoot." His face was almost unreadable. None of the earlier sadness remained. Just a matter-of-fact expression.

"Is Lucy okay?" Tabby asked.

He nodded. "Better. Going to take her a little bit to adapt." He glowered at the rod in the backpack. "Better get that thing out of reach."

"We're way ahead of you. But for now...." I hopped up, walked across the room, and grabbed the rod from the backpack. Why it had no effect on me, I didn't know. Maybe because my soul was connected to my body? Of course, it didn't do anything to Tabby either when she touched it. It had to be the spirit. It was called a fleshing rod, after all. Jesus, I needed a manual.

I shoved it on the shelf in the top of my closet. At least it was out of the way of prying eyes, and, hopefully, that would prevent Lucy from even thinking to look in the closet for it. Though I suspected that she probably would never touch the damn thing again. 'There. That should do for now."

"And later?" Doc asked.

I sighed. Sometimes, it seemed like nothing I ever did was good enough. "Tabby and I are working on that."

We headed downstairs. I couldn't help but shake the feeling that this wasn't so different from when it all began at Sorrow's Point. We were trying to get the demon out of her then and it hadn't all gone well. I felt the creepy-crawlies dancing up and down my spine. Something was off. I smelled something bad... like rotten meat.

I took the lead. No sense in making Tabby see things if they were truly awful. I tried not to psych myself out. I drew in a deep breath, stepped off the staircase, and peered into the living room. At first, nothing seemed amiss. I saw Lucy in spirit form standing very still. She was back in her little white dress. That was okay. More normal than not. But then my eyes drifted downward and I saw it. A pile of skin lay on the floor. She had been wearing a meat suit. Blood and mucus pooled around the little pile of skin. It was sad, disgusting, and...wrong. I forced myself not to gag.

"Is it bad?" Tabby asked.

I closed my eyes and didn't answer. This was going to take some doing. I didn't want to make it seem like a walk in the park, but I had to think of the kid's feelings too. This wasn't Lucy's fault. I needed to be strong for her. I stilled and then stepped forward. "It could be a lot worse."

I focused on Lucy. "Are you okay?"

Lucy shifted her head toward me very slowly. Her mouth quivered as if she were about to cry. I opened my arms. Her little spirit body rushed to me. I felt a bit of coldness. I reached up and tried to pat her head, but my hand passed right through her. This sucked. "I'm sorry, honey."

I could hear her sobs, but no wetness emerged. Nothing. Poor thing. It was one of those times when something so cruel happened that you never would have even imagined or thought about it, unless you'd seen it with your own eyes.

"You've still got us," Tabby said from in front of me. I hadn't even noticed that she'd come over. I smiled at her.

Lucy glared at her. "Don't let that happen to me again."

THREE

EVERY ROSE HAS ITS THORN

NEEDLESS TO SAY, our day was shot. Boxes littered the place. Tabby and I hadn't had the chance to unpack yet. I sent Tabby and Doc upstairs with Lucy to keep her occupied while I got rid of the mess. No sense in traumatizing the kid more than she already had been.

Isaac was trotting around the mess, being ever so careful not to step in any of the goo. That would have been yet one more disaster to add to the list. Yeah, gooey, bloody kitty pawprints all over the house. Yuck.

"Thanks for the help," I said to him.

He chirped back at me, seemed to glare in fact, which gave me the impression that he would roll his eyes at me if he could. Then, he turned his tail and walked into the kitchen. I could almost swear that animal was reincarnated from someone. Jesus.

"Thanks a lot," I said. I gaped at the mess. The goo had soaked into the carpet. I was so screwed. Where was the paranormal cleanup company when you needed them?

I went into the kitchen and got one of those big black lawn and leaf bags. I also grabbed an oven mitt. The less contact I had with it all, the better. I made a mental note to keep around some of those rubber gloves that people use to do dishes by hand. That is, if I could find any to fit my big mitts.

I headed to the living room with my goodies. Taking a shallow breath, I tried to ignore the smell, which was a combination of unwashed ass and rotting flesh.

"Okay. Let's do this." I tried to amp myself up. It wasn't working.

I shook the trash bag and set it outside the goo. After that, I gloved up my right hand with the oven mitt, grabbed what had once been Lucy's physical head, and adjusted the mouth of the bag. I held my breath and got the sack of skin into the bag as fast as I could. It was drippy, wet, and plain gross.

I stared at the floor. It was going to take a hell of a lot more than bleach to get rid of the mass of mucous and blood. It was going to have to be me to fix it. I needed a damn assistant.

"Shit." I went back for paper towels and started the disgusting task of soaking up all the fluid. It sort of helped, but it was like herding snot.

All in all, it took two rolls of paper towels to get it all up and I was still left with a giant ugly fucking stain. Nothing like old mustard-colored carpet with a giant reddish-brown stain in the middle. Sure, no one would notice that at all. I sighed. Hopefully, the carpet-cleaning crap would prevent it from stinking. I'd about had enough.

"Tabby!"

"What?" she yelled from upstairs.

"Can you come down here for a minute?"

Soon, I heard the pitter-patter of her feet on the stairs. Not that her feet were all that small, but she had a way of carrying herself that made her sound lighter than she was. Maybe it was all those years of ballet training.

"What do you need?" she asked as soon as she hopped off the stairs.

"How do I take care of this?" I pointed at the stain. It now seemed kind of brown. Technically, it still should have been red, but nothing about this was normal.

"Shit. I don't know. I'm not a magical cleaning fairy, you know."

I tapped my foot for a minute. "Got any of that anti-pee stuff for felines?"

She laughed. "You mean that pet smell stuff?"

"Yeah."

"Somewhere, but you need to do more than that." She leaned over, peered at the stain more closely, straightened up, and shook her head.

I sighed. "So any ideas?"

She tapped her fingers against her leg. "I'd get one of those industrial carpet cleaners you can rent from the store."

It was a damn good thing I had money in my account again. No way did I want to put this on the Order's credit card. It would cause too many questions.

"Okay," I said. "Don't let Lucy down here until I get this all cleaned up."

Tabby nodded. "Buy spot remover too. I have a feeling this is going to be a multi-step process."

"Great." I tied off the bag. No way would I let that sit in my garbage all week. I needed to find a dumpster. "Tabby, is it illegal to use someone's dumpster without asking?"

She shrugged. "I have no idea. Probably. I mean, the business has to pay for the trash removal, and since you're dumping your trash without paying them for it, it's almost like theft."

'That's what I figured. Shit. Looks like I'm going to have to be creative." Which is what I normally did, but that was beside the point.

She laughed. "Aren't you always?"

"Thanks a lot." She didn't have to agree with me.

She went back upstairs and I surveyed the damage. All I could do was hope that the garbage can outside Wally World was empty. That, and that the Order was out to lunch.

Driving in the car with that bag was worse than smelling a dead deer rotting alongside of a roadway in the heart of summer. Even though it was only forty degrees, I drove with the windows down. It was that disgusting. Part of me wished I still had the rental, but logically I knew this stench would cause a hell of a fee. The last thing I needed was to have to answer more questions for the Order.

I got a parking place as close to the front door as possible. Sadly, this meant roughly in the middle of the lot, but it wasn't like I had much choice. I carried that gnarly garbage bag as best as I could up to the trash bin. I did not want to get any of that crap on my hands. At least the bag wasn't leaking—yet.

The can was one of those that had the spring-loaded top. Lovely. I probably should have expected it. But it would have been nice for luck to me on my side for once. The dumpsters were nowhere in sight, probably to prevent exactly what I was doing.

I shoved the bag in, top first. Still, nasty liquid squelched out onto my hands through the small opening that was left after I tied off the bag. I gagged. But I got the damn thing in the garbage. I felt sorry for the guy who was going to have to take care of that later.

I looked around frantically for the disinfectant wipes they kept out front   and I was in luck; the container was full. I scrubbed up my hands and arms. I got a few odd looks, but I ignored them. No way was I going to have that crap on me any longer. Let them deal with the shit I'd been through the last few months. Finally, I tossed the wipes in the receptacle and headed into the store.

I almost felt like I was readying myself for the zombie apocalypse instead of going after cleaning supplies. This was what my life had become.

When I arrived back at the house and got the carpet cleaner hauled in, the odor assaulted my nose again. I had almost lost all trace of it from the car, thank God. But now, here it was. If all of this didn't work, I was going to be in a real mess. I guessed I'd have to completely re-carpet the living room and hope that took care of the smell. Now I wondered what serial killers did to keep from getting caught for so long.

Part of me expected for the cops to show up at the house at any minute for dumping body parts. It would be my luck, after all. I did have the argument that I didn't dump body parts, just a pile of skin, but somehow I didn't think that they would be very sympathetic.

The Order probably had it all on video somewhere. I'd considered it before, but now, it seemed a plausible idea. They'd been in my house, after all, to deliver the tablet. Yet I doubted my house was bugged—simply because I couldn't imagine them leaving Lucy alone, but there was part of me that wondered if they wanted to see how long it would take for me to hang myself. Then again, with the Devil popping in for chats, I seriously doubted they had the stuff inside the house. No way would they pay me if they knew that. They seemed just as uptight as the Vatican.

I should have buried everything in the back yard and hoped for the best. Nah. Then I'd end up with some old, gnarly, blood-dripping tree like in that version of *Sleepy Hollow* with Johnny Depp. Man, I was losing it.

I hooked up the carpet cleaner as fast as I could. It wasn't hard to get the solution going or anything. I wanted it all to be done and over with. Soon, the noise of the machine blotted out everything else. Maybe there was something to the "white noise" machines. When I had the time, I was going to have to look into one. My sanity could use a breather.

By the time I was done, most of the stain was gone. It was still dark in the middle, but now, at least, it didn't look like someone had been murdered on my carpet. I would have to see about the smell.

I switched off the machine. "I think everyone can come downstairs now."

I said it loud enough for them all to hear upstairs. It wasn't long before both Lucy and Doc popped right in front of me. Doc was his usual self. Lucy's eyes, however, brimmed with tears.

"I am so sorry," Lucy said.

Dammit. I needed her to calm down. It was an old carpet. Shit. I shook my head. "Don't worry about it, kiddo."

Tabby came downstairs. "What do we need to do now?"

I stared at her. "Wait until the carpet dries and see what else we need to do."

She nodded. "I guess we still have research to do."

Might as well. Standing here watching the carpet dry wasn't going to help us with anything. "I guess so."

We needed to know the implication of the rod. We sure now knew what it was capable of, but we needed to know a lot more. Thinking about it gave me chills, but it wasn't like that ever stopped me before.

"Who would know about stuff like this?" I asked. I couldn't go to the Order about it. And ordinary people wouldn't have a clue.

Doc cleared his throat. "You ain't gonna find anything 'cept probably at the Vatican."

I blinked. He'd been able to find out information before, so I wondered what made this so different.

"What do you mean?" Tabby asked.

"No low-rent Devil-worshipper is going to get one of those. It's the real deal." He scratched at his chin for a minute.

"He has a point," I said.

"What do we do?" Tabby asked.

I took a deep breath. Sometimes it would have been easier if she could have read my thoughts, but she wasn't that type of witch. "We do what we were going to do before—get a case for it. Then, maybe when I'm all in research mode, I can dig through the library over there and see what I can come up with."

"Wow. That sounds like an actual plan," Tabby said.

I laughed. "Smart-ass."

She didn't have to seem so damn smug about it.

"Can we talk about something else now?" Lucy asked. Her voice sounded nervous and I didn't like it. We needed to pay attention more to how all of this was affecting the kid.

I sucked at this whole parenting thing. I crouched down. "Whatever you want."

We ended up going out to a fast food restaurant. Even though she couldn't eat it anymore, Lucy wanted to watch us eat. It was such a small request that I didn't think much of it. Hell, I'd have probably bought her anything under the sun if I thought it would do any good.

As it was, there wasn't much at all I could do for the kid and it broke my heart. At least she had Doc, but she needed more and I didn't know how to get it for her.

"Get a chocolate milkshake," Lucy said to me after I shoved a French fry into my mouth.

If I was going to start eating for Lucy, too, I was going to have to do some road work or some type of exercise to offset the extra calories. I needed a stiff drink. "Okay."

I laughed. Who was I kidding? There was no way I had time for road work. Granted, an exorcism was a hell of an ordeal, but I was hoping I didn't have to perform those all that often.

She smiled slightly.

I got out of my seat and walked to the counter. There was a girl with black hair and a lot of piercings manning the register. She couldn't have been more than twenty.

"I'd like a chocolate shake," I said.

"How'd you end up with her?" the girl asked and motioned with her chin toward where we'd been sitting.

I glanced over. Tabby wasn't there. Maybe she'd gone to the bathroom. Lucy was staring out the window, watching kids play on the playground. I glanced back at the girl. Now I was really confused.

"The ghost?" she asked.

I almost choked. I'd never met anyone else who could see Lucy like that. Even Tabby had had to work at it. "It's a long story."

The girl nodded. "You've got her happy though. That's hard to do."

I leaned closer. "Just how many have you seen?"

"Enough. I've always been able to see them." She headed to the back and I heard the mixer whirring to make my shake. She came out again and handed it to me.

"Here," she said.

"How much do I owe you?" I asked.

"Nothing. It's on me."

I'll admit it; there was part of me that wondered if she'd put something bad in my drink, but I didn't get that type of vibe from her. I smiled. "Okay. Thanks."

Her eyes grew sad. "No, thank you."

I walked to our table in sort of a daze. I wasn't sure if she was a marker, or even if she knew what we were, but she sure as hell was what people tended to call "sensitive." Yet another thing I was going to have to look out for.

Tabby was standing there with her hands on her hips. She did not look happy. "Who was that?"

I stepped forward and leaned in close to her ear. "She could see Lucy."

Tabby blinked. "Well, at least Doc went off to do God knows what. I can't imagine what she would have thought of him."

I laughed this time. "I'm not sure. She gave me the impression that she sees a lot of ghosts."

Tabby shrugged, and then looked over at Lucy. After a minute she motioned toward Lucy with her chin. "I feel so bad for her. I think she got her hopes up."

I put my hand on Tabby's shoulder. "Yeah. I wish I could make everything right."

"Me too," she said.

By the time we got home, Doc had returned. He was sitting on the sofa, watching Isaac chase a catnip ball. Luckily, he didn't seem worse for wear or anything. Just pensive.

"Everything okay?" I asked him.

He cleared his throat. "Depends. I got some information for you."

That could be good, or it could be very bad. Either way, I was nervous as hell. "All right. Let me get everything settled and then we'll talk."

He nodded.

I deposited Lucy in front of the TV. Well, more like I switched the TV on for her and she sat down in front of it. Her having been flesh and its rejection seemed to have weakened Lucy a bit. In Arizona, she'd been able to control the TV a little herself. Now, not so much.

I paused inside the kitchen doorway and motioned to Doc. Tabby headed toward me and Doc followed. Soon, all three of us were sitting around the small table.

"Whatcha got?" I asked quietly. It wasn't like Lucy wasn't eventually going to find out, but it was better if she focused on the TV for now.

He kept his voice lowered. "That stick is pretty highly prized. Throughout history, they have been used to give flesh to demons. Let them invade our world."

The words "holy" and "shit" struck notes in my head.

"And Lucy?" Tabby asked.

Doc shrugged. "I'm going to guess it didn't stick because she isn't demonic. Though the Devil was right about one thing—they are useful."

"How?" I asked. In the wrong hands, every evil entity in the world could be made flesh. But that was of no help to me at all. And that seemed too easy somehow. Why would the Devil want Tabby to have that power?

"Since you're the owner of the rod, the demon you could give flesh to would be beholden to you. In other words, you would own him. He would be your servant. That's what the legends say, of course. Not sure how much stock you can put in it."

I leaned back in the chair. Now, that was interesting. He was wrong about one thing–the rod belonged to Tabby, so all the demons would be her servants, not mine. But it made me wonder if it would make it easier to dispatch them if they were controlled. I wasn't sure if I wanted to find out. Since the rod wasn't mine, none of these thoughts mattered that much. Big Red had made it for Tabby. Again, I had to wonder what his agenda was for giving her this power.

"Where did you get the information?" Tabby asked.

Doc smiled, then disappeared.

"Son of a bitch!" Tabby crossed her arms.

"Guess I don't have to research *that* at the Vatican."

Her eyes flashed for a second, and then she laughed. "Small favors, right?"

"Why do you think Big Red wanted you to have that rod?"

She shrugged. "Maybe he likes me."

I rolled my eyes. "Smart-ass."

She swatted me on the arm. "Since there is nothing going on for half a minute around here, help me finish unpacking."

I saluted her. "Yes, ma'am."

I slept like the dead. Dreams flitted in and out of my subconscious until finally, my inner self landed in a black expanse. My brain evidently wasn't big on sitting still. Kind of interesting. There was nothing as far as the eye could see but sheer darkness, and yet my feet felt solid on a floor. I was reminded of this book I'd read once about a haunted house that had more space inside than out. Suddenly, I heard a voice. I looked up and there he was, dressed in his red regalia. Maybe it was the Devil that didn't care about the setting.

"So life has been interesting has it, Mr. Holiday?" the Devil asked. His fangs glinted in an unseen light. Whole place was odd. Maybe I was actually in part of his domain and not in my head.

"You could call it interesting. Stressful, too," I said. This had "wanting something" written all over it. The question was, besides the obvious, what?

He smiled. "Things are in flux, changing. Whatever you do, keep my gift safe. It wouldn't do for it to fall into the wrong hands."

I gulped. With what Doc had told me, and with what I already suspected, I knew the rod was major bad news. "No, I guess it wouldn't."

"And your messenger should check his sources a little better."

I blinked. Did this mean that Doc was wrong? "What are you talking about?"

He laughed. "My gift isn't so easily explained."

He disappeared from in front of me, and very faintly, I heard his disembodied voice say, "Beware."

As soon as it faded to nothingness, my eyes popped open. I was alone in the bed and the sun was shining. I need sleeping pills.

"Holy shit."

Things connecting with me in my sleep made me uneasy. It was the second time it had happened. The first had been Lucy at

Sorrow's Point. But the Devil doing it was not cool. Maybe a sleeping pill wouldn't be a good idea. What if it trapped me wherever the dream was occurring?

I got up and headed downstairs. The house seemed almost too quiet. There, on the carpet, was the mess. The blood and glop was back, as well as the smell. I glanced around for Lucy's spirit. It was nowhere to be found. I got that odd feeling spread through the nerves in my body, like I'd bitten down on a piece of foil while having an aluminum filling.

Not cool.

I spun around and there was the meat suit, standing there looking at me with those empty eye sockets. The eye sockets dripped with blood. It reached toward me and I screamed. I closed my eyes and screamed some more. I felt its hands on me. Shaking me. I wanted the fucking thing off me. I lashed out, but it seemed like I wasn't hitting anything. Still I felt the touch of it.

"Please, stop." I kicked and screamed.

Something slapped me across the face.

"Goddamnit, Jimmy. Wake the fuck up!"

My eyes popped open again. Doc and Lucy stood in the doorway to the bedroom. Tabby was on her knees in the bed, waiting to give me another shot if I needed it. Fuck.

"Jesus Christ." I sat up. I was going to have to do something about these dreams if they continued. This was starting to verge on night terrors. Maybe stuff was affecting me after all, but I didn't show it all that well when I was awake.

"What the hell is wrong with you?" Tabby asked.

I scanned the room. Nothing was weird. Everything was fine. I shrugged. "Bad dream."

"He came to see you, didn't he?" Lucy asked.

I blinked. The way she could sometimes sense things caught me off guard. I glanced over at her and nodded.

"Who?" Tabby asked.

"Big Red," I said. "Told me not to let anyone else have the rod. Also, said something about not believing the stuff Doc found out about it." I scratched my arm and thought about it all some more. Maybe, Big Red wanted Tabby to have it because he planned to use her for something. The question was what.

Doc glared. Then huffed.

"I know. Believe me."

"Just remember you can't trust the Devil," he said.

"Well, it's not like you tell us where you go on these information expeditions Jimmy sends you out on," Tabby said.

Doc snorted. "I go to the places that make the most sense. Come on, Lucy. Let's go where we're wanted."

He winked at me, then led Lucy out of the room.

I chuckled. "Yeah. Though sometimes I wonder if what Doc goes after is as reliable as I've been thinking it is. I rely on him too much."

Tabby sighed. "It isn't like you have any other choice. Not really. Besides, has he led us wrong yet?"

I scratched my eyes with the back of my hand. She, as usual, was right. "No. It could be more like the Devil has more information—which is entirely possible."

"Exactly."

"And apparently, we are to keep the damn thing out of the wrong hands." I watched for her reaction. Her eyes went from wide to narrow.

"How are you supposed to know whose are the right hands?" Tabby asked.

That was a damn good question and one for which I had no answer.

FOUR
BLACK HOLE SUN

NONE of us got much sleep. Doc, Lucy, and Tabby all settled in with me in the bedroom. I couldn't help but be reminded of the library of Blackmoor, but this time, it was not the house that was haunted, it was me. I was going to have to figure out how to fix it, but for now, I had other problems.

About seven thirty, when the sun rose, we all headed downstairs. The light from the living room window was highlighting *the* part of the floor. The carpet was stained, but the chemicals had done their job pretty well. No smell. Thank God. At least my dream hadn't come to life.

"We can try the bleach today," I said. It couldn't hurt. Maybe it would do something.

"What?" Tabby asked from behind me.

"On the floor." I pointed.

"Oh. Yeah. Sure." She stepped around me and wandered into the kitchen. She had pulled her hair up in a loose bun today. I preferred it flowing down her back.

"She needs her coffee real bad this morning," Lucy said.

I looked at her and laughed, then sat on a chair at the dining room table. I patted the chair next to me. Lucy climbed up. The poor kid was still wearing the white nightgown I'd always seen her in. Well, prior to the fleshing. When that had happened, we had gotten her some clothes, but her spirit seemed stuck in the clothing she had been in when she ended up in this state. It was sad. I doubted she could change it. Doc hadn't.

"How are you doing, kiddo?" I asked her.

She shrugged. "At least it doesn't hurt anymore."

"That's good." I wanted to give her more, but there was nothing. Just about the only thing I could do was make her feel loved and I was trying to do that.

"Here," Tabby said, handing a steaming mug toward me.

What did I do to deserve her? Damn. I took it. The caffeine would do me some good.

"Sit down," I told her. "We've all had a rough night."

I didn't have to tell her twice. She plopped in the chair opposite me. She looked exactly like I felt—completely exhausted and tired of all the bullshit. Her hair was flying around her head after having escaped her bun.

"Damn, Jimmy," she said.

"What?" It wasn't that I didn't want to say the same thing, but her meaning behind it could be completely different, and I could come out of this looking like a total jackass again.

"If you have any more dreams like that, I swear."

I snorted. Well, sort of what I was thinking, but not exactly. I'd been right not to assume. "What are you going to do?"

"Probably beat you with my broom."

I laughed. "Just don't pee on my head and use it as a coconut."

"What?" Doc asked. His eyebrows were raised up so high on his head I thought they might pop off.

Tabby turned to him. "Old Voudou saying. To get evil spirits out of your home, you take a fine coconut, place it on the floor. Then, open the doorway to your house. You squat and pee all over the coconut. After that, in the most forceful voice you can muster, you scream, 'Get the fuck out of my house!' And you kick the coconut out into the street."

Doc scratched his hand through his hair. His hat he held in his other hand. Rarely did he even set it down. I wondered if it had some power of its own, but so far, I hadn't seen anything out of the ordinary pertaining to it. It was probably because, long ago, men wore hats all the time and you never wanted to lose yours since they cost money. It would be like me leaving behind something that made me, well, me. Maybe the hat was the 1800's version of the cell phone. He could never leave it alone or put it down.

Lucy laughed. I mean really laughed. If she had a body, her belly would hurt.

"That's one of the weirdest things I've ever heard and I've been around a while," Doc said.

Tabby chuckled. "I never tried it myself, but it is unique."

Isaac hopped up on the table and head-butted me. Hard.

"Ow." I glared at Tabby. "You feed him yet?"

Tabby laughed. "No, I forgot."

That figured. Ack. I glanced back at that cat. "Okay, Mr. Man. Come on."

After breakfast, I attacked the carpet again.

"I'm sorry," Lucy said.

I glanced up. Poor kid seemed like she was going to cry. It was a fucking carpet. If she didn't get over it soon, I was going to go crazy. Even if I had been poor, the worst that would happen would be that I would tear the damn thing up and live with the subfloor until I could afford to replace it. "Don't worry about it. It was an old carpet anyway. When stuff calms down, we'll get a new one."

"Okay," she said, still looking sad.

"Here, come help me," I said. She needed a distraction and fast. Good thing I was good at coming up with stupid shit.

"Do what?" she asked.

I motioned for her to follow me. I walked into the kitchen and dumped the bleach out of the squirt bottle into the sink. Then I rinsed it out really good. After that was done, I peered down at Lucy. "Want to have some fun?"

She nodded her head slowly. Her eyes were as wide as dinner plates.

This was going to be a blast.

I filled the bottle with water. Then I crouched down. "Okay. I'm going to hide right behind the edge of the doorway here." I pointed to the doorway of the kitchen. "Now, what I need you to do is to go get Tabby and tell her that you really need to show her something. Then lead her down here."

Lucy giggled and jumped up and down.

I loved hearing her laugh. "Okay. Ready?"

She nodded, almost quivering in anticipation. I couldn't stop myself from grinning. "Go!"

She disappeared in a pop. Was Tabby going to be pissed? Probably. But it was worth it to cheer up Lucy. Besides, it wasn't like this was going to hurt anyone. And the worst that could happen would be for Tabby to beat my ass. I could handle that. In fact, that might be kind of fun too—in a twisted kind of way.

Soon, I heard footsteps coming down the stairs. I waited until I saw her arm, and when I was about to strike, the doorbell rang. I shoved the bottle on the table and stepped out of the kitchen as Tabby opened the door. Plan foiled yet again.

"Yes?" she asked when she opened the door.

The postman handed her a thick envelope and walked away. Damn, I was starting to think there was something sinister about getting mail. Especially after getting the flask from Arizona that led me to Vespa and his fake possession.

I looked over her shoulder. "What's that?"

I watched her analyze the address.

"It's for you," she said, handing the envelope to me.

It was from the Vatican. If that wasn't enough to make my

asshole grow tight, I didn't think anything would. Images of being carted away in an old black sedan filled my head. It was all nonsense, but my brain went there.

I flipped the envelope around in my hands. I knew what it was. I let the breath I'd been holding out. "These are my acceptance papers."

I walked over to the dining room table and opened the envelope. There was a letter and some sort of guide. I chose to read the letter first.

Mr. Holiday,

We are pleased to invite you to our school of Exorcism. Your class will start on 1 May, 2015. An interpreter will be provided for you.

Enclosed you will find the booklet. Please pay careful attention to the rules.

Fr. Luca Rossi

"I start May first," I said. That gave me a little time to prepare. For that, I was thankful.

Lucy crawled up beside me in a chair. "Can I come?"

I glanced over at her and smiled. "I don't know how I'd leave you behind."

It was true. She was tied to me. It was one thing to leave her at the house while I went to the store. Another thing entirely for me to be a whole continent away.

"What was it you wanted to show me, Lucy?" Tabby asked.

"Never mind," she said in a sing-song voice.

Later that evening, after dinner, I sat at the dining room table looking over the class stuff. Most of it was the regular church info. The rules were something else. I was almost reminded of that movie with Brad Pitt and Ed Norton. "First rule: never talk about fight club."

I'll admit it, there was a big part of me that wanted to waltz in there like John Bender from *The Breakfast Club*, smoking a cigarette and wearing old ripped-up doo rags on my boots. But I couldn't. It would be an insult to God. Granted, the church did a lot of shit that wasn't cool, but it wouldn't do any good for me to do something that was an honest affront. I was better than that. Plus, there were plenty of places where I could get my Bender on. Heh.

I refocused on the class. One thing: I had to dig into my old work clothes. Because I was no longer a priest, I didn't have to wear the uniform, but I was expected to present myself in a certain way. I guessed khakis and a nice shirt were good enough for the Lord. The most important thing I knew was that I was going to have to keep my mouth shut. It wasn't going to be easy. A lot of the stuff I'd learned since starting all of this was probably not with the program. And having an exorcism ritual written by a witch was definitely not on the Vatican's list of crap to do. But maybe, if I was lucky, they could teach me something. If I could be a good boy, that was. That part was questionable.

I could almost head the bass line of "Inna Gadda Da Vida" in my head. My ability to be humble to an authority figure kind of went out the window when I was kicked out of the church. Being surrounded by muckety-mucks all day was a recipe for disaster. I needed to keep it all tamped down though. Especially since this trip wasn't cheap and the Order was trying to help me for once.

I wasn't even a church employee at all anymore, so their politics meant nothing to me. I simply needed to be respectful. Just as long as no one was an asshole, stuff would be fine. I hoped the Order knew what they were doing. Of course, with the way crap had been, so far they'd let me fly by the seat of my pants. That could be the biggest mistake of their lives.

"What are you thinking?" Tabby asked me.

"That this is going to be an epic fail." I knew I was eventually going to fuck this up. The only question was how bad. Maybe I could hope that my "issues" would not present themselves until I was back from Italy.

"How do you know that?" she asked.

I sighed. "Because I won't be able to stop myself from speaking. I don't have the patience anymore. I'm not sure I ever did."

She patted me on the arm. "Just keep in mind that it isn't these people who chose for you to be a marker."

She had a very good point. God had given me the ability to mark the souls of the possessed before they died during the course of an exorcism. The only one who had the ability to take any of that power away was God. Screw all the rest. If I could deal with demons, I could manage to keep my mouth shut long enough to make it through the class. The insides of my cheeks were going to be bloody, but so be it.

"So I've got to be on my best behavior," I said. "What are you going to do?"

Tabby leaned back in her chair. "How long is this class again?"

"Six weeks."

"If it wasn't for the fact that I know you very well, I'd go back to school. But something is going to happen."

I rolled my eyes. "Thanks for the vote of confidence. Anyway, why don't you do something with your Mom?"

She shrugged. "Maybe. More than likely, I'll just get this house in order."

"You could get the carpet replaced." It was an idea. And something that was easy. She could go pick it out and pay to have it installed.

She laughed. "I could."

"That settles it then." Suddenly, I got this feeling I couldn't shake. Before I knew it, my mouth was moving faster than my brain. "When I get done with all this shit, will you marry me?"

Tabby looked at me for a minute like I'd grown another head. Hell, I was shocked myself.

"You're serious?" she asked.

"As a heart attack." And I was. No other person on this Earth was going to be willing to put up with my weird bullshit.

"Okay," she said.

I almost swooned. Seriously.

Later that night, I sat up in bed, looking at the packet again. I figured I might as well memorize the damn thing. At least, then I'd know what rules I'd be breaking. I knew me too well. If I behaved like I normally did, I'd break every one of them. Most of the time without meaning to. I did have a tendency to bumble through life that way. Hell, if I was honest, I'd been bumbling through the exorcisms I had performed too.

"You know you've looked at that same page for ten minutes," Tabby said as she rubbed lotion on her elbows.

I shrugged. "I don't want to do this."

It was true. I had no real desire to set foot in the ruling paths of the church again. Going to Mass once in a while was fine. Dealing with bureaucracy was not. Hopefully, I could avoid most of it as much as possible.

She started laughing. "All you've been doing since you started this was bitch because you didn't know what you were doing. And now that they are actually going to train you, the only thing you can do is complain about that too? You amaze me."

I shrugged my shoulders.

.She had a point. Every exorcism I'd had to do, I'd performed with instinct, mistakes, and a lot of luck. I was a novice at best. It was time I manned up. I was getting what I had asked for. I needed to remember that, in the future, it would be best if I were careful in what I wished for.

"What, you aren't going to say anything?" she asked.

"Nope." Why would I? She'd nailed the whole thing.

"Why not?"

I leaned over and kissed her on the forehead. "Because you're right."

She sat back, eyes wide. "Are you sure you're okay?"

I laughed. "Yes."

"Did you ever get back in touch with that other priest who wanted to meet up with you?"

"Yeah, told him the meet-up would have to wait. Too busy."

She nodded

"Now, why don't we try to get some sleep?"

She glared at me sideways. "If you say so."

The next morning, I made myself get up at a decent hour. There was so much to do. I had to find out who was handling my reservation for the school. Honestly, I hoped they were going to do it because I didn't know a damn thing in Italian. If I had to make my own reservations, I'd probably end up in the slums or something.

It was 6:30 a.m. and Tabby was snoring softly next to me. Her long red hair was scattered all over her face in a tangled mess. Part of me wanted to move it, but I was afraid I would wake her up. Still, I couldn't imagine being comfortable with hair all over my face, but maybe that was me.

"Jimmy," I heard someone whisper.

I glanced up and Lucy was there in the doorway with her finger over her lips. I crept out of bed and followed her. She led me downstairs.

I couldn't imagine what this could be about, but since she didn't seem upset, I tried not to worry.

"Look," she said once my feet hit the living room floor. She was pointing at the spot where the stain had been, but it looked like it had never happened.

I closed my eyes and then peered again. The stain was still gone. No way in the world was this natural. "How did this happen?"

Lucy shrugged. "I don't know. I was watching TV and I heard this weird noise. When I went to look, it was gone."

It took me a minute to make sense of what she said. I looked down at the floor. Even the bleaching was gone. I'd been involved with this shit long enough to know that something like that was reason to worry. There was more to it than a noise. A lot more to it.

I glanced back at Lucy. "And all you heard was that sound?"

"Uh-huh."

There was something about what she was saying that left me feeling like she was holding back. Almost like a little kid lying about something they'd done that they knew I wouldn't be happy with. I wasn't about to accuse her of anything though without more proof. "Well, put a call out for Doc. I'm not liking this at all."

Lucy nodded. "It didn't feel bad, though."

Well, that was something at least. Every time she felt bad before, there was something for me to deal with. Her not feeling something bad…well…it could be that she was still weak, or that whatever took away the stain wasn't malevolent. Kind or not, I wanted to know what was helping me and what it wanted in return. If there was a spirit helping us, that was. Nothing in return would be way too damn easy. I was pretty sure she'd done something, but I still didn't want to create resentment.

With nothing else to do, I headed into the kitchen and began making breakfast. Tabby was going to have to check her wards. Somehow, whatever this was had gotten through, and I wanted to know why. If Lucy did have something to do with it, she was going to get a hell of a talking to.

I pulled out the eggs and began scrambling them in a pan with a little butter. It wasn't long before I heard footsteps. I smiled. Nothing like the smell of food to wake people out of a deep sleep.

"Making breakfast?" Tabby asked from behind me.

"Yep. See the living room?" I asked.

She froze. "What do you mean?"

She must have been tired. That, or she wasn't as obsessed with the stain as I was.

"Go look at the floor," I said. It was easier for her to see it than for me to describe it. Plus, I wanted to find out if her reaction was the same as mine.

She turned around and backed away. Soon, she ran back into the kitchen. "How?"

"That's the problem. I don't know. Lucy came to me this morning and told me about it." I proceeded to tell her exactly what Lucy had said about the strange sound. I still wasn't buying that there wasn't more to it, but Tabby's reaction confirmed my suspicion that this was very wrong.

"So," I said. "You'd better check your wards."

Tabby walked over to the back door, stood in front of it for a minute, and glanced at me. "They're fine. Remember, I set the wards to only let in things that meant us no harm."

I paused. Meaning harm and paying a price were two entirely different ideas. I was still uneasy. "Still doesn't explain what did it."

"No, but at least it did something helpful."

"I guess." Granted, it might not be a bad idea to think positively about all of this, but I'd had too much bad shit go down to not be suspicious.

She came up to me and hugged me. "You worry too much."

"No, I don't like things in my house I don't know about."

Tabby laughed. "You'd better get used to it. The other world knows who you are. It makes perfect sense for them to seek you out."

"So very comforting."

She punched me on the arm. "Finish breakfast. I'm going to get a shower."

I saluted her. "Yes, ma'am."

FIVE

MAN IN THE BOX

AS SOON AS I set all the breakfast food on the table, Lucy trotted up and crawled up in a chair. Isaac followed her and sat on the floor next to Lucy's chair. I don't know if Isaac knew she'd killed her own cat or not, but I still found myself watching Lucy now and then to make sure she wasn't going to do something like that again. I did give her the benefit of the doubt because she'd been possessed at the time, but once a demon puts its claws in you, nothing is certain.

"What are you guys doing today?" I asked Lucy.

"Isaac says you shouldn't be so nervous," she replied.

I raised an eyebrow, and then stared down at the cat. Isaac was licking his balls. I glanced back at Lucy. I seriously doubted he'd said that just then.

"Does Isaac know what fixed the carpet?" It was an odd hunch. I had no explanation for it. Of course, I had hunches about a lot of shit. It didn't mean any of them were right.

Lucy nodded.

"So?" I asked.

She fidgeted. "He said something about horses with gifts."

It was times like this, when she messed up a phrase, that I remembered she was only six. I had a feeling that she was grafting what she was telling me onto Isaac, when she really wanted to let me in on everything. "Tell him that isn't good enough. I need to know."

Lucy laughed. "Isaac isn't just a cat, you know."

I plopped in the chair opposite from her. This was different. "What do you mean?"

"What's going on?" Tabby asked from behind me.

I jumped. "Jesus Christ!"

Lucy snickered behind her hand.

"Damn, Jimmy. I didn't mean to scare you." Tabby parked herself in the chair to my left and began spooning eggs on a plate. "You didn't used to be this jumpy."

"I also didn't used to be an exorcist." I chuckled. "It's okay. You caught me off guard."

"So go on," Tabby said.

I shoveled some eggs onto my plate. "Lucy was explaining to me that apparently Isaac has something to do with the clean floor."

Tabby froze. "Like what?"

I looked at her. "She won't say."

Tabby pointed a fork at Lucy. "Okay. Time to spill it."

Lucy shook her head. "Uh-uh. He won't let me."

"Wait," I said. It felt like the temperature in the room had dropped several degrees. "Who won't let you?"

Her eyes got serious. "You know."

Then she hopped off the chair and ran upstairs.

Tabby looked at me. "What did that mean?"

"I honestly have no idea." And I didn't. There were probably about forty million possibilities. I was guessing, but as far as I knew, there was no way to document every single demon that existed throughout history. Was there?

As I got my shower, my thoughts drifted to Isaac. I'd always known he was Tabby's familiar, but I guessed that meant more than him being just a cat who wasn't afraid of magic. I still figured the crap she was telling me about the floor wasn't from the cat's mind. As far as I knew, Isaac didn't actually help Tabby's magic at all. She'd done plenty of it without him around. More so, I think he kept watch over things and, if he thought something should be done about it, he acted. I still remembered in Arizona when he tried to get me to go on the ghost tour. Thinking back on how things ended up, I probably should have listened.

Yet, someone telling Lucy she couldn't tell anyone about the whole thing—that sat wrong. If it was Isaac, I could handle it, but I had a sinking suspicion that Big Red had his hands in more than one cookie jar and I didn't like it. Granted, again, there were lots of possibilities, but with the weird visit-dream from Mr. Man, that put him in the running for the number one culprit. And I'd rather not tell Tabby about that yet. It was better for me to wait until I was sure. No sense in making problems where there weren't any. It wasn't like I was going to march down to Hell and demand an answer, so I was stuck.

Best to concentrate on the things I could fix, like figuring out how I was going to get to Italy. Too much dwelling on all of this crap was going to drive me bonkers.

After I got dressed, I went into the bedroom and grabbed the iPad. I went ahead and plugged it in so it would have a good charge; then I powered it up. I jotted off a message to the email address of the Order and asked about flights, etc. Hopefully, they would get back to me soon. If the shit that had happened in Arizona was any indication, they seemed to reply when they felt like it. I had a feeling that it might take a while for me to get an answer, which was why it was so important to contact them now. I didn't want to leave any of this until the last minute.

I shut down the tablet and left it on the bed to charge. Then I headed downstairs to try to make some sense of everything and make sure we had a decent day for a change.

We'd spent the day finishing up all the unpacking that needed to get done before I left for Italy. We were all tired, but it was a good tired. Nothing weird happened, and in my book, that was a plus. After dinner, and after all the trash was taken to the garage, Tabby and I sat on the sofa and watched TV with Lucy for a while. It was some survival show. I could deal with that compared to her love of horror films. Maybe she wanted mindless stuff too. "Why do you think she likes TV so much?" Tabby asked suddenly.

I shrugged. "You'd have to ask her."

"What?" Lucy asked as she turned around to face us.

"Why do you like TV so much?" Tabby asked her.

I almost expected some sort of bizarre story dealing with the space-time continuum and Isaac's love for tuna fish.

Lucy paused for a minute. Her eyebrows scrunched together. After a bit, they relaxed. "It lets me see things I never see when I'm here."

"And the scary movies?" I asked.

"Oh, those are fun because they are so fake."

I laughed. I should have smacked myself. She did have the mind of a six-year-old. I don't know what the hell I was expecting. "Guess you'd know."

Lucy's eyes darkened. "We all would."

Sadly, she was right.

Doc popped in. "Seems to me that life is easier without all those thingamagigs."

He was holding his hat in his hand and grinning.

"You're probably right," I said to him.

He sat effortlessly at the dining room table and set his hat on the table top.

Lucy walked over and hopped up on Doc's lap. "I feel so much safer when you're here."

In a way, it was kind of sweet, but it also made me feel like chopped liver. I had to wonder exactly how much she remembered about being possessed. If she remembered a bunch, God help me. I still had nightmares about Lucy propositioning me back at Sorrow's Point. I had to hope that, over time, the memories would fade. That was, if she was stuck like this for a while. Hopefully, she didn't remember that much, though my funky detector said otherwise.

Suddenly, my phone rang. The timing could not have been better. I picked it up. There was a string of numbers I did not recognize. I shrugged and answered it, getting ready to use my telemarketer spiel.

"Hello?" I asked.

"Mr. Holiday. This is Father John." His voice was deep, but not quite baritone.

I paused. I'd never heard of him before. He hadn't even been mentioned in any of the emails. "Okay."

"I am with the Order of Markers," he said.

"Oh, okay." Glad we cleared that up. I rolled my eyes. "Is this about my email?"

Ol' Johnny Boy coughed. "I'm afraid not. This is about something more... unsettling."

I paused. It did not sound good. I had a feeling I was in deep shit. "Okay."

"The girl who was part of your first experience, Lucy Andersen?" he asked.

My heart started hammering in my chest. "Yes?"

"We received word that she left this life very early this morning."

My eyes darted over to Lucy, sitting in front of the TV. She seemed fine. My stomach felt very heavy, like I'd swallowed something made of cast iron.

"Is there a way I can pay my respects?" I asked.

He cleared his throat. "We never provide that information. Just know that her family is upset, but doing well. They've had a long time to adjust."

I couldn't even imagine what all Will and Tor had been through. The time had been hard on them. There had been so many times I'd wished I could give them an update. Something. But I'd never been able to make contact. The Order, apparently, had made sure of that. "That's true," I said. "Thanks for calling."

"Yes, we thought you should know," he said, and then he hung up.

I set my phone on the dining room table and glanced at Tabby. I needed to talk about this. Part of me felt like my soul was breaking. "Will you come upstairs with me for a minute?"

Tabby gawked at me, puzzled.

Dammit. I didn't want to have to explain anything in front of Lucy. I pleaded with her using my eyes.

Then I glanced at Doc. "Don't let Lucy watch any scary movies."

Doc chuckled.

"I'm sure we can find something to do, can't we, Lucy?" Doc asked her.

She giggled.

I motioned for Tabby to follow me. Then, I led her upstairs into our bedroom, and once we both were inside, I closed the door.

"What is this about?" She stood there, hands on her hips.

I practically fell onto the bed and patted the mattress beside me. She joined me.

"Lucy's dead," I said.

"What?" Her eyes were wide and I watched as her body started to shake slightly.

"That was the Order. I guess her poor body finally gave out." I could feel the wetness creeping into my eyes.

She took a deep breath and stopped shaking. "Do you think she knows?"

I shrugged. "I think with what happened this morning she does know, but maybe God put it in such a way that it didn't upset her."

It was the best I had. Anything else was going to have to come from other sources. Just about the only thing I had in mind was a stiff drink.

"So the weird sound?" Tabby asked.

That was the question, wasn't it? Was it just a magically cleaning spirit, or was it something more? The fact that Lucy hadn't been bothered about it still left me feeling a bit odd. There were so many possibilities that I found my head swimming.

"I think it was what was left of her soul leaving her real body," I said finally. It was the only thing that kind of made sense. For the sound anyway, not the carpet cleaning.

SIX
HATE ME

OUR EVENING WAS PRETTY MUCH RUINED by that point. I couldn't make myself pretend everything was fine when it wasn't. I suppose part of me had figured that, as long as Lucy's real body was still alive, she'd be fine. But I'd been wrong. I felt like an epic failure. No kid should have to die that way. And fuck, Lucy had died twice.

At least Lucy was still here though. Her soul was safe. I'd done something right. Not that it had happened because of anything I'd done specifically. I had a feeling that the Good Guy was a lot more active than he let on. Didn't mean I wanted visits from him either. Still would be better than visits from Big Red.

Too bad that wasn't very comforting at the moment.

Tabby poked me with her fingernail. "You know you are going to have to talk about it eventually."

I sighed. "Yeah, but I want her to have at least one more normal night."

Tabby shook her head. "We already figured out that she knows. I don't think she's ever had one normal night around us."

On the normal part, she was probably right. But having to prod Lucy about her feelings? It could wait. Tabby's prodding nature was one thing that drove me crazy about her. She could never let stuff rest. I'd rather have all my teeth pulled from my mouth with a rusty set of pliers than talk about this, but I could tell I wasn't going to get an opinion.

I went downstairs and paused in the doorway. Doc and Lucy were watching a nature show on TV. It was interesting that he was such a good influence on her. Doc wasn't exactly known for being a nice guy. He'd been a gunman in the Old West, for Christ's sake.

I took a deep breath. "Lucy?"

She spun her head around to face me. "Yeah?"

"Come here a second." I motioned her over with my hands. This would all be so much easier if I could hug her. Dammit.

She got up from the floor and walked over to me. Doc watched her, glanced at me, and nodded.

When she was next to my leg, I began. "You know that phone call I had a while ago?"

She nodded her head.

I looked into those innocent blue eyes and silently cursed Tabby for making me do this. I was going to get my revenge... somehow. "You didn't lose your fake body."

She ogled at me for a minute, and then blinked. "I know."

I shook myself. I felt like someone had pulled the emergency brake on the roller coaster ride. "What?"

"My real body died when I got rid of the fake one. They just didn't realize it with all of the machines." She shrugged.

Tabby had put me through this for nothing. I was so confused. If she died when the meat suit did, then the weird noise and subsequent cleaning wasn't connected to it at all. It was like I'd thought before—something else I didn't want in my house. Great.

"What about the weird noise? Was it Isaac?" I asked.

She laughed. "No silly. Isaac can do a lot, but not that."

Like what? Dress in drag and do the hula? Well, I would have liked to see that, but oh well. I needed to focus. "Then who?"

Her face got very serious then. "I already told you, I can't tell you."

I decided to leave it alone for now. No sense in upsetting her for no apparent reason. Nothing bad had happened here. Not yet anyway. But I wasn't willing to press my luck either. "Okay, Lucy."

I could let it go for now. I was back to having that funky feeling. Even though whatever it was meant no harm, the Devil hadn't exactly meant for Lucy to have her accident either. I was so fucking confused. If all this shit weren't happening, I would spend some time in the dark cave of my bedroom eating chocolate and hiding from the world. But that wasn't an option.

Later that night, while I was lying in bed, and Tabby was in the bathroom getting ready for the night, Doc suddenly popped in with a serious expression on his face. Doc being serious was starting to feel like the times when Lucy had a bad feeling. I needed a drink.

I sat up in bed. "What's wrong?"

Doc came a bit closer. He floated. I didn't even think his "feet" were touching the ground. Usually, he gave the impression that he was walking. This time, however, he didn't bother. "I think Lucy made a deal."

"With who?" I asked.

Doc rested on the bed. "It might not be a deal per se, but I think she felt so bad about your carpet that she asked for help from someone you don't use for help."

I put my head in my hands. This was it. Dammit. I'd suspected it before, but the fact that Doc was here talking to me, well, that kind of pointed toward it. If it looked like a duck, walked like a duck, and quacked like a duck, it was probably a duck. "Please don't be telling me she made a deal with the Devil."

He nodded. "That's exactly what I think. Now, I don't think the death of her body had anything to do with it. But there's something there. I'm sure of it. What he wants, that's the question."

"Shit." I scratched my head. Then, glanced back at him. "Thanks for letting me know. Kind of explains the feeling I've had about all of it."

Doc nodded. "I'm going back to her now. I'm going to try to stick to her like glue for now on."

"I appreciate it." I was kind of sad that Lucy needed a full-time sitter and not for the usual kid stuff either. I couldn't help but imagine what her parents would think about all of this. Tor, Lucy's mom, would probably have a heart attack.

"Who are you talking to?" Tabby asked as she walked out of the bathroom. She had on this pair of pajamas that had ducks on them. I almost laughed.

I looked up. "Doc."

She sat on the bed and threw the covers over her feet. "What did he have to say?"

I sighed. "Oh, nothing. Just that Lucy made a deal with the Devil."

"What?" Tabby gaped at me. Then she opened her mouth as wide as a bass.

"For the fucking carpet." Who would have thought that a stupid old carpet would be this much trouble. Had I known that, I would have put down hardwood. Jesus Christ.

"Oh, no." Tabby slumped her shoulders. "What are we going to do?"

"I guess I have to figure out what the hell the terms of their agreement are. Doc said he isn't going to leave her alone again." I hoped she hadn't promised something stupid. If she had, my head was going to explode.

Tabby nodded. "That's probably a good thing."

"Yeah. So any ideas how to contact the Devil?" I was partly joking, but not really. I needed to get to the bottom of this and fast.

Tabby laughed nervously. "Not anything without risk."

"Shit." Nothing with the supernatural was without risk. I needed to get drunk. It wouldn't solve anything, but it would be a hell of a lot more fun.

"Yeah." Tabby leaned into me and gave me a hug.

I needed that.

It probably wasn't hard to figure out that I had a hell of a time getting to sleep. The only thing I could be thankful for was that what dreams I had were normal stress dreams and nothing supernatural. It was a nice change of pace, and I'd had enough stress for one day. I guessed the beasties felt I had too. Nah. They weren't paying attention. For all I knew, they were hanging out in a bar in Hell. Heh.

I spent most of the night tossing and turning. Just trying to find a comfortable spot. But as soon as I moved, my brain started rolling again. I eventually fell asleep because by the time I woke up, Tabby was gone from the bed.

I got up and shuffled downstairs. I found Tabby in the dining room with Lucy beside her looking at Tabby's laptop. Not exactly what I expected to see, but I could take it. It was something normal for once.

"What are you guys doing?" I asked.

"I thought Lucy might like her own room," Tabby said.

Lucy grinned.

I sat in the chair opposite from Tabby. She had a point. Now that Lucy was going to be living with us...well...for a while, she might as well settle in. If I was honest with myself, I should have done it sooner. A little girl has toys and stuff. I could have made her feel at home. I was an idiot.

"You're going to paint?" I asked.

Lucy nodded. "I get to pick the color."

I grinned. It was so awesome to see her happy about something. Granted, there were still issues, but it was nice to see her smiling.

"Besides, we need a good project while you're gone," Tabby said.

I didn't even bother to ask where the money was going to come from. The paycheck I was getting from the Order was more than I'd ever had in my entire life. I knew I needed to start saving away retirement funds and crap, but I hadn't exactly had time to breathe either. Yet another thing that needed to be put on the list of crap I had to do. Maybe the Order would have someone I could go to about setting up an IRA or something.

"Do you think we should make Doc a room too?" I asked. I mean, shit. If Lucy was going to have one, it was only right. I wasn't about to start playing the spirit favorites game.

"I don't need nothing like that," Doc said suddenly from behind me. "I got a whole house to roam around in."

Lucy laughed.

Part of me felt for Doc. At least I didn't have to worry about playing favorites now. He seemed happy enough. Of course, before we'd gotten in contact with him, he'd just been hanging around Tombstone watching Vespa. At least now we gave him something to do. Our lives were anything but boring.

I thought that, if Lucy weren't a kid, this would all be a lot easier. But in a weird sort of way, she was my kid now. That changed stuff a little. She was going to have whatever she wanted—within reason, of course.

"I'm going to make breakfast." I stood up. They were too busy staring at the computer. I shook my head and headed into the kitchen. Let them do fun stuff. It didn't bother me at all.

As soon as I pulled the eggs out of the refrigerator, I had a weird feeling again. The leaves of the trees outside the window were frozen in place. Fuck. He was here. I set the eggs on the kitchen table and waited. Soon he walked into the kitchen.

Today, the Devil was back to wearing his black suit and a blood-red tie. Nice way to seem non-threatening—not. I wanted to kick him right square in the ass for making a pact with Lucy. I kind of wondered if that was against the rules somehow. Then again, it would help if I knew what all the rules were in the first place, but the higher powers hadn't provided me with those either.

"What do you want?" I needed to find out what the hell he had planned.

He paused in front of me, pulled out a chair at the table, and sat. "To talk."

Now, I was really uneasy. There was never "just talk" in a situation like this. Everything had meaning with him and I wasn't stupid enough to fall for it.

I pulled out the other chair and sat too. No telling how long this was going to take. "What do you want to talk about?"

He looked up at me. His eyes flashed red for a minute, then settled on dark brown. "I have a warning for you."

I raised an eyebrow. This was different. I'd expected it to have something to do with Lucy. Evidently, I was wrong. "Okay."

"Things are coming that will not be easy. Things that you will not like." His voice was steady, not too deep, and definitely not high-pitched. And yet, it had this creepiness to it. Not what you'd expect, but not nice either.

Again, the demons were under his control, so if they were the threat, then he was behind it. I wasn't that easily deceived.

"Again, I have to ask, what is it you want?" I wasn't about to assume a damn thing.

He laughed. "You can't blame me for trying."

I nodded my head. At least I'd gotten something honest out of him. "True."

Isaac popped his head in the doorway. One look at Big Red and his eyes narrowed as he hissed, and then he darted away. How in the hell he wasn't stuck in the Devil's thrall, I had no idea. Maybe Lucy was right. I didn't understand all of the things that cat could do. And maybe Tabby didn't even know what her familiar was capable of. Not that it really mattered, but Isaac was definitely more than a pet.

"I've always liked animals," the Devil said.

I laughed. "They sure like you."

He smiled, coldly. "They simply do not know me better. Not yet."

I felt a chill travel up my spine. Yeah, best not to forget who I was talking to. "So what did you do to Lucy?"

His smile waned. "Nothing. It was not my intention that the fleshing rod be used on her."

That made me pause. I'd expected something much more sinister. More stuff was afoot than I realized. "What is your intention for it?"

He adjusted himself in the chair. "As I told you, it is for your safekeeping. Or rather, your safekeeping as well as use by your witch. Little Lucy was an accident, so I made it up to her."

"For what price?" This was it. I was going to get the rub.

"None. It was I who owed her." His odd morality set me on edge. It was almost as if he was more predator than anything else. Maybe that was why he was so hard to understand.

"You aren't any closer to collecting her soul?" I could almost kick myself for asking such a thing.

He laughed. "Oh, I'm not worried about that. I'll collect hers when I collect yours."

My asshole snapped shut. "What?"

He disappeared in a loud whoosh.

That figured. My life had gotten more fucked up than I thought was possible. And leave it to me to ask the questions that could very well make it all worse.

"I thought you were going to make breakfast?" Tabby asked from the doorway. I was still sitting there, stunned.

"Something came up," I said. Granted, that was an understatement, but whatever. I was tired of having to explain.

"Obviously." Her hands were on her hips and she was giving me that look.

I peered up at her. "He was here again."

"Who?"

Did I have to whack her over the head with a stick? Who else came to visit and left me all discombobulated? Jesus Christ.

"Who do you think?" I asked.

She glared at me. "There is no sense in being like that."

Great. I did not want to start an argument on top of everything else. This was getting worse and worse. I got up from the table and pulled her into my arms. "You're right. Forgive me?"

"Maybe."

I nuzzled her for a minute. I was lucky she let me.

"What did he have to say?" she asked.

I let go of her and swallowed. "He fixed the carpet because he 'owed' Lucy."

"What?" Her eyes seemed like they were going to pop out of her head.

"Yeah. Because he hadn't meant for her to use the rod," I said. That part still felt wrong. Like usual, there was more to it than that.

Tabby scratched at her head. "That makes some sense, I guess."

"I asked him if it put him further to claiming Lucy's soul, and you know what he said?"

Tabby shook her head.

"He said he wasn't worried about it because he'd be claiming her soul when he claimed mine." That still had me freaked out and it probably always would. If I kept my cool and played by the rules I knew were right, I should be okay. That was, if my brain wasn't trying to trick me or anything.

Tabby glared at me. "What have you been doing?"

"That's just it. I haven't done anything." Well, except do exorcisms and flounder around in my usual fashion. Nothing damnable there. I was actually a pretty decent guy.

She tapped her fingers against her hips. "He could be trying to get your goat, you know?"

"It's possible. Before I even asked about Lucy, he had an answer waiting for me." It was almost as if he could read my mind, but I didn't even want to think about that too much. It wasn't like I had special powers or anything to stop him if he did.

"About what?" Tabby asked.

"Just that things were changing." I suppose I should have been grateful that he warned me, but the fact that he was behind the changes kind of negated the kindness of the whole thing. I was probably overthinking everything.

She shrugged. "Guess we'll find out."

"Guess so."

A few hours later, Tabby, Doc, Lucy, and I were in the car. The house had started to feel too closed in, so we figured we would get out for a while. It would probably do us all some good.

"Where are we going?" Lucy asked.

"To Tamarack," I said. "It's an artist colony with shops and stuff. I thought we could look for some stuff for your room." I glanced at her in the rearview mirror. She was grinning. Score. I needed to do crap like this more often.

I drummed my fingers against the steering wheel. "Well, they have all those quilts, right?"

Tabby leaned across the car and hugged me. "I love you."

I chuckled. "For what?"

She shook her head and settled back into her seat. This had the makings of being a good day after all.

"You folks done with all the lovey-dovey stuff?" Doc asked.

I laughed.

Lucy giggled. "Yeah. No kissing."

I smiled. Part of me wondered if this was how she was with Will and Tor before Blackmoor. It didn't seem fair somehow. They were left with a broken heart and I ended up with their daughter. Not fair at all. Still, I was viewing it as the gift it was. Unless something changed drastically, I would not be having kids of my own. Maybe Lucy was my chance.

SEVEN
BE LIKE THAT

QUILT PROCURED, we ended up going to a Waffle House to grab a late lunch. Tabby had a hankering for pancakes. I didn't care. Food was just food at this point. It was all tasting the same to me. I needed to start getting off my ass and making something.

It pained me to see Lucy sitting in the car with Doc, but it was the most humane thing to do. I mean, how kind would it be if Tabby and I ate in front of her like that? Especially something sweet? I supposed that she'd eventually adapt again, but for now, since it had been so short a time since she'd eaten normally, I wasn't going to put her through it. At least Doc was in the same state, so she had someone to complain to who could understand.

"What are you getting?" Tabby asked.

We were sitting at a booth near one of the windows. We could see my car from there. Doc was talking to Lucy about something. Neither one of them was smiling. Not good.

"I don't know." I picked up my menu and glanced at it. I didn't feel like eating. I wanted to go home and hide in my closet for a while. It wouldn't solve anything, but maybe it would make me feel better. Sort of, anyway. That was, until the closet monster came out of his hiding place. Now I was being stupid.

The waitress came over and took our orders. Tabby got her pancakes. I ordered a breakfast sandwich.

"You need to snap out of this," Tabby said.

I looked up. "How am I supposed to do that?"

She rolled her eyes. "You could at least fake it."

"Like Lucy wouldn't see through that in two seconds." It was true. That kid was more astute than most adults.

She crossed her arms. "Don't you think you'd be better off killing the pity party? It isn't like you don't have a lot to do."

I sighed. "I know. I have to prepare for Italy."

Since Lucy was going with me, she would be taken out of the house and the stuff that seemed to be happening there would be over soon enough.

"Do you even know where your passport is?" she asked.

I laughed. "I'm not that stupid. It's in my desk drawer. I renewed it a couple of years ago."

"Okay. Okay." She waved her hands as if to admit defeat. "You just seem to have your head up your ass."

I raised an eyebrow. Maybe she was lashing out because of what had happened to Lucy, but I didn't want to start an argument in the middle of the restaurant. Best to do it at home where no one was watching. My eyes darted back to Lucy and Doc in the car. Yeah. Right.

"Fine," I said. "So it isn't okay for me to grieve for Lucy?"

She gaped out the window. "That wasn't what I meant."

The waitress arrived with our food. Nothing like timing. Damn, I needed some hobbies. Maybe then I would have something else to talk about.

"Anything else?" she asked. She was dressed in a brown uniform and had this silly hat on her head. I felt sorry for her. These companies needed to think about the shit they were making their employees wear. Jesus.

"No, this is great," I said. No sense in dumping all of my crap on her. She didn't do it. I wanted to give Tabby a piece of my mind, but my desire to not make a scene outweighed that urge for the moment.

The waitress nodded and left.

Tabby dug into her food without saying anything. I didn't bother to try to insert conversation. Things had gone badly as it was. No sense in making it worse. Maybe by the time we got back home, the stress would have calmed down and the fight wouldn't happen. I had to hope for something. I needed a vacation from my problems.

I picked at my sandwich. Part of me was daring her to say something, but she didn't. Frankly, I knew Tabby was more adult than me, even though I was almost ten years older than her. Still though, I was used to fighting for what I wanted, and believed, so it was hard to stop—even when it was over something fucking stupid.

Needless to say, it wasn't long until we were climbing back into the car. Amazing how lack of conversation can make a meal pass quickly.

"Ready to go home?" I asked Lucy and Doc.

"Yeah," Lucy said.

I nodded, put the car into reverse, and backed from the parking lot.

Tabby kept quiet. This was turning out to be a fun day. I should have known not to be optimistic. Maybe one day I'd know better.

When we got home, Tabby went upstairs. Fine. She could be that way. I did have better crap to do than spend the day being all pissed off. Frankly, now she was the one being childish, though I wasn't stupid enough to tell her that.

I settled on the couch and watched TV with Lucy and Doc for

a while. Nothing like mind-numbing entertainment to help me block out everything else. Maybe that's why Lucy liked watching TV so much. It was something to think about.

About an hour later, Tabby came downstairs. Her hair was wet. She sat on the couch beside me, grabbed my arm, and wrapped it around her. Maybe I was misjudging her again. I needed to stop assuming shit and just take in the facts.

"You okay?" I asked.

She snuggled into my chest. "Are you going to check on your trip tomorrow?"

I stroked her hair. "I'll power up the email tonight before I go to bed to see if I got a reply yet."

"Okay," she replied.

Lucy spun away from the TV and looked at us for a minute, then she went back to the TV.

"Everything okay, Lucy?" I asked.

She spun toward me. "Yeah. I'm just kind of bored."

She didn't admit that often, so I knew it was really bad. Time to try to fix it. "Anything you'd like to do?"

"Can we play a game?" she asked.

I smiled. "We can play any game you want."

She scooted closer on the floor. Tabby sat up.

"Any game?" Lucy asked.

From the mischievous look on her face, it was starting to seem like not so good of an idea.

"What do you have in mind?" Tabby asked her.

"We all can tell a story about something that scared us most. The one that is the scariest wins."

Okay, now I wasn't liking that at all. One, Lucy had made a deal with the Devil, even if it was loosely formed. Two, after dealing with the demonic this long, there was no way I was going to vocalize what scared me most. So I was caught. Did I tell her no and make her choose another game? Or did I lie? It was a conundrum.

Technically, I could lie about the thing that scared me most, but that wouldn't be fair to Lucy. Plus, I didn't lie lightly. It was one of my pet peeves.

"What if we choose whether to tell a scary story or a funny story?" Tabby asked.

Leave it to Tabby to step in. I wanted to hug her so hard.

"Okay," Lucy said.

I could tell she wasn't happy about it by how rigid her body went, but she didn't vocalize it. Maybe the poor kid was happy we agreed to play a game with her at all. Kind of sad. We needed to include Lucy more instead of having her tag along. This sudden parenthood business wasn't doing any of us any favors.

Doc cleared his throat. He'd been sitting in the chair on the other side of the sofa. Lucy and Tabby gaped at him. Kind of amazing he could get them to listen by clearing his throat. Me? I was chopped liver. I guessed you had to have a presence or something.

"I think there's a reason Miss Lucy wants to know what you're afraid of," he said.

Okay. I'd bite. It wasn't like I had anything better to do. "Okay, Lucy. Are you afraid of something?"

She nodded her head very slowly.

Sometimes getting information from her was like pulling the teeth out of a cat. "Okay. What are you afraid of?"

She adjusted and sat cross-legged. "I don't want to lose you."

It was really fucking sweet. I nodded at Tabby and looked back at Lucy. "We aren't going anywhere."

Lucy blinked. "What about when they decide where I'm going?"

There was no way I could see her either place unless I was dead too. And there wasn't anything I could do about that. It was out of my hands to make any decisions with that much importance behind them. I didn't want to lie to her, so I presented it in the only way I could. "Lucy, all we can do is the best we can. Who even knows when we'll have to worry about that. It might be a very long time."

"Okay," she said.

That was all it took. I thought it was going to be a hell of a lot harder than that. "Next time, just tell us if something is upsetting you, okay?"

She got up, ran over to me, and hugged me. I felt a slight bit of pressure this time. Maybe all the stress was getting to her too. I wished there was some way to make all of this a lot easier on everybody.

"I love you," she said.

I smiled into where her hair would be. "Love you too, kiddo."

Later that night, I peered at the iPad. Still no word from the Order. Hell, it was possible I wouldn't even be told until the last minute. With the way they'd done everything else, it wasn't out of the question. Yet, I wasn't too worried. It was on their dime after all. If it had been coming out of my pocket, I'd have been throwing a shit storm.

"What are you doing?" I asked Tabby. She seemed to be staring off into space.

"Thinking," she said.

Okay. Now I was interested. There was a lot of stuff I loved about Tabby and a big one was her brain. "About what?"

"Coffee."

Jesus Christ. Here I thought she was having some sort of major epiphany. I rolled my eyes. She had this unhealthy obsession with those crappuccino things. "You know those are bad for you, right?"

She looked at me and rolled her eyes. "Like bacon isn't?"

I laughed. "Hey, bacon is wonder-food."

She laughed back at me. "If you say so."

I shrugged. No way was I going to back down from that one.

Meat had nutritional content. Besides, my father had eaten it every day of his life along with his morning oatmeal and his cholesterol was great.

"What are we going to do tomorrow?" Tabby asked.

I noticed how she was slyly trying to change the subject, but I chose not to call her on it. "Well, I think I'd better check the airline rules and crap so I can make sure I have everything I need, just in case they tell me at the last minute."

She flopped over on her side, facing me. "That's actually not a bad idea."

"Thank you so much for your faith in me." Sometimes I wondered if she thought I deserved to walk upright.

She smacked me on the arm. "That's not what I meant and you know it."

I grinned at her. "We still need to find a box or something for el rod-o."

"Any ideas?"

My brain bounced around about fourteen different items at once. Most of them from old movies I'd seen. "We could go old-school Mafia-style and get a violin case."

Tabby laughed. "You are interesting, you know that?"

I chuckled. "You have to admit, that would be interesting to go through security with. Here's a violin case. They put it through the x-ray machine and it is not a violin. So they open the case for further examination and–dum dum dum–find a stick!"

She shook her head. "What am I going to do with you?"

I shrugged. "Keep me around, I guess."

"Turn off the light," she said and reached toward me.

"Yes, ma'am."

The next morning, I didn't wake up until eleven. Part of me was happy for the sleep. The other part was afraid that I'd wasted too much of the day. I needed to start setting an alarm or something so I wouldn't waste so much damn time. Not having regular hours was fucking up my system. The old body needed more rest.

I got up out of bed, grabbed a quick shower, and then lumbered downstairs.

I heard nothing, which was odd. Usually, the TV was on and I could hear voices.

I peeked into the living room and the place was spotless. It was so wrong. I knew Tabby had to have been the one picking up. It sure as hell hadn't been my lazy ass. When I'd been by myself, the house had been lucky to get cleaned like once a week.

I went into the kitchen. The only evidence that anyone had been there was the dishcloth draped over the sink. It was wet. At least I knew they hadn't been gone that long.

I stared out the window.

Tabby was sitting cross-legged in the middle of the back-yard. Her eyes were closed and she was in what I called her "meditation pose." Lucy was copying the same pose, but the only difference was that she was hovering in mid-air. Doc was leaning against a tree, watching them. Probably a good thing that very few people could see them. Other-wise, our street would become the haven for rash car crashes in the area. That, or misinformed Goths trying to connect with their inner supernatural. Were there even Goths anymore?

I opened the back door and walked over to Doc. The grass felt cool against my feet.

"How are they?" I asked him.

"Okay, for now. They decided you needed some rest."

I laughed. Maybe I'd been crankier than I realized. "They did, did they?"

Doc chuckled. "Mentioned something about you being entirely too grumpy."

Suddenly I felt something warm and furry land on my foot. I looked down and Isaac stared up at me. That damn cat.

"Guess this is your version of man time?" I asked him. He meowed back.

I looked back up at Tabby. Her eyes were still closed and it was almost as if the sunlight was bursting from the highlights in her hair. Damn, she was beautiful like that. With the sun glowing around her, I could almost see her special powers.

"You got yourself a mighty fine filly," Doc said.

I blushed. It was ridiculous, but I did. "Yeah. She's something else."

Doc grunted. "Better take good care of her."

"That's the plan."

Hell, I'd been doing better this time than I had before. We didn't fight as much. I wasn't sure if it was because I was older, or if I had mellowed out any. Or, maybe, Tabby and I just had the ability to deal with each other better.

"Jimmy!" Lucy floated across the yard toward me.

I waved. "Hey, there."

"Tabby's been teaching me to…to…medi-something."

I grinned. I couldn't help it. She was so damn cute sometimes. "I see."

"Remember what I said about rule #1?" Tabby asked. Her eyes were still closed. The corners of her mouth were quivering like she was trying not to laugh. I wondered how long it was going to be until she gave up.

Lucy stilled. "Be very, very quiet."

Tabby opened her eyes and grinned. "That's right."

I snickered. It was so great watching them interact. I could almost imagine Tabby actually being Lucy's mom.

Tabby put her finger in front of her lips, got up from the ground, and walked over to the rest of us.

"Finally decided to get up, did ya?" she asked me.

I laughed. "Guess so. I haven't slept that well in a while."

It was true. Maybe we all needed to talk about crap more

instead of jumping in and trying to fix everything. And I knew I was one of the worst culprits of this, but we all needed to take a step back.

She nodded. "That's why I let you sleep."

I plucked a strand of her hair out of her face. "Want to grab some lunch, then hit the antique shops?"

"Sounds good to me."

"What are we going there for?" Lucy asked.

I glanced at her. "To find a protective case for the rod."

She stood on the ground and stopped hovering. "I promise I'll never touch it again."

Her lips were quivering, and I could almost see tears forming in her eyes.

Dammit. Either she was too sensitive, or I was a fucking idiot. Frankly, the jury was still out. I needed a manual or something. "No! We know you didn't mean it. It was an accident. We're just going to get a box for it so that doesn't happen to anyone else."

Her eyes were so large, looking at me like that. "Really?"

"Yup. Besides, we have to keep it safe, don't we?"

She nodded again.

I waved my hand toward the back door. "Okay, everybody inside. Let's get ready for the road trip."

They followed me like a herd of geese.

I was getting tired of driving, but hopefully, after this trip, I wouldn't be doing any traveling until I had to leave for Italy. If everyone wanted to do something, we'd do it closer to home. That, or I'd have Tabby drive, though I would imagine even she was getting tired of spending so much time in the car.

I don't know what possessed me to go to antique stores. One —who knew there were this many in southern West Virginia? I lived right on the border, right past Bluefield into Virginia. Not much was there on the Virginia side, so West Virginia it was. Two—everything was overpriced. And three—no one had any violin cases. I was ready to give up. I should have gone to the local music store, but I hadn't been thinking. And apparently, Tabby hadn't either. I wasn't blaming her or anything. It was just something we both normally would have caught. I think we both needed some more rest.

We were sitting in the car outside the last store. Doc and Lucy were in the back seat as usual. They'd stopped going into the stores after the third one. I didn't blame them. This sucked lime-green donkey balls. I didn't even mention the music store. Frankly, I didn't want to pay two hundred dollars for a good hard case.

I glanced at Tabby. "Got any other ideas?"

She leaned against the headrest. "Does it have to be a violin case?"

"No," I said. "Not really. Just would have been cool." Hell, at this point I would take something made out of duct tape. Well, not really, but I was tired.

"Well, all you want is something that can be secure, right?" Tabby asked.

"Yeah."

She stared out the window for a minute, and then suddenly turned to look at me. "What about a gun case?"

I paused. It was a pretty good idea. You could get them in various sizes. People would know whatever was inside was dangerous. Better yet, the hard cases locked.

"Any idea how much they cost?" I asked.

"Around a hundred dollars for a good one," Tabby said. She adjusted herself in the seat.

That was better than the violin. I put the car in gear. "Okay. Sporting goods store here we come."

I didn't go to one all the way down there. I drove us back home first. No sense in waiting to get rid of the long drive when we had sporting goods shops close to the house. It was Virginia, after all. Hunting was huge here.

Once I got there, Doc and Lucy stayed where they were. In fact, Tabby did too. That shocked me.

"You aren't coming in with me?" I asked Tabby.

She shook her head. "I'm feeling kind of tired."

Welcome to the club. But whatever. It wasn't like this wasn't something I could do myself. "Okay. I'll be back as quick as I can."

I closed the car door and walked into the store. It was your usual chain sporting-goods store. Helpful clerks standing here and there—mostly looking bored. I didn't bother taking any of them away from their cell phones. It took me a little bit to find the cases. But soon I found what we needed. It was a hard black case with silver metal clasps. It was designed to let you carry your gun broken down. It was a little wide, but the length left enough room on each end to keep the rod safe. Best of all, it was on sale.

The clerk didn't even look at me twice on the way out. She was more interested in staring at the clock. After a while, I could imagine how mind-numbing her job was. Made me thankful for the one I had—and that's kind of sad.

I walked out the store and held up the bag. I was about to show Tabby the prize when I realized she seemed a little too still. Oh, shit.

I ran over to the car and threw open the door. It was like everything alive had been sucked out of the car. Even the air inside it smelled stale. Doc gaped at me and tried to speak, but I couldn't hear a word he was saying. His mouth moved, but nothing was coming out. Not good.

Next thing I knew, everything went black. And the bag with the case in it? It was gone from my hand.

"You didn't think it would be so easy, did you?"

The voice was tenor. Not bad and not good. Just there. I opened my eyes. The place I was in felt wrong. Like it was a little too hot. The walls were a red color. I wasn't sure if this could get more cliché or not. I was starting to feel like Scrooge felt in that 1970's musical.

I looked around. Standing over me was the man himself. Big Red wore flowing black robes that seemed to undulate between lightness and darkness. Just one problem. The voice wasn't exactly how I remembered Big Red's to be. That was a big problem. Something was off.

"What did I think was going to be easy?" I asked him.

"Your debt."

Now I was confused. I had made no deal with him at all. In fact, I hadn't done anything. Plus, he'd said himself that Lucy didn't owe him anything, so this wasn't making any sense.

"I believe you are mistaken," I said.

He laughed. Heartily. "How easily you mortals forget."

I sat up on the floor. My head was spinning. This seemed like Big Red, but his mannerisms were different. His voice was different. Either the man I knew as Big Red was a hoax, or this one was. I suspected the latter.

"Who are you?" I asked.

"Now, why would I tell an exorcist my real name?" he said.

Big Red wouldn't have worried about it. When he'd been around me, he'd shown no fear at all. Well, that's because he was a bucky badass and didn't have anything to prove. This idiot...yeah.

"Well, that makes a lot of sense," I said. "You might as well drop the façade. I know you aren't who you are pretending to be."

It laughed. The face slowly changed shape. It almost undulated like something from an old werewolf movie. Soon, the transformation was complete.

His hair had turned white. I don't mean blond either; I mean white. His eyebrows and eyelashes were white too. His eyes had the odd red hue that many albinos possessed. His ears were pointed like an elf. No wonder he was such a pissant.

"You're one of his sons, aren't you?" I wasn't sure how I knew that, but it fit. Especially since the last dealing I'd had with one of the sons had been so great.

He smiled. His teeth were pointed, like his father's.

"What debt do I owe to you?" I knew that there wasn't any damn debt, but I needed to know what the hell he was claiming before I could counter it.

He walked over and sat on a great marble throne that randomly appeared out of nowhere. "You were young at the time, but any age will do."

"I still don't know what you are talking about," I said. Also, his ability to randomly have stuff be suddenly there made me think this wasn't the actual place per se. More like he'd taken my soul somewhere or he was somewhere in my own mind. No matter what, though, I didn't like it. I should have control over my own damn soul, thank you very much.

"The man who hurt your sister. You damned him to Hell, did you not?"

I stood up. Oh, hell, no. He was not taking this there. If there was one thing that was going to piss me off, it was trying to blame shit on what happened with my sister. He'd run into a fucking buzz saw. "First, how do you expect me to remember something I said when I was a kid? And second, plenty of people damn others to Hell and they don't owe a thing."

He leaned forward and sneered at me. "Those people are not markers."

"And third, preying on something that makes me rather emotional was a big fucking mistake." I was tired of this shit. "There is no contract because I didn't even know I was a marker. I had no way of knowing that. Besides, I didn't even have the power back then, so I suggest you try to fool someone else."

"Not knowing makes no difference. A pact is a pact."

"That makes no difference? I'll show you a difference in a minute." I was gearing up to beat his ass, but then I thought better of it. I didn't know if I even had any powers where we were, so it was better if I played it cool. "No, send me back or I will alert your father."

He smirked again. "And how do you expect to do that?"

I reached down and held out my mark. I began strumming my fingers over the top of it as if I were playing a harp. Shit, I didn't know if that did anything, but the important part was that neither did he.

"Dare me," I said.

In a flash, I was sitting on the concrete in the parking lot. Tabby was screaming at me. Doc and Lucy were hovering nearby. The bag with the case in it was sprawled at my feet.

I glared up at Tabby. "I'm okay now, but someone has a hell of a lot of questions to answer."

Tabby wiped her forehead with the back of her hand. "Who?"

"I need to invoke the Devil."

EIGHT

WITCHY WOMAN

TABBY GOT me loaded into the passenger seat of the car. Apparently, I had only been unconscious a few minutes, but it felt a lot longer than that. She was probably right that I wasn't fit to drive. I didn't argue with her either.

She loaded the case in the trunk and then sat in the driver's seat. The whole time, she didn't say one word.

"You can't be serious," she said finally. She put the car in gear and headed toward the house.

I didn't want to fight with her, but apparently I had no choice. "I am perfectly serious. No way in hell am I letting some bratty devil kid get the best of me."

"I agree with Tabby. This sure doesn't sound like a good idea," Lucy said.

I spun around in my seat and looked at her. I was going to get nowhere if I made the kid cry again.

"Have any better ideas?" I asked Tabby.

"You could research demons, you know? Try to find out who it is that way."

I glared at her. "How did you know this was what this was about?"

She slammed on the brakes and turned to me. Her eyes grew wide. "I don't care."

"Okay. Let's get the fuck home. We'll figure out what to do then." If she wasn't going to help me—fine. I would figure out how to do it myself.

"And I am blessing this car," she said a bit too loud.

"Okay."

To be honest, maybe carrying the meat suit in the car had something to do with it, but nothing bad had happened and it had been a couple of days. Not to mention that we were still using that car. For the car to be cursed, it was pretty fucking light. Hell, we'd even taken some road trips. Granted, this last one had ended in disaster, but not by way of an accident or anything.

As soon as we got home, Doc and Lucy got out of the car, and I went around to the back to get the case.

Tabby stepped up and put her hand on the back hatch of the car. "No, leave it. I'm blessing that fucker too."

"Okay...?" If she thought it would help, then by all means.

"You were handling it before you went down. That smells fishy to me," she said.

Okay. We were back to being concerned. All right. I held up my hands. "You're the expert."

I went inside and laid on the couch. It didn't take long before she was heading back outside. Why was I going to interrupt her now? It was better to let her get it done; then, we could talk about what we were going to do. That was if I felt like running it by her. She was overreacting in my opinion. But then maybe demons were a lot scarier to her than they were to me.

I didn't think that the car was haunted at all, but if blessing it made her feel better, so be it. Now, the gun case could possibly be compromised—possibly. But I had my doubts about that too. It was probably just the son having more powers than he needed. And going behind Daddy's back. I had my doubts that Big Red would operate that way. He'd snatch what he wanted, not mess around with all of this bullshit. He had better things to do.

I knew better. Demons, if they wanted to have dealings with you, they'd just come. They didn't need a special invitation like a vampire. All they had to do was get you open enough to notice them. And of course, I could see them, which meant they could see me too.

Whatever; maybe having the case for the rod blessed would make it less noticeable or something. It couldn't hurt.

By the time Tabby came back inside, it was me, Doc, and Lucy sitting side-by-side on the couch—waiting. I don't think any of us expected her to lose it like this. Though, in her defense, it wasn't every day I threatened to invoke the Devil either.

I had to wonder—was that a sin? It was possible. But the fact that it wasn't for a bad reason somehow made me think it wasn't. I wasn't exactly operating on church rules anyway. Whether that was a good or bad thing remained to be seen.

I shrugged it off. No sense in worrying about it. If I already had a mark on my head—however tremulous, I needed to know how to get rid of it. And the Devil needed to rein in his children. Unless driving me crazy was his plan all along. I knew God and the Devil were playing a giant game of chess. The question was what piece was I standing in for?

"I want you to know I don't like this," Tabby said as she came inside carrying the gun case.

Well, at least she wasn't going all batshit-crazy on my ass now. That was improvement. I still felt a little loopy, so when she caught me off guard, I almost fell off the couch.

She set the case on the floor and crouched down next to me. "You really aren't okay, are you?"

I rubbed my head. "This time? I guess not."

"Do you think the demon did something to you?" She was parting my hair with her fingers, almost as if checking for bugs.

I shrugged. It was hard to say. It could be the stress of being pulled down to Hell, then sent back that left me like that. Or him being in my head. I still wasn't entirely sure what had happened. All I knew was that I had a whopper of a headache.

"Well, we need to do something," Tabby said.

I nodded. "Which is why I need to invoke Big Red. He has the answers. It's his kids who keep fucking with me. I think it's time to stop it all."

Tabby sighed. "Are you even in any shape to do this?"

"Nope, but that never stopped me before." It was true. So far, bumbling through all of this shit worked out okay. I had no reason to think that this would be any different. It was my talent.

"Sadly, I know that's true." Tabby pulled her hand away from my head and stared at me.

"So," I said. "How does one invoke the Devil?"

Tabby shook her head. "I have no idea. That's not something I even ever wanted to touch."

I leaned on the sofa and scratched my head. I did what I always did when I was left with something I didn't know. I winged it. "Hey, you! Dude. Devil man. Guy that gave me that nifty present—or rather gave it to Tabby! I have some questions for you."

Tabby gaped at me in shock. "Jesus Christ, Jimmy. Warn me next time you decide to do that."

I laughed.

Suddenly, there was a thunderclap. Big Red stood in the

middle of the living room dressed in another suit. His tie was dark green. I had to admit that he was a snazzy dresser. Isaac darted underneath the sofa. I didn't blame him.

"I come out of sheer curiosity, Mr. Holiday. I believe that was one of the most ridiculous incantations I have ever heard. And for your personal information, in order to invoke a demon, you need to use their true name." He smiled quickly and flashed his teeth at me.

"Well, it got you here, didn't it?" One thing I noticed about this time was that no one was frozen. Maybe it was because I instigated this visit. Or maybe he just didn't bother. It was hard to tell.

"What is it that you need?" he asked.

I sat up on the couch straighter. "A few questions answered."

The Devil motioned toward one of the dining room table chairs. It glided over to him and he sat. "Begin."

"One—is there a mark on my soul?"

The Devil laughed. "Of course there is. Everyone has them. What do you think allows God to measure how many sins you've performed in your lifetime?"

Okay, that wasn't exactly comforting. But I wasn't about to stop now. "Oh," I said. "What about marks that *mean* something? Have I ever made a contract with one of your sons?"

The Devil sighed. "Is Leviathan trying that business again? I do not have a son that is more power-hungry than he."

I blinked. If this was his opinion, he needed to pull rank and fast. I had a sneaking suspicion that he wanted this stuff to happen. It put him in contact with me after all.

"So he has no contract with me?" I asked.

The Devil shook his head. "If he did, you would have a mark bearing his name. You do not."

I knew the Devil was the father of lies, but that rang true to me, so I relaxed. Some.

"Okay," I said. "Did he do anything to me?"

The Devil glared at me. Then, he stood. "Do you mind if I try to find out?"

"Go ahead, but no funny business." Hell, if he could fix it and it wouldn't cost me anything, then why not?

He laughed and held his hands over me. Soon, I felt warmth, as if I were standing under a heat lamp spreading warmth throughout my body, and then it stopped. The Devil backed away.

"Do you feel extremely tired?" he asked.

I nodded. "Yeah. And a little dizzy."

He nodded. "A weaker person would be under his thrall. Consider yourself fortunate, Jimmy Holiday."

"He didn't do anything?" With the pain in my head, I was kind of surprised.

"Not because he didn't want to. He tried and he failed."

I guessed my hard head was good for something after all. "Will he try again?"

"Most certainly. But he will come at you from a different direction."

"Why not just stop him?" Tabby asked.

He turned to her and laughed. "Now, why would I do that? The world is ever so much more interesting when the lot of you are scrambling."

"Gee, thanks a lot." Though at least I knew I was appreciated.

Big Red winked at Tabby. Then he disappeared. Like usual.

Tabby rubbed her arms. "Do me a favor? Never ever do that again."

I glanced up at her. "I'll try not to."

"I miss pizza," Lucy said long about dinnertime. Every time I turned around, she broke my heart. The hits kept on coming. It was a good thing I was a stubborn bastard or I would have needed therapy by now.

She was in her usual spot in front of the TV. Poor kid. I wished we had hidden the rod or something, but that wasn't exactly something we could have prepared for. We still didn't even know what it did. Not really. It took Lucy touching the damn thing to figure it out.

"I know, Luce," I said. "If I could fix it, I would."

Doc started making a sound like he was clacking his teeth together. "I have an idea."

I raised an eyebrow at him. "Okay. I'll bite."

"Sometimes, I can smell very strong smells. It's almost as if they drift through what's left of me," he said.

"Okay...?" I had no idea where this was going, but whatever. If he knew of some way to make all this shit better, then by all means.

"Maybe if we put down some food and Lucy stands right over top of it. Maybe, just maybe, she could at least smell it." He scratched his head, and then smiled.

I didn't know if that would be crueler or not but, shit, it was worth a try. The kid needed something to hold onto. "What do you think, Lucy?"

She hopped up. "I would like to try."

"Okay. That's settled."

Isaac came from under the couch and rubbed against Doc's leg, or rather where Doc's leg should be. The man reached down and scratched the cat on the head for a minute.

If it weren't for the fact you could see Isaac's fur through the tips of Doc's fingers, it would have been kind of cute. But instead, it was weird as shit. That's what it was. I was still trying to get used to seeing all this crap on a regular basis, and I wasn't doing a very good job of it. Every time I tried to make a difference, something new would happen.

"I'll go let Tabby know what we're doing for dinner," I said.

Doc looked up. "Good idea."

I went upstairs to our bedroom. Tabby was sitting on the floor with the fleshing rod nearby, a bunch of her witchy stuff around it, and the case. I did love watching her work. It was amazing what she could make from a few herbs.

"What are you doing?" I asked.

"Warding the case so that only you and I can open it," she said.

I took a deep breath. Granted, it was a good idea. I was just uneasy about being one of the keepers for that damn thing. But I was stuck with it. Shit, even the Devil felt the thing was co-owned by Tabby and me. I was seriously fucked. Though, honestly, I couldn't think of anyone else better suited to keep the damn thing. Also, I had to wonder if the Devil had actually made it for Tabby for a reason other than safekeeping. That didn't make a lot of sense. Why make it at all, then? There had to be a reason. Still, no sense in rambling about it all now. I had more important stuff to attend to.

"Lucy wants pizza for dinner," I said. I didn't mean to blurt it out like that, but it could have been worse. Besides, pizza was the least of our worries.

Tabby tilted her head to the side like a dog.

Was I really being that weird lately? I didn't feel any stranger than usual. "Doc thinks he's come up with a way for her to at least smell it."

She leaned back a little and blinked. "Okay. That's fine by me."

"How much longer are you going to be witchy?"

She shrugged. "Not long. Why?"

"Want to go with me to pick up the pizza?" I thought we

needed some alone time. Maybe it would give us a chance to calm down some.

"Why not? I'll be down when I'm finished."

I saluted her. "Okay. Take your time."

Doc and Lucy played a game with Isaac while I waited. Doc would make a light glow on the wall, Isaac would jump up and try to catch it, and Lucy would giggle. They did it over and over. It was amazing what types of things could entertain a kid for hours. I wished I had that ability now. The best I could do was read a story in a silly voice. The ability to make something glow was a much better superpower.

It felt good to hear her laugh. My mind drifted back to the girl at the fast food restaurant talking about how I was doing a good job—that Lucy was happy. My question was: compared to what? Lucy was going to be seven eventually, and even though her body couldn't show it, all the crap she has had to put up with had to weigh on her. She was never going to be a normal kid and she could partly thank me for that. The fact that I managed to give her some sort of home counted for something, but there was only so much I could not erase.

Tabby came downstairs and grabbed her purse. "You want to order or should I?"

"Go ahead. I didn't do it because I didn't know how long you were going to be," I said. I also didn't want to make a mistake and order the wrong type or something. Granted, the standard was pepperoni and sausage, but she might want something different.

"Okay." She pulled out her cell phone and headed into the kitchen. Lucy and Doc continued their game.

As I watched them, I thought about my sister and how the

room always seemed to light up for me when she smiled. I knew that when she was happy, everything was going to be okay. I missed her. Candy had been my protector when I was little. She was the one I wanted to be, not Dad. Dad couldn't keep his head out of a bottle long enough for me to get to know the real him.

But Candy, she kept it all going. Had I known that asshole down the street was attacking her, I would have killed him myself. Leviathan's claim that I'd called to him and damned the man to Hell was false. The bastard had damned himself.

Though I did find it interesting that as many of the Devil's children were after me. Ares had wasted most of my time. Granted, I'd known him as Vespa for the most part, and still thought of him that way, but his father had been the one to expose his true motive. I still had to thank him for teaching me something though—don't get cocky. Investigate everything. And ask all the questions. I wasn't about to make those mistakes again. At least I learned something, which was probably counter-productive to what they had intended.

"You ready?" Tabby asked from the kitchen doorway.

"Yep." I glanced at Doc and Lucy. "You guys be good while we're gone."

Doc nodded. Lucy ignored me.

I let Tabby go first. I closed and locked the door behind us. I had a feeling that this was going to be an interesting evening.

Tabby insisted on driving. I think she was afraid I'd have a fit or something, but I was honestly starting to feel better. Maybe the Devil had done something to me to lessen the effects. It was possible. He didn't seem to want me taken over by one of his sons, and that's exactly what Leviathan had tried to do. He'd tried to possess me. Good thing I was as goofy as I was.

"Are you sure you're okay?" Tabby asked.

I patted her hand. "I'm fine, so okay per se. Takes more than a Devil visit to take me out."

She rolled her eyes. "Sometimes, that's what I'm afraid of."

"You think Lucy is going to be okay?" I asked. What happened to me didn't matter so much now that the crisis was over. Time to go back to thinking about what was important.

"Of course."

It kind of made me uncomfortable that she was so nonchalant about it. "How do you know?"

Tabby glanced at me from the corner of her eye. "Because she has to be. What good would it do her to be a mess forever? Even we don't know how long she'll be in limbo."

She did have a point, but Lucy was still six. She always would be. Spirits didn't age. "Yeah…Just been trying to figure out how to make it better for her."

Tabby pulled into the parking lot of the pizza place. It was this little mom and pop shop that would even put prosciutto on it if you asked for it. It cost a lot extra, though, so we usually skipped that part.

"That's what we're doing right now," Tabby said.

"It seems like so little." And it was. It was a fucking pizza for Christ's sake, and that was all we were doing to make a kid happy. It verged on ridiculous.

She sighed. "To us, maybe, but to her, we're giving her everything we have the ability to give. For a child that's more than enough."

Sometimes she was so damn smart. I needed to stop over-thinking things.

"Stay here," she said and started crawling out of the car.

"Come on; I can at least pay for pizza." I was starting to feel a little worthless.

She finished getting out and leaned into the car to look at me. "Nope. Jimmy, let me take care of you for once."

I sighed. "Oh, all right."

She grinned and closed the door.

This was going to be a lot harder than I thought it would be.

Back at home, Tabby did at least let me carry the pies into the house. I guessed I'd proven to her that I wasn't going to fall down every two seconds. I let her open the door for me and I walked inside.

Doc and Lucy were back to watching TV. I needed to come up with some stuff that would get Lucy away from the TV. It wasn't healthy.

"Get the plates," I told Tabby as she passed me. She saluted.

"Smartass," I said.

I walked into the living room and set the pizzas on the floor. Lucy crawled over near the pies. The TV was on yet another bad horror film.

Doc floated down from his perch on the recliner.

Tabby came in and sat on the floor, plates in hand. I lumbered to the floor and felt my knee pop. I was getting too old for this. If I kept this up, I could see myself in a wheelchair doing exorcisms and swatting at demons with my cane. I was destined to be crotchety.

I opened the box and put a slice on a paper plate Tabby handed me. Then, I set it on the floor in front of Lucy. This was the moment of truth.

"Okay, kid. Give it a try," I said. It was going to be weird as shit, but whatever. Weird had been the norm around here for a long time.

She stood up and positioned herself right overtop the plate. At first, she seemed kind of confused. Then, suddenly, her eyes lit up with light. "I can smell it!"

Tabby, Doc, and I all clapped. Ectoplasmic tears of joy ran down Lucy's face.

"Congratulations, kid," I said. It was bizarre, but who cared.

She darted across and grabbed me in a huge hug. I could feel her denser now. More real. It was nice to feel that again. I'd missed it.

"Thank you, Jimmy," she said.

I smiled. "You're welcome, Lucy."

Thank heaven for small favors.

NINE

FLY LIKE A BIRD

WHEN WE WENT UPSTAIRS to bed, the first thing I did was turn on the iPad. I'd almost gotten out of the habit of checking it and that was probably a bad thing. Especially since there was a note waiting for me. Whoops.

> Mr. Holiday,
>
> Please review the following visa forms to make sure that they are correct. We will be making all reservations for you. Relax.
>
> Fr. Martin

At least, it was an answer this time. Maybe they were getting used to me and my way of doing stuff. Although this was also a new guy. I was starting to wonder if their secretarial staff cycled around that much or if I was being considered a "special snowflake."

"Tabby?" I asked.

She popped her head from the bathroom door. "What?"

"Do you have any experience with visa forms?" It was something out of my league. I'd never done anything outside of the country besides vacation.

"Credit cards?" she asked.

"No, immigration stuff." I sighed. Nothing like paperwork to put a damper on things. I'd known it was coming, but I'd been avoiding thinking about it like the plague. And I'd been kind of preoccupied.

She stepped out of the bathroom. "No, not really. Why?"

"The Order sent the forms that I have to have filed to stay in Italy for the length of the course."

She shrugged. "Oh. Well, print them out and we'll find someone to look at them tomorrow."

Leave it to her to simplify everything and make it seem manageable. I needed to calm the fuck down. "Good idea."

I forwarded the email to my usual address. I had no way of accessing my Order email any way except on the iPad, and since I'd never figured out how to link my tablet up to the printer, emailing the file was a lot easier. And I had to admit, I was sort of lazy. It was easier to climb the stairs than fuck with networking.

I got up, ran downstairs, and started booting up my laptop. The spirits were in their usual spots: Doc in the chair and Lucy on the floor in front of the TV.

"Everything all right?" Doc asked.

"Yep. Got some paper from the Order I gotta print out," I said.

He grunted and went back to watching TV. Lucy was focused on some old 1980's sitcom. I could handle that a lot better than her unhealthy obsession with scary movies. It wasn't that I had a thing against scary movies, or even against kids watching them. It was that she'd lived through enough horror, so why add to it? But if she liked them, and wasn't afraid of them, there wasn't much else for me to do. Maybe she was just a weird kid. Hell, I certainly wasn't anything you could call normal.

I got the files printed and flipped everything off. Then I went back upstairs.

Tabby was in bed, flipping through a magazine. She glanced up when I entered the room.

"That could have waited until tomorrow, you know," she said.

I nodded. "Technically, yes. But if I didn't get it done, I would drive myself crazy thinking about it all night."

She shook her head. "You really are an odd duck."

I laughed. "And you're normal?"

She smacked me with her magazine. "Normaler than you."

I crawled into bed, put my hands behind my head, and lay down. "It's weird how fast your life can change."

Tabby stared at me. "If we'd be honest, we were destined for this, though."

I couldn't deny that. My life was steamrolling ahead and I wasn't sure when it was going to stop. "Ever think about what it would have been like if we'd never split up the first time?"

She put down her magazine and glanced toward me. "We probably would hate each other."

Thinking back to how it was...she was right. I hadn't been willing to believe in her, not her religion anyway. Now, I had a hell of a lot more open mind. Encountering the demonic had a tendency to do that.

I leaned over and switched off the lamp on my side of the bed.

"It's only ten," Tabby said.

"Go ahead and stay up. I'm tired."

I felt her adjust in the bed. "Are you sure you're okay?"

I nodded. "Yes. I'm just tired. Can I go to sleep?"

She sighed. "Go ahead."

I almost expected to have a weird sort of dream, but there were none. I got up and looked at my cell phone. It was after seven. At least I hadn't slept the day away. I needed to do something about my stress level though. And, well, the crap my brain picked to worry about wasn't helping either.

I glanced over and Tabby was still snoring softly. No sense in waking her up. She deserved to sleep in once in a while. Especially with my crazy ass driving her up the wall.

I crept out of bed and made my way downstairs.

Lucy was perched at the dining room table. Isaac sat near the doorway to the kitchen. I was honestly surprised that she wasn't watching TV. I didn't know where Doc had wandered off to.

"Where's Doc?" I asked.

"When he heard you get up, he said he had to go take care of something," she said.

I shrugged. It wasn't like I owned Doc or anything. He was with us because he wanted to be, not because I had any hold on him. Still, I felt a little uneasy not knowing what all the man was involved in, even thought I was probably better off not knowing. He'd promised to keep an eye on Lucy for me. Granted, I hadn't been awake all that long, but I would have rather he waited until I was downstairs. Oh well.

"Lucy, what do you want to do today?" I asked.

She shrugged. "Maybe just have a normal day."

I plopped down beside her. One thing was sure: she was going to have to come with me to Italy. I wasn't sure if this meant Doc, too, but I had a feeling I could only be away from her for so long before the bad stuff happened. If that was worse than what happened when I was with her, then I didn't know what I would do. She would have to get used to hanging out with me again.

"How do you feel about going away with me?" I asked.

Her eyes got big. "Go where?"

"The Order wants me to take exorcist classes. And the only

school is in Italy." I watched her expression very closely. She didn't seem upset or anything.

"Is Tabby coming?" she asked.

"No." I shook my head. "She will be staying here."

Lucy's face kind of drooped. Damn. Had I thought about it earlier, I might have been able to do something, but I never would have guessed that Tabby staying home would be a problem.

"Can Doc come?" she asked. Her face was a little brighter.

I shrugged. "I don't know. You'd have to ask him."

It was true. I had no idea if his ghost was somehow tied to somewhere and had a certain reach or not. I knew he'd said something about recharging once in a while, but I wasn't entirely sure if he meant what I thought he did. I had read a couple of ghost-hunting books where the entities followed the people, but I couldn't remember if any moved that far away and still had experiences. It was one more thing to add to the list of stuff I needed to research. Good thing that, as far as I knew, I'd be a marker for life. So there should be plenty of time for research.

"Jimmy?" Tabby asked from upstairs.

"Yeah?"

"Want to go out for breakfast?"

"Sure." I was getting tired of eating out, but I didn't feel like cooking either. So laziness won.

Lucy crawled off the chair and sat in front of the TV.

I went upstairs to grab a shower. I still didn't know how Lucy felt about the whole thing. She hadn't told me. But then, I hadn't given her the chance, either. I was going to have to be more thoughtful when it came to her.

"You got everything?" Tabby asked next to the front door. Doc still hadn't returned. Lucy was standing next to Tabby.

"I think so," I said. Surely we could make it to breakfast and back without any bad shit happening. At least I hoped it would be that way. I needed a spiritual bodyguard.

"Even your papers?"

"Oh, shit." I swear, I was starting to wonder how I even functioned when Tabby wasn't around. I probably was more alert because it was always my own ass in a sling.

I went over to the desk, grabbed them, and shoved them in a folder. "Now, can we go?"

My stomach was starting to make enough noise that I thought it was going to eat itself. The pull of food was strong.

Tabby opened the door and we all piled into the car.

"Where do you want to get breakfast?" I asked.

"IHOP," Tabby said.

I was surprised she let me behind the wheel, but I guessed I must have seemed normal enough now. "What do you want, Lucy?"

"I can have something in the restaurant?" she asked.

I shrugged. "I don't see why not. Not many people can see you anyway. You tell me what you want and I'll order it."

"Yay!" She was grinning so wide I thought her mouth might split.

Tabby glanced over at me and smiled. I nodded back. Maybe I wasn't such a bad parent after all.

We didn't make it back to the house until around noon. We'd taken my papers over to the university to talk to their travel coordinator. She said everything was in order. I was glad to have at least that part done. Now, all I had to do was reply to the email. It was nice to have something simple work out. All it had taken me was a little time.

As soon as I got close to the front door, I knew something

was wrong. I heard Isaac yowling. My brain went to the idea that some sort of demon was in our house again. Or someone was trying to hurt him, like what happened in Arizona. I looked around for a weapon, but there was nothing. I was going to have to use my fists and hope for the best.

I threw open the door and saw nothing. I heard Isaac's yowling, but I couldn't see him. That wasn't good.

"Oh, Jesus Christ." Tabby ran past me and up the stairs. At the top, there was a little bit of railing where the steps angled around. Isaac had his head stuck between the railing and the wall.

I let loose the breath I'd been holding. It was sad that I was relieved that his distress was from a normal problem. I still felt sorry for him, but the lack of the supernatural was a welcome surprise.

"Dammit," Tabby said. She reached for Isaac's head and he tried to bite her.

"A little help would be nice," she called down the stairs.

I dropped the keys onto the table and walked up. Time for me to come to the rescue. I hoped I was up to the challenge.

He was wedged all right. "How in the hell did you do this?" I asked him.

He made an angry chirp at me.

"He was chasing a cricket earlier," Doc said.

I looked up. He walked toward me from the room that was going to be Lucy's. Shame he couldn't have prevented the damn cat from doing something this stupid, but oh well.

I turned my attention back to Isaac. "Okay. Let me help you." Isaac stilled.

At least he listened. I gently took hold of his head. "Now, move with my hands. Don't struggle." I twisted his head sideways and pushed it through. Isaac shook himself and sauntered off. He didn't even stop to thank me. Cats.

"I swear, that cat," Tabby said.

"What are you talking about? I thought we had another

demon." There was a pause where laughter would normally be inserted, but neither one of us felt like laughing. Things were getting way too strained. We went back downstairs.

"Is Isaac okay?" Lucy asked. She was still in her usual spot.

"Yep. Just got himself caught in the railing," I said.

Lucy shook her head. Doc came down the stairs and Lucy squealed. Again, I had to remind myself how old she was, but damn. I was not used to squeals in my house.

"Doc, where did you go, if you don't mind me asking?" I asked.

"Had to recharge. Nothing interesting," he replied.

I didn't poke further. I had a feeling that there was more to it than that. I imagined part of it he didn't want Lucy to know. The other part, well, it technically wasn't any of my business. Perhaps, in the future, he'd let me in on his secret. But it seemed awfully quick for him to go and come back if he really was recharging.

"Don't you have an email to write?" Tabby asked.

Good thing she was keeping me on schedule or I would have been totally screwed. "Yeah. Right."

I left them all to whatever it was they were going to do, went upstairs, and flipped on the iPad. A bright red alert popped up. I tapped on it and a video played. A video of me dumping Lucy's skin at Walmart. Fuck. Suddenly, I was staring at another priest. This dude had gray hair.

"So, Mr. Holiday," he said. "What is this?"

I didn't even want to think about how long he'd been sitting there, waiting for me to turn the thing on. It was not a good feeling. My asshole was so tight I didn't think anyone could even drive a nail into it.

"I was getting rid of trash," I said. Might as well call it that. It was better than saying it was the skin sack from the spirit of a six-year-old.

"Soupy, foul-smelling, organic matter is not normal trash," he said.

I shrugged. There wasn't a damn thing I could say to counter that. He was right. "No, it's not."

"Mind explaining what the substance was in the bag?" he asked.

Evidently, the skin melted into something else. What, I was not sure exactly. It was a boon for me. I could keep Lucy safe. No sense in giving away more information than needed.

"Gosh. Um. Ectoplasm would be part of it," I said. "Not sure what else. All I know is that it was gross."

The priest nodded. "And how did you come by it?"

That was the tricky part. I couldn't very well lie to the man. It would be so wrong on so many levels. "It was in my house. My living room to be exact. Had to rent a rug doctor to get the rest of it out of the carpet."

I knew he could look and see that was true. My own conscience felt better because I didn't bullshit him. Leaving out stuff wasn't lying. At least in my book.

"You are very lucky that humans do not normally know what ectoplasm is made of. From the stench, they thought you'd thrown away a body." Then he chuckled.

I felt so damn uncomfortable. "Is that all you wanted to know?"

"Yes, that will about cover it. Allow me to introduce myself. I am Father Nicholas Martin, your assigned adviser."

Apparently, they'd passed the buck enough that he'd gotten stuck with the problem case. I kind of felt sorry for him. "Nice to meet you, Father. Oh, and I got those visa papers looked at. Seems fine to me."

He nodded. "Good. I'll have them sent to the proper channels. One more thing, Mr. Holiday."

"Yes?"

"Remember–we're always watching."

The screen blinked out. Great. It's hard to tell what all they had footage of. Probably a lot of me talking to myself. They could look at that as much as they wanted. Hell, I'd talked to myself long before becoming an exorcist. Still, though, I didn't like being told how extensively they were following my every move. But I did now have complete proof that they were not filming inside the house. If they had that, I would have been shown it. Still though.

"Motherfuck."

I should have known that Big Brother was watching, but I'd allowed myself to be lulled into a false sense of security. I needed to reexamine how I felt about all of this next time. Being a marker was hard enough without all of this going on as well. Besides, what business was it of theirs what I did in my private time?

I put the device away and went back downstairs. My mood was betrayed by my look because Tabby started in right away.

"What's wrong?" she asked.

I sighed. No sense in hiding it now. "Let's just say that we weren't as discreet as we thought we were and leave it at that."

"Eek. Are we in trouble?" Her eyes grew wide.

I shook my head. "No, we're both lucky I am full of bullshit."

She leaned back on the sofa. "Now what?"

"We relax. The guy that read me the riot act was apparently my 'case worker.' So he's the dude I had to tell about the visa anyway." I sat down next to her on the couch.

"I swear. Every time we relax, something happens," Tabby said.

She had a good point. We needed to change the way we did stuff.

"You know how to solve that, right?" I asked.

"How?"

"We never relax."

TEN

GIVE IT TO ME

WITH THE FEELING that I was being watched hovering over me, I kept looking over my shoulder, almost expecting a priest to be there shaking his finger at me. Of course, no one was there. It was completely psychosomatic, but I couldn't help it. I probably should have been more worried about the demons...I wasn't.

"I need to do something to get my mind off all of this," I said.

Tabby tossed me the remote. "Watch a movie?"

I threw myself back into the sofa. "Like what?"

"I know! I know!" Lucy jumped up.

Her excitement had me worried. If this were a normal kid, we'd be watching pink princesses or something. But this was Lucy. I'd better prepare for something monstrous. "Okay, Lucy. What movie?"

"On the pay-for channel thing, there's a new movie," she said.

I could almost imagine what type of movie it would be. Something bloody and gory and completely inappropriate. I wasn't complaining. It kind of fit my mood. "What movie?"

"Turn on the thing and I'll tell you. The name is too big. I can't remember it." She stared at the TV screen.

"Okay." I grabbed the remote off the coffee table and hit the button for the pay stuff. I entered the movie section.

"Click on the scary movies," Lucy said.

I rolled my eyes. I knew it. Maybe seeing the fake stuff comforted her. I entered the horror section. It was my fault anyway. If I wanted to watch something else, I should have picked it.

"I think it starts with an 'e.'"

I followed Lucy's directions and started scrolling.

Tabby was watching me, and every so often, she would smile. I wasn't sure what amused her more, Lucy or me dealing with Lucy. Probably both.

"Stop," Lucy said.

I obliged. "This one?"

It was highlighting a movie called, "The Exorcism of Annelise." Great.

"Are you sure you want to watch this?" I asked her.

She nodded.

I glanced at Tabby. "What do you think?"

Tabby spoke to Lucy. "Do you find any of these movies scary?"

Lucy shook her head.

Tabby turned to me and shrugged.

With that resounding endorsement, I bought the movie. So much for getting my mind off all of this shit. It wasn't going to do a thing to stop me from thinking about everything. I already knew how the movie ended. Or a close approximation at least.

Annelise Michel was a young girl from a farming community in Germany. Her folks were devout Catholics. When they didn't believe their daughter's problem was epilepsy, they brought in the local priest who pronounced her possessed. Her bout of exorcism lasted for several years until she died.

I couldn't help but think about the similarities between her and Lucy. Part of me was now afraid that the authorities were crazy. Annelise could have been possessed. And maybe the priests who were working with her were not strong enough.

It was something to ask about at the Vatican school.

I turned my attention back to Lucy. She was enthralled. I watched the movie for a while, but there was so much wrong with it or flat-out stupid that I ended up watching Lucy instead. Sometimes, she was captivated. Other times, she smiled or rolled her eyes. Not once did she seem afraid. It was something, at least.

After the movie was over, I said, "What did you think of the movie?"

"It was okay. Some of it was really silly."

I nodded. "Why do you like scary movies so much?"

She shrugged. "They're fun. And I keep hoping someone will get it right."

"Wouldn't that scare you?" I would have thought there would be some sort of residual PTSD or something.

She shrugged again. "I don't know."

I motioned for her to go on her way and sunk into the sofa. Did I believe that her watching scary movies would set her up for possession again? No. If it were that simple, there would be millions of people walking around possessed. It still left me uneasy. Her parents had never mentioned her love of scary stories. All they talked about was the cat they'd had and how much Lucy had loved it. Before she killed it.

I feared her being possessed had changed her in a way no one suspected. Technically, I could have asked her. But there was something telling me not to and I wasn't sure what it was.

The next morning, I came downstairs about five. I needed some alone time, or at least as alone as I could get, and that meant Lucy watching TV with Doc while Tabby slept. No sense in driving anyone crazy but myself.

I'd made a decision right before going to sleep. I was going to try to find Will, Lucy's dad. If I had a kid, and she died yet was still around in some way, I'd want to know about it. I hoped he wouldn't want to kill me. It felt like the right thing to do. I didn't care if I got in trouble or not. It was about time I was proactive about something.

I switched on my laptop and typed Will Andersen into the search engine. I didn't know why I had stopped at social media listings before, except that I knew that while part of Lucy was alive, he'd want nothing to do with me. The search engine came up with a good number of listings for Will. But the latest thing I could find was from 2011. It was like he'd dropped off the face of the Earth.

Just for fun, I pulled my cell phone out of my pocket and searched there too. It was possible they'd added something to my computer, but my phone would be harder. Granted it'd searched before, but it had been in the middle of Arizona, and I could have missed something.

I typed his name into the phone and got the same results.

"What are they, the holy witness protection program?" I was tempted to throw something. If this kept up, I was going to need a heavy punching bag. I needed something to relieve my tension.

"What?" Lucy asked from the other side of the room.

I shook my head. "Never mind."

"Okay."

I didn't like this. Not at all. I couldn't imagine Will abandoning his entire life, his career. His ego had been too big for that. I had a big feeling that the Order had done something to him. The question was what.

Still, I was left with nothing. For now, I'd file it all away for the future. I was going to get some answers. Even if I had to force them out of somebody.

By the time Tabby came downstairs, I had mopped the kitchen floor and dusted and vacuumed the living room. It was amazing what all I could get done when I was annoyed. I probably needed to get annoyed more often...well that or be less lazy, but whatever.

"To what do I owe the extra help?" Tabby asked.

I chuckled and put the sweeper away in the closet. "I couldn't sleep and after what I found this morning, I couldn't sit still."

"Explain?" She sat at the dining room table.

"There is nothing online about Will at all past 2011."

She shrugged. "I thought you researched that before."

"Sort of. But it isn't right. There wasn't even an obituary for Lucy."

Tabby's eyes grew wide then. "That is a little odd, but maybe they're going to wait a while. That happens sometimes."

I sat beside her. "Do you really think Will could abandon all of his accolades?"

She drummed her fingers against her knee. "Okay. I'll admit that seems a little fishy."

"I just want to know what's going on." I didn't care about the Order's need-to-know basis. I needed to know.

She paused for a minute. "You know, before this, we had never heard of the markers or the Order."

"True." That in and of itself wasn't all that bothersome—mostly because anything supernatural was kind of hidden. I was used to how the church worked.

"There's one thing that would make Will abandon everything," Tabby said as she set a glass for me to dry.

"And what's that?" I asked.

"Money."

It was possible, but it didn't feel right somehow. "I'm not sure I'd buy that."

"Think about it. All of their money was tied up in that damn house. Will had nothing. Everything belonged to Tor."

The more I thought about it, the more it seemed probable. "You know, you have a point."

"Ever try searching about Blackmoor?"

I froze. Then I checked my phone again. "Not since we left it behind."

I entered Blackmoor into the search engine and waited. After a little bit, I knew why. "Hey, Tabby. Look at this."

It was an article dated roughly around the time we left for Arizona. "Fire Demolishes Historic Home."

"Maybe he did buy his freedom," I said.

"Though it's kind of nice to know that damned place is gone," she said.

"Well, as long as someone doesn't build on the site." I had visions of countless ghost movies rolling through my head.

Tabby swatted me on the arm. "You had to say that, didn't you?"

"Well, it's true. That place had enough bad for forty houses, let alone one." Hell, all it took in *Poltergeist* was a graveyard that hadn't been moved. Blackmoor had way more bad mojo.

"What do we do?" Tabby asked.

"Nothing. There isn't anything we can do. It's yet another place where the supernatural can get in."

She patted my shoulder. "Still sucks."

"Hey, there's always the chance that the fire cleansed the ground and got rid of the badness." I was trying for hopeful, but I knew it didn't even come close.

"Gotta love that wishful thinking."

"Why do you worry so much?" Lucy asked.

I glanced up from the book about the Centralia Mine Fire I'd been reading. I'd figured it would be better for me to read about something that had nothing to do with what was happening now. It wasn't working very well. "I just do. Tabby always said I think too much."

Centralia was the loose basis for the old video game and movie, "Silent Hill." Basically, the town burned up and the government allowed it because it was cheaper to cause cancer and screw the residents than to fix it and not give the government officials raises. While nothing supernatural happened there, plenty of real-life devastation occurred.

"Oh," Lucy said. "Doc thought it was something else."

I glanced at Doc. He seemed a bit tired, which wasn't normal for a ghost. It was yet more proof that he hadn't been truthful with me. Still, I wasn't sure if I had the right to know what he was doing every waking minute. If he wanted to tell me, he would.

"What's up, Doc?" I asked.

"I think you have to worry in order to keep everything together," he said.

"That's possible." I didn't think I'd ever made it two weeks without worrying about something.

"But that's not what I wanted to talk about." He adjusted his hat in his hands.

I nodded and put my book on the coffee table. "I thought not."

"I figured I might go home once you and Lucy head off," he said.

"Any reason why?"

"I forgot how much energy a kid takes. Wouldn't hurt to fully recharge. What I've been doing has been in fits and starts, and it truly isn't enough. Besides, I can't go across the pond."

"And your 'recharge' was what exactly?" I asked.

"Something you need not trouble with. But the fact now remains that I have to do it whether I like it or not."

Lucy was staring at him. "Why?"

He crouched down in front of her. "You are different, Lucy. Your soul is tied to a human. That means you can go where he goes. I'm tied to a place. And while I've gotten strong enough I can wander, there's only so far I can go."

Lucy sighed. "Will I ever see you again?"

Doc laughed. "Course. I'll be able to sense when you're close enough. Then I'll come back."

She turned to me. "How long are we going to be gone?"

I sighed. "Over six weeks."

I knew it was a while, but it couldn't be helped.

"But that's like forever."

I forced myself not to laugh. Six weeks was a while, but it wasn't that bad. I'd forgotten how kids view time. They had no ability to see how fast it truly traveled. "Look at it this way: after this, I shouldn't have to go there again."

She frowned. "I hope not."

"Come. Let's go play a game," Doc said and took her by the shoulder. They went upstairs, I supposed to the room that Tabby was making Lucy's.

I hoped I hadn't lied to the kid. Some days, I couldn't do a damn thing right.

"What are you brooding about?" Tabby asked that night in bed.

"Everything." I needed for my brain to shut down for a while, but it wouldn't comply. I needed a "sleep" button.

"I take it," Tabby said.

"It's this whole thing sucks. First, Lucy dies here, and then her body dies. Now Doc's leaving and I can't find her parents." I needed to figure out a way to let myself off the hook when shit didn't work out, but I couldn't help it. It was kind of like if I thought it should happen and I failed at getting it done, then all I'd done was waste everyone's time.

"But all of that is out of your control." Tabby untucked the blanket from around her legs.

I punched my pillow. "Doesn't seem like it."

Tabby scooted closer. "Keep in mind that if you were doing a bad job, Lucy wouldn't like you."

Isaac hopped up on the bed and took the space between Tabby and me.

"Guess with him the jury's still out," I said.

Isaac meowed.

Tabby laughed. "Tomorrow, I don't want you leaving this bed until I'm ready to get up."

"And when is that?"

"You and lack of sleep doesn't mix. If you don't start resting, you're going to drive yourself crazier than you already are." She pushed my head down onto my pillow.

"Okay. I'll stay in bed," I said.

"Besides, there might be a very good reason for you to stay in bed," she said and wiggled her eyebrows.

I playfully bopped her on the nose. "You are something, you know that?"

She grinned. "Yup."

ELEVEN
ONE THING

I DIDN'T HAVE to worry about beating her out of bed. I slept until half-past ten. I crawled out of bed and popped my back. Then, I shuffled downstairs. One of these days, I was going to fall down the stairs with all of my shuffling, but oh well.

I heard them before I saw them.

"Can we, please?" I heard Lucy ask.

"For the umpteenth time, let's wait for Jimmy," Tabby said.

I chuckled and stepped into the living room.

"Wait for me for what?" I asked.

"I made the mistake of mentioning to Doc that Blackmoor had burned down," Tabby said.

I blinked. "Why?"

"Because Lucy was talking about it and I remembered hearing something about it somewhere. And now, Lucy wants to go check it out."

The giant hole in my stomach made its presence known again. Kill me now. This was not what I wanted to wake up to. "I don't think that's a very good idea."

Lucy blinked. "Why not?"

I crouched down in front of her. "Because I'm afraid too. I

don't know what will happen, and I'd rather not risk losing you."

"I don't think that would happen," she said.

I fought not to roll my eyes. Kids always thought the bad stuff would never happen to them...again.

"Why don't we compromise?" Tabby said. "We could have Doc go and make sure everything's okay."

I watched Tabby. While I liked that idea a lot better than me taking Lucy, I worried about what would happen when a powerful spirit like Doc got around that place. Would it absorb him or would it change him? I didn't want to find out.

"Where is this place?" Doc asked.

"Down in Sorrow's Point, Virginia. Blackmoor was the huge mansion house of the coal baron who lived there," Tabby said.

He nodded.

I gritted my teeth together and rubbed my arms. I still didn't even like to think about that place. "Be careful."

Doc tipped his hat to me. "Always am."

Then, he disappeared.

"What are we going to do if this turns out to be a giant epic fail?" I asked. Maybe I'd seen too many horror films too, but my brain was full of evil demigods trying to take over the world. And, well, if it was possible for a spirit to absorb another spirit, we were all seriously fucked.

Tabby shrugged. "We'll deal with it like we always do."

Lucy shut off the TV.

Shit. I knew the kid wanted some connection to home, but that was one place I wished I could forget. Hell, I wished she would forget it. Maybe I was being too pessimistic.

Suddenly, my phone chimed. I picked it from my pocket and glanced at it. It said I had email, but the notification wasn't my usual email notification. They'd been in my phone too now. The notice contained an icon that looked suspiciously like my mark.

"I'll be back," I said.

"What's wrong?" Tabby asked.

No sense in hiding it. "The Order."

I ran upstairs and powered up the iPad. The email notification popped up immediately and I opened my inbox. It was my travel itinerary. I took a deep breath.

Mr. Holiday,

I hope to find you well. Attached is your travel itinerary, flight information, and hotel reservation. Please inform us if something does not meet your expectations. I'll look forward to meeting you—in person this time.

Fr. Martin

I was leaving in two weeks. This was actually happening. Holy shit. I took the tablet with me and ran back downstairs. I needed to get this crap printed as soon as possible.

"What's up?" Tabby asked.

"Got my deets."

She raised an eyebrow at me.

I laughed. "I'm leaving for Italy in two weeks."

Tabby grunted. "Better find that passport."

I grinned at her. "I'm on it."

Finding it wasn't as easy as I thought it was going to be. I tore my desk apart, dug through my bookcases, and even cleaned my kitchen junk drawer. It was that bad. I checked my personal safe just in case I put it there. But I had to dig that out of the closet first, and it was covered in dust. Needless to say, the passport was not in the safe.

I started digging through my desk again. I knew if I didn't find it, I'd have to file an emergency rush or something like that, and then hope it would turn up in time. After rooting around in the drawer, I grabbed a plain white envelope. My passport was inside. I glanced around the room. It looked like a tornado had passed through it.

"You know you are going to clean this up, right?" Tabby asked.

I raised up and shuffled the envelope in my hands. "I hadn't actually thought that far ahead, to be honest."

She laughed. "Give me that."

She motioned for me to hand her my passport. I did.

"Before you put it somewhere stupid, I'm making you a trip folder," she said.

I snorted. "You act like I couldn't function when you weren't around."

She stopped. "Well, I didn't mean it like that."

I took a deep breath. "Let's just start over. It isn't going to do any of us any good to get into a fight." I could so see this becoming a huge thing that could result in something neither of us wanted. It was a good thing I wasn't quite as hot-headed as usual.

"Okay," she said. She quietly walked from the room.

"You look like you need a hug," Lucy said.

I smiled at her. "I'd love one."

She wrapped her arms around me as best she could. I could feel her cold energy wash over me. It felt good in an odd sort of way. At least somebody loved me.

"You're a good kid, you know that?" I asked.

She stepped back and grinned. "Wanna see what I taught Isaac to do?"

"I'd love to."

At least it wasn't something freaky. It looked like she'd had

Tabby draw a piano keyboard. Interesting. Then she pointed to it and Isaac walked over and sat down.

He meowed.

I was reminded of the funny pet tricks that happened on late night TV.

"Now, Isaac," Lucy said.

The cat glared at her. And if I hadn't been there myself, I wouldn't have believed it.

He chirped out, "Fuck you."

I lost it. What the hell it had to do with a piano, I had no idea, but it was funny as shit. "Next thing I know, you'll have him flipping the bird."

She giggled.

"But," I said, "keep this between us. We have enough eyes already."

She put her hands on her hips and stuck out her tongue. "Uh. Duh."

I held up my hands in defeat. "Just trying to help."

I could imagine Lucy somehow making herself visible and performing this trick to some unsuspecting neighbor…and us ending up with a visit from child protective services.

"Okay," Lucy said.

"You know who is going to love that?" I asked.

"Who?"

"Doc."

She sighed. "I hope he comes back soon."

"So do I, kiddo. So do I." I wanted to reach out and pat her on the head, but her being incorporeal sucked sometimes.

As soon as Tabby came back from wherever she'd gone with my passport, she headed straight for the kitchen and I heard pots and pans on the stove. My ears pricked. This could be a very good thing.

I left Lucy playing with Isaac and went into the kitchen.

"What are you making?" I asked as I looked over the top of the pot she was stirring.

"Fudge. I want some fudge."

I wasn't about to argue with that. We'd had so much crap happen that something sweet wasn't a bad thing. "Mind if I sit here and keep you company?"

"You can if you want."

It was a lot better than being told, "Fuck, no." I was still treading lightly. I didn't want to leave for Italy with stuff being all weird between us. If I did that, I'd probably come home to an empty house. Besides, I was better than that.

"If you want, when you're done, I'll do the dishes," I said.

She shook her head and turned around. "Stop. Okay. Just stop. What I said was shitty. Now you're here acting apologetic, and I should be the one apologizing. Just let it go."

I blinked. Wow. That was different. "I'm sorry...but I still want to help."

She took a deep breath. "Okay. You can stir."

Having fudge for dinner was kind of fun. Granted, it was probably the worst thing in the world in terms of nutrition, but who cared. Heck, some of my favorite dinners as a kid were when my sister, Candy, would announce that we were having ice cream for dinner.

"Mommy never made candy for dinner," Lucy said.

"Well," Tabby said. "Your Mommy is a hell of a cook."

"Oh, I don't know, I think you're pretty damn good too," I said, thinking about her chili made my mouth water.

Tabby smiled shyly.

"When's Doc going to be back?" Lucy asked.

Tabby's face fell. "I don't know, honey."

Lucy stared at the carpet.

Had I known it was going to take this long, I wouldn't have even recommended he go and would have come up with something else to distract Lucy. Damn. "Hey," I said. "I bet he's just researching things really good."

Lucy shook her head. "It didn't feel like this before."

She wasn't the only one who was worried, but there was nothing else to do about it. If he didn't come back after a few days, I was going to have to make a trip.

"Well, all we can do is wait. Hopefully, we'll know soon," Tabby said.

"Keep in mind that Doc is crafty. He might even be cooking something up. After all, we don't know what he's into when he isn't with us." I reached down and scratched Isaac behind the ears. He meowed.

I needed to be positive for Lucy. Hell, I needed to stop coming up with worst-case scenarios about everything.

"That's true," Lucy said.

"Why don't you see if you can find another movie?" Tabby asked.

Lucy grinned and walked over to the TV.

"If he doesn't come back, I don't know if I'll be able to forgive myself," Tabby whispered.

"No sense in inviting trouble where there isn't any. Try not to freak out until we know something." Even though I said it, I didn't believe it. Most of the time, Hell was coming. It was only a matter of when.

"But it's so hard. "

I nodded. "I know."

I kept waking up all night long in the hopes that any little sound I heard was Doc coming back, but it was just the house settling. If Doc didn't show up soon, I'd have to concede defeat. Granted, I'd probably try to rescue him, but how does one rescue a ghost? I guessed I'd do what I normally did, get me a supply of holy water and hope for the best, but I wished I had something to help me out.

Around five, I gave up and went to the bathroom. When I got out, I heard someone saying my name very softly. I glanced around the bedroom, but there was nothing there. Then I peered into the hallway.

I could faintly see Doc's outline. Not good.

"Are you okay?" I asked.

"I've been better. Gotta go recharge early. I already told Lucy." I couldn't even make out his face. That's how weak he was.

"Okay. Thanks for letting me know," I said.

"Not a problem, but that isn't why I'm here."

"Okay?" He grunted. "Don't ever say I never gave you anything." A small piece of paper fluttered to the floor and Doc disappeared. I picked it up. In Doc's spidery handwriting, two items were written:

Will Andersen
Crazy88@xxorder.xx

"Holy shit."

I crept back into my bedroom and grabbed the iPad off my nightstand. I stared at Tabby for a minute to make sure I hadn't woken her up. Luckily, I hadn't. Then, I went into the hall and sat on the top step.

I fired it up, opened the browser, and loaded my personal email account. I took a deep breath and started typing.

Will,

I had to write when I found out Lucy passed. I am so very sorry. I may be able to help though. Feel free to give a call.

555-778-4213

Jimmy

It was the only thing I could do. In a way, I would have rather gotten the story about Blackmoor from Doc, but this was the right thing—even if the Order didn't view it that way. I was pretty much done with living my life inside a bubble. I should have the choice whether I wanted to contact an old client or not, dammit.

I heard a chime. I looked down. Will had replied.

Is this a joke?

I didn't know if he thought it was a dummy account or what. I didn't blame him. As far as he knew, I'd dropped off the face of the earth.

No joke. Had to jump through some hoops to get your email address.

I waited. After a few minutes, he replied again. It seemed like his sleeping patterns were matching mine.

I'll call in five.

I hopped up, almost dropped the iPad, ran into the bedroom, and grabbed my phone. Then I closed the door to the bedroom and sat on the step again. I put the tablet on the floor. In a way, it was kind of funny, sitting there, holding my phone like a school-girl waiting for the boy she liked to call. I couldn't help but be excited. There was so much that had happened.

Finally, my phone rang.

"Hello," I said.

"Jimmy."

His voice sounded gruffer than I remembered. Sadder too. "Hi, Will. I'm glad you called."

"Maybe I can get some answers for once. Those people you work for have made living hard."

I could only imagine, with the way he'd had to put himself under the radar. Hell, he was probably living under an assumed name now. I felt sorry for him. I took a breath. Might as well give him everything I had.

"What would you say if I told you that I might be able to let you talk to Lucy?"

It was silent on the other end for a long time.

"So it's true...what they told me?"

"Depending on what that was. I have no idea what they told you," I said. How could I? I hadn't been there, and it wasn't like the Order was great at giving me info.

"That you were special. That you made sure Lucy was safe."

Okay. I could live with that. It certainly didn't tell the whole story, but there was time for that now. "That's true. I'm also the keeper of her soul. For now, anyway."

He was silent again. He cleared his throat. "A few short months ago and I'd think you'd gone crazy."

"And now?" I asked.

"Now, I'm scared."

Damn. I wanted to give him a beer and tell him to relax. "If it helps at all, Lucy is her old self."

He started sobbing. "If only Tor had known."

I froze. "What are you talking about?"

He hiccuped. "Tor killed herself. She couldn't take knowing Lucy was gone."

"Jesus, Will. I'm so sorry." I felt like such a fucking heel.

He took another deep breath. "You said I could talk to her?"

It was worth a shot. I mean, I could hear her and Tabby could. I hadn't tried it with anyone else. "I'm going to try. Listening to her is a little different."

"That's okay."

"Okay, Will. Hold on." I went downstairs and found Lucy in

her usual spot in front of the TV. I grabbed the remote and muted it. Then, I put the phone on speaker.

"Lucy?" I said. "Your dad would like to talk to you."

She ran over. Her eyes sparkled. "Daddy?" She asked the phone.

"Oh, my God. Lucy, baby, it's so good to hear your voice."

She twisted her body back and forth, almost like she was about to spin around. "I miss you, Daddy."

He sobbed again. "Oh, honey, I miss you too."

She bowed her head over the phone. "Don't cry. Jimmy and Tabby are real nice."

He chuckled a little. "Yes, they are."

Then, she sauntered away. I shook my head.

"I guess she's done," I said. I would have thought that she would have wanted to talk to him longer, but I was wrong. I was wrong about a lot.

Will laughed. "She never did like talking on the phone. Can I call again sometime?"

"Any time you want. I'll be going to Italy in a couple of weeks and Lucy has to go with me. Might be a little hard, but you can call and Tabby will keep you updated."

"Jimmy?" he asked.

"Yeah?"

"Thanks."

And he hung up.

"Daddy shouldn't be so upset about Mommy. She knows I'm fine now." Lucy was perched in front of the TV again.

My eyes grew wide. "Lucy, you never cease to amaze me."

She grinned. "I know."

Then she turned the sound back on the TV with a flick of her hand. I had a feeling there was a lot I needed to learn about Lucy.

TWELVE

AWAKE

TABBY CAME DOWNSTAIRS a couple of hours later. Her hair was wet from her shower. I was watching some home improvement show on TV. Lucy and Isaac were lying on the floor in front of it.

"How are you all today?" Tabby asked.

"Okay. Doc's gone," I said. I still hated he'd drained himself so much to get details for me, but at least it seemed like Lucy was going to be better for it.

She paused. "What do you mean?"

"He came back last night to say that he was leaving for home early. Something happened that had to do with Blackmoor, but I don't know what. Only that Doc had a present for me that turned out to be Will's email address."

Tabby pulled out a chair from the dining room table and sat facing me. "So what happened?"

I shrugged. "I emailed him. He got back with me almost immediately."

Lucy turned her head. "Yeah. Daddy's upset that Mommy died."

Tabby stared at me questioningly. "I gave Will my phone

number and when he called last night, I let him speak to Lucy. Tor took her own life after Lucy's body passed away."

Tabby glanced at Lucy who had gone back to watching TV. Sometimes, I wondered if everything affected Lucy as little as it seemed, or if the kid was good at hiding it. If it was the hiding, we were going to have to try to figure out something to get her to open up. Spirit or not, it wasn't good to hold in that much stuff.

"Damn," she said.

"Yeah. So when Lucy and I go to Italy, keep my phone charged. I told Will he could call you for updates."

"Okay. That makes sense. What else do you need to do for your trip?" she asked.

"Little toiletries, a power converter. That will get me started at least. Anything else I need, I can either buy or have you ship it to me." I wasn't fretting about it too much. I'd traveled before.

"Where will you be staying?"

I shrugged. "I forget. I need to print all that and figure out how to print from the iPad."

Tabby laughed. "It can't be that hard."

I got off my ass and powered up my computer. Then I searched it. The problem was that it used a wireless printer which I did not have. Oh, well; it wasn't that big of a deal to email shit to myself.

"Well, that takes care of that," I said as I leaned back in the chair.

"What?" Tabby asked.

"I'm stuck forever emailing this stuff to myself. Or, well, until I decide to upgrade everything." And I was too lazy to do that—especially when everything was still working.

"Yay! One more thing I can get done while you're gone."

I could almost imagine her clapping her hands. Jesus. I got up and walked over to her. Then I kissed her on the head.

"Update the whole house for all I care," I said. "But don't touch my refrigerator."

She laughed. "Most men have a favorite chair. You have a refrigerator."

I shrugged. "Where else would I keep my bacon?"

She swatted me on the ass. "Go get your shower. We aren't going to stay inside all day."

Days passed. Tabby, Lucy, and I fell into a sort of routine. I helped Tabby pick paint colors for the entire house. Lucy finalized everything for her room. Doc did not come back. At least, this time, as far as I knew he was fine. There was no danger of him going home.

The night before the trip to Italy, I pulled Lucy aside. Well, sort of. I asked her to step outside with me.

She followed me into the backyard without a word.

I closed the door behind us and turned to look at her. "I know it is going to be hard to do this, but while we're in Italy, you'll have to be quiet."

"Why?" she asked. Her eyes were wide as she stared at me. It kind of gave me the heebie jeebies.

"We don't know who will or won't be able to see you or hear you. I want to draw the least amount of attention to you as possible. If it wasn't for the fact that I don't trust the safety of hotel rooms, I'd just have you stay there."

"Because of Arizona?"

I nodded. "You'll be going to class with me. It is going to be hard, but maybe you can help by watching for stuff you find unusual."

"I have to be quiet all the time?"

I shook my head. "Only when we are in class or at the school or around anyone we don't know. So in restaurants and at the hotel, everything should be fine. There's so much noise in those places that no one should notice."

"I'll miss Isaac."

I sighed. No way would I get away with taking a cat with me. He would probably have to be quarantined and everything else. "I know, but he'll be waiting for you when you get back."

She wiped at her nose. "Why didn't you want Tabby to hear this?"

"Because she worries too much." Granted, she didn't vocalize it, but I noticed the dark circles under her eyes that weren't going away. My bullshit was getting to her. Maybe me going away for a while would be a good thing.

"That's why you are letting her fix up the house?" Lucy asked.

"Yup."

Suddenly, Tabby opened the door. "What are you two doing out here?"

"Preparing for Italy," I said. She didn't need to know much more than that.

She grunted.

I held up my hands. "I swear, it was nothing bad."

She laughed. "Okay. Okay. Hurry it up, though, because I'm bored."

I laughed, then turned to Lucy. "You ready to go inside?"

"Yeah."

I herded Tabby and Lucy back into the house. Now that that was out of the way, I could concentrate on getting my shit ready to go.

The airport was crazy. Somehow, it seemed more hectic than when we went to Arizona. Maybe because Tabby wasn't there. She kept me grounded. Now, I was on my own.

"I think the gate is over there," Lucy said, pointing.

I followed her finger and there it was. Maybe it was a girl

thing. I wasn't quite ready to admit that I couldn't handle this without them, but I'd sure be a lot more bumbling about it.

"Thanks, Luce." I headed toward the gate and Lucy trotted behind me. I sat in a chair to wait and set my carry-on bag in front of the chair next to me so Lucy could sit down.

"I like airplanes," Lucy said.

I inwardly groaned. The last time had been a stressful mess for me. On our way to Arizona, she flitted about the place like a bumblebee. I kept expecting disaster to strike, but it never did. But ever since that girl at the fast food restaurant admitted to seeing Lucy, I'd been pretty uneasy.

I could only imagine the types of shit she could get into on a transatlantic flight. It could be an epic disaster.

"Lucy," I said out of the side of my mouth. "Remember not to do anything crazy on the flight, okay?"

"Uh-huh." She was looking out the window at the big plane coming in.

This was going to get interesting.

I was surprised. As far as plane rides went, Lucy mostly sat at my feet. I was thankful for the little bit of legroom. Maybe she was as nervous about it as I was. It was still nice to know that she was listening to me finally. I knew it wasn't an easy thing for her to do, but the minute I got the chance, I was going to do something special for her. I didn't know what. Hopefully, inspiration would strike.

The first thing I did when we get to the hotel room was check for bedbugs. Tabby had given me a checklist of stuff to watch and that was at the top of the list. Luckily, it didn't have any. I brought my suitcase into the main part of the room and sat on the bed to relax. All I wanted to do was sleep, but it wasn't happening yet.

"We're staying here for six weeks?" Lucy asked.

"Yep." The room was one of those hotel apartments. It had a single bed, a small table with two chairs, and a kitchenette. The bathroom was serviceable, and I was thankful we were staying in a place where there wasn't a communal bathroom for the entire floor. Those were common all over Europe. I wasn't ready to get that close with other people.

It was fancier than the room I'd had in seminary, but it wasn't luxurious either. The most important part? I could work with it.

"Where's the TV?" Lucy asked.

I looked around. She was right. I guessed either the Order didn't feel it was important or TV in a hotel room wasn't a necessity in Italy. Either way, Lucy was going to have to figure out something else to do. Shit. More and more I was starting to wish I could have left her at home. This was not going to be a fun trip for her.

"Guess we don't get one. I'm sorry," I said.

She shrugged. "It's better than staying in a car for days."

In Arizona, we'd been left without a choice as far as that went. The supposedly possessed dude had forced us into staying with him. It hadn't been pretty. Plus, since he was actively contacting and dealing with demons, it wasn't good to have Lucy there. So Tabby had warded the car and Lucy had stayed in it with Doc.

"I'll get you some books and anything else you might want tomorrow when we go out. Right now, I need to get some sleep." My eyelids were starting to close on their own and even blinking a lot wasn't stopping them.

"Okay," she said.

I lay back on the bed and my eyes slammed shut almost as soon as my head hit the pillow.

I didn't wake up until almost noon local time. Starting tomorrow, I was getting up at seven. According to my packet, the classes for Exorcismo E Preghieri Di Liberasione started at nine. I was thankful they brought me over a few days before-hand. Otherwise, this exercise would be a disaster.

It was Friday morning. Class started Monday. I crawled out of bed and went to the bathroom. When I came back, I sat down at the little table and peered outside. Lucy was sitting opposite me, very still.

"What are you looking at?" I asked.

"Nothing. Everything. It's almost as good as TV."

I chuckled. "Well, that's good. I'm going to get a shower. Then, you and I are going shopping."

She turned to me, grinning. "Okay."

It was the least I could do. Maybe I would find her some toys or games to help her occupy the time.

The first thing I did was to buy myself a cell phone and minutes to use while I was there. If I ran out of minutes, all I needed to do was buy a new SIM card. So much easier than in the States. If it wasn't for the fact that I was used to the way stuff was in America, I would consider relocating. But I wasn't sure if Europe could stand that much of me.

Lucy and I sat at a little café. I was programming Tabby's number into the phone when Lucy gasped.

I glanced up. "What?"

"He's gone now, but there was a guy that looked like Mr. Black."

I peered in all directions, but there was no one there. I sighed. Chances were it was a fluke, but I knew better than to count on stuff to go the way I wanted them too. "Well, keep your eyes open. If you see him again, let me know," I said.

"Okay."

The waiter came and took my order. I got a cappuccino and had to stop myself from calling it a crappuccino. I also ordered a breakfast pastry platter the waiter recommended. And people complained about Americans being obsessed with sugar. I wanted to laugh.

After he walked away, I stared at Lucy. "Want to talk to Tabby?"

She shook her head. "Not today."

"Okay." I shrugged. I guessed Will was right about Lucy and phones. Oh, well. I dialed Tabby's number.

"Hello?" I heard her answer.

"Hey, wanted to make sure you got my number while I'm here," I said.

"How's Lucy?" she asked.

"She's okay. No TV in the hotel room, so after breakfast, I'm going to get her some books and toys."

I heard her sigh. "This house feels too empty."

I was starting to feel sorry for her. I'd figured she'd be happy to have the house to herself. I assumed wrong yet again. "At least you know the date we'll be back."

"True. And I'm counting on it."

The last bit, the way she said it, was almost angry. Not like Tabby at all. Maybe she was having a bad day.

"I'll let you go now, looks like the guy's coming with my food." The waiter had a tray piled high.

"Okay. Love you."

"Love you, too." I hung up.

The waiter deposited my pastries in front of me. "Anything else?" he asked in halting English.

I shook my head. "No, thanks."

After a few misunderstandings, I found how to get to a bookstore that was close by. I bought Lucy several picture books and as many coloring books as I could find. They even had these cute little bird dolls and I bought her one of those too. It wasn't TV, but it was something at least.

We caught a cab back to the hotel room. As soon as we were up in the room, Lucy visibly relaxed.

"It is really hard to not say stuff," she said.

I wanted to ruffle her hair. Poor kid. This was sucking for everyone. "I know. I wish it wasn't so bad."

She nodded.

"Want me to set up your books here on the table?"

"Yeah."

I got all of her stuff organized. Then I set myself up on the bed. I'd brought along both my Bible and my copy of the Roman Ritual for the sole purpose of brushing up on information before class on Monday. I imagined that they would be referring to both often. At least that's how everything in seminary had been. No reason to think this class would be any different.

It had been quite a while since I'd read either one. And well, this was the Roman Catholic Church. They didn't do too well with unconventional. I could imagine how well me and Tabby's ritual would go over with them. The fact that it worked would only make them more pissed.

"Jimmy?" Lucy asked.

"Yeah?"

"What are we going to do if they can sense me?"

I stared at her. Dammit. She shouldn't be fretting so much. "Who?"

"The people in the class."

I sighed. And they all wondered why I worried about stuff so much? There was no guarantee; I'd already learned that. "We'll deal with that if we have to. God wouldn't have put you in my hands for no reason at all. Try not to worry."

She sighed. "Okay."

Getting to class Monday wasn't as easy as I thought. Rome had all of these twisty, turny streets with names I had no way of remembering. I thought about using the GPS on the phone, but who knew if I even had enough data for that. Best to be frugal and try something else.

I ended up getting the directions via the iPad. I honestly wasn't surprised at all to find that it worked there. So far, the Order's network seemed to be everywhere. In a way, that was unsettling, but now, it made it all a lot easier. I was going to have to start being thankful for the little things.

Lucy almost floated behind me as I rushed through the streets. Just getting to the bus stop was an adventure with the morning thrall. I hated the traffic, and unlike the States, most of it was people walking every damn place. It was complete chaos.

Eventually, I found my way to the school. It was the campus of the American Catholic University, but the exorcism class was part of their offerings. I stopped at the big map located near the elevators and found the classroom.

I hopped onto the elevator and rode silently up to the proper floor. Lucy was being good and quiet. I wished that there was something else I could do for her, but there was nothing. The only consolation was that I was probably going to be as bored as she was.

I got to the classroom with about a half an hour to spare. There were a few students waiting there already. Among the mix were priests, a nun, and one man dressed in a suit. Good to know I wasn't the only oddball in the class. Or at least the only one dressed in regular clothes. I was probably the weirdest person there no matter what.

As the minutes ticked by, more and more students crowded around. On a good note, not one of them appeared to notice Lucy. That made one less thing to worry about. And if Lucy got bored and wanted to make silly faces, she could. In fact, I would have to try to encourage it.

My imagination wandered and, suddenly, I found myself wondering what would happen if someone dropped a giant pack of fireworks in the middle of the hallway. I had to keep from smiling. These people were entirely too formal. I could almost see one of the nuns pulling out a ruler to smack me.

I mean, granted, this was a class about how to do an official exorcism, but shit, even the demons laughed. Looking at the stoic faces around me, I had to doubt if they'd even seen a demon. I, however, probably had too much experience with them at this point. I should have been given this class as soon as I was "welcomed to the family." Not now when I had already performed exorcisms, discussed evil with the Devil, and dealt with a fucked-up changeling.

Soon, a man dressed in a black robe came and opened the door with a large set of jingling keys. I chose a seat in the back. No sense in drawing more attention to myself and, well, maybe I could whisper to Lucy now and then from up there. Surely, the teacher wouldn't be looking in the back all the time?

The dude in the black robes went to the front of the class-room, and began turning on lights and firing up computers. It was kind of nice to see the Vatican was high-tech. I should have known, though. The Order certainly had plenty of fancy doo-dads.

He said something in Italian. I raised my hand. I needed to see about the translator they had said I would have. I hadn't seen him anywhere. It was possible one of the guys dressed like a businessman was my translator and hadn't been given my picture or anything.

"Che cosa?" he asked.

I cleared my throat. "What about my translator?"

"Lo non parlo inglese," he said.

I figured that meant he couldn't speak English. Great. This was going to be fun.

I pulled my iPad out from my bag and held up my hand with my index finger up. I hoped he'd recognize I was wanting him to wait. As soon as it loaded, I pulled up a translation app and had it say, "Traduttore."

The guy paused for a minute, then said, "No."

Well, at least I had confirmation. Either the Order had lied, or there was a fuck-up. I let the guy ramble on. He started passing out papers. I sent off an email to Father Martin about my lack-o-translator. Hopefully, they could get it sorted out as soon as possible.

There wasn't anything else I could do. I leaned back in the chair and let him drone. Every so often, he'd put up a picture that was supposed to be scary, but since it had no meaning to me, it didn't touch me. None of the photos were very graphic either. I had the American insensitivity in my favor.

I finally got my piece of paper passed up to me. It was in Italian. I could get it translated, but there was a big part of me wondering why should I bother. If I couldn't understand the lecture, the notes from it wouldn't help all that much.

Every so often, I thought I understood something because it was similar to Latin, but I couldn't be sure.

After class, Lucy and I hit a café nearby for lunch. I needed something good after that fiasco.

"How are you supposed to learn anything if you don't understand?" Lucy asked.

I shrugged. "My point exactly. I mean, they could have set me up with some of those headphones they use at the UN or something at least, but no. I got squat."

"Can your thing do it?" She pointed at my bag.

I blinked. "What, the iPad?"

She nodded.

"Well, it could if he was close to me, but being that far away, even if I sat in the first row, it wouldn't work. I honestly can't see them hooking him up with a microphone for one student."

Lucy twirled the ends of her hair in her fingertips. "That sucks."

"Yeah. Even worse, I know the Order isn't going to be getting back to me all that quickly. This isn't an emergency."

She sighed. "I think they need a 911 instead of this silly email thing."

I laughed. "I'll be sure to tell them that."

We went back to the hotel after that. There wasn't any reason to stay near the school. Lucy went to her coloring books. I plopped on the bed to try to translate the damn paper. I hadn't bothered to look at it too closely before.

After a bit, I realized what it was—a syllabus. But the second page made my asshole grow tight. There were, from what I could tell, a list of dates of the class, and there were a hell of a lot more than six. More like ten. Either this was yet another fuck-up or the Order only wanted me to take part of the class. I wouldn't know anything until they got off their asses to talk to me. Great.

I pulled out the phone and called Tabby. She answered on the third ring.

"Jimmy."

"Hey, how is stuff going back there?" I tried to keep my voice upbeat, but it was damn hard.

"Okay," she said, sighing. "I got everything moved out of the living room. I plan on painting that tomorrow."

"That's good." I drummed my fingers against the bed.

She was fiddling with paper or something. I could hear rustling.

"How was the first class?" she asked.

"I have no idea. The translator is nonexistent." No sense in lying about it.

"Oh, no! What did they say?"

I sighed. "No response from the Order yet. I swear. One of these days I'm getting a phone number."

She groaned. "That is if they'd answer your calls."

"Yeah. True."

"What are you going to do?"

That was the question. "Hell if I know. Even their estimate was wrong. The syllabus says ten classes."

"Maybe the Order only had a few classes they want you to go to."

I was reminded of how much Tabby and I thought alike at times. But I wasn't about to jump to conclusions. "At this point, a clerical error seems more and more possible."

"When's the next class?" she asked.

"Next week. Each class is like four hours long."

"Shit."

I heard some thumping.

"Yeah. It isn't just Lucy who is going to be going crazy from boredom." I made a couple of faces at Lucy. She smiled slightly.

"Don't be stupid. There are so many cool things to do in Italy. So do them."

I laughed. "Okay. Okay. I will."

"Good." She hung up.

She was right. Why spend the entire trip in the damn hotel room? It was time Lucy and I explored Rome.

Exploring Rome with a spirit was interesting. Everything was fine until we ran into one of those little carnivals. Lucy forgot to be quiet and kept begging me to let her ride. It was partly my fault because I had told her that restaurants were okay to talk in, and there was food at the carnival, but this was a disaster. I kept trying to motion for her to shut up, but she wasn't having it.

"No," I said quietly. If I tried to buy her a ticket, I'd be carted off to the nuthouse.

"I want to ride!"

Shit. Her scream exploded the guy's iPhone next to me. I jumped back. Glass sprayed out like mist from an aerosol can. The man dropped what was left of the phone onto the pavement. Blood ran down his face and cheek.

I stared at him, not even knowing how to ask if he needed an ambulance, but luckily none of the blood seemed to be coming from his eye. I dug in my bag and handed him a handkerchief. He nodded his thanks. A few other people came up to help.

I took a deep breath.

Car alarms were going off. Motherfuck.

Lucy's eyes went as wide as snowballs. I walked away as soon as I was sure the guy was okay.

It was best to get the hell out of Dodge. As soon as we were several streets away and no one was around, I turned and glared at Lucy. "Do you see why you have to be quiet, goddammit? What if you killed someone? Hell, you hurt that guy. Was it really worth it?"

Her eyes welled up and her chin quivered. "But I didn't mean it."

"That's all well and good, but we talked about it. You are going to have to start thinking a bit. And I'd like to know how I'm supposed to buy a ticket for a ghost?" I hadn't meant to be so damn mean about it, but she needed to learn. Being nice wasn't working.

She started to cry. "I'm not a ghost."

"Yes, you are. That's what you became when your body died." I knew it was a shitty thing to say, but I had to do it. I hunkered down, my anger gone. "Here, even more than America, you have to be careful. People believe in the supernatural in this part of the world. The last thing I want is for us to be hounded by some fanatics."

"What's that?"

"What's what?" I crossed my arms over my chest.

"The Fat. Fant. Thing?"

"A fanatic?"

She nodded.

I was going to teach her how to read as soon as I could. She needed to learn more of these words. Shit. "A person who uses their religion or a religion to hide their own crazy beliefs. Like the Jihaddists in the Middle East."

"Who are they?"

I kept forgetting that I was being faced with her six-year-old brain and it was difficult. I was getting ready to give up. "They are the guys who were behind the two thousand and one bombings in New York."

"The twin towers?"

"Yes."

She bowed her head and shuffled her feet. "Why do people have to be mean?"

I sighed. "I have no idea. Let's go back to the hotel, okay?"

"Okay."

One thing was for sure, there would be no more exploring with Lucy in Rome. It was shitty, but I couldn't risk it.

Once we got back to the hotel, Lucy was quiet. I hadn't meant to yell at her like that, but shit. What she did wasn't cool. It made me uneasy as all hell. It was one thing for electronics to stop working, but another thing entirely to blow them up and hurt someone. Six or not, she was going to have to grow up before her special powers killed us. It was almost like being the guardian of Godzilla.

"I think room service would be a good idea for dinner," I said once we were back in the room.

Lucy ignored me, sat in her chair at the table, and peered out the window.

I shrugged. She could pout all she wanted, but I was not going to give in. What she'd done had been wrong.

I never thought about having kids, and what it was like to make them atone for their actions, but now that I was having to do it, I didn't like it. It wasn't the punishment part. It was the fact that her childishness could have hurt someone way worse than she had and her little kid brain didn't fully process it. She felt worse about my damn carpet at home than she did about this—probably because she didn't get what she wanted. And that didn't sit well with me at all.

I didn't have the patience for it. I could see now why my parents had spanked me when I was a kid. Today, that would get you brought up on abuse charges, but I had to admit, corporal punishment made sense to me. Whether I felt it was right or not, it didn't matter. There was no way to spank a ghost. My hand would go right through her.

"Do you want to talk about anything?" I asked.

She turned around and glared at me. "No."

"Well, I think we should."

She rolled her eyes.

"Do you understand why I was mad?"

She shrugged.

"Don't you care that you hurt someone with your stunt?" I felt my blood pressure rising.

"But you wouldn't listen to me."

It was taking everything I had not to blow up. "I was listening fine. I just said no. You are not always going to get what you want."

She frowned. "But I never get what I want."

I sighed. "What is it you want?" I held up my hand stopping her from speaking. "And don't say to be alive because that ship has sailed. Hell, it sailed when you were no longer connected to your body. So before you speak, think about it."

She frowned some more. "Okay. I didn't want Doc to go away."

"I didn't either, but he had to recharge like you've had to before. I'm sure he'll be back."

"I wish Isaac were here."

I nodded. "If Tabby could have come, that could probably have been done, but with that class, and since this was only for me, there wasn't much I could do."

"Guess I have to get used to forever being like this," she said.

"Pretty much."

"Are you still mad at me?" she asked.

"A little, but I think you understand better now." I was calming down too. Though I was starting to think that Tabby better be the disciplinarian from now on. My tendency to get really mad wasn't a good thing.

"Can we call Tabby?"

It was a little request, and if I needed another SIM card, I would get one. "Yes, we can."

I set the phone to speaker and left it in the bathroom. I figured Lucy would want some privacy. As far as I was concerned, she could talk to Tabby as long as she wanted.

"Go ahead in. I have it dialing. Just let me know when you're done," I said to Lucy.

She hopped off her chair and went into the bathroom. The door closed by itself behind her. It still took some getting used to, seeing stuff like that. It was the stuff of horror films. But it was my life. Good thing I'd never been the type of person who got easily scared.

I loaded the iPad to see if there was any response to the email. Unfortunately, there was none. At least the next class wasn't until the following Monday so there was time for them to rectify the problem. But the longer I was here, the more I had a bad feeling about the whole thing.

THIRTEEN

ON THE DARK SIDE

THE NEXT MORNING, I woke up grumpy. Maybe it was the way stuff had turned out the day before or maybe it was the fact that the class was four weeks longer than I was told it would be. Hell, grumpy didn't even cover it. I was a bear.

Even Lucy wasn't as opaque as she'd been the day before. Most likely, it was because she'd had that fit. I got all my stuff together and paused by the door. "You coming?"

"Where are you going?" Lucy asked.

"Library."

She got off her chair and followed me out. It probably wasn't a great idea taking her anywhere now, but I couldn't leave her by herself either.

On the way to the library, I simply watched the people meandering around the sidewalks. I was heading to the NAC or the North American College. I knew it had a good library and I hoped to read up on some stuff about exorcism I hadn't been able to find back in the States.

The building was massive, but you'd never have known it was a college by looking at the outside of it. All that betrayed its purpose was a small bronze plaque beside the front door.

As soon as we walked inside, Lucy moved slower.

"What's wrong?" I whispered from the corner of my mouth.

"Feels funny here," she said.

I looked around, but nothing seemed amiss to me. I felt nothing, but she was a heck of a lot more sensitive than I was, so I left it at that. There was no sense in getting caught talking to thin air.

Luckily, since this was an American college, the signs were written both in English and Italian, so I had no trouble at all finding the library. The biggest advantage? This library had the largest number of English books in Italy. If I couldn't find what I was looking for here, it probably didn't exist.

I walked up to the circulation desk. "Where can I find the books on exorcism?"

She was this older lady who looked like she could have been my grandma. I could only assume that she was a nun. While a lot of the nuns in Italy still wore habits, not all of them did. The church, it was changing.

"Are you in the class?" she asked.

I nodded.

"Wait right here. I'll get them." She slowly got up from her chair, grabbed a little cart, and left. I couldn't help but be reminded of the library at Sorrow's Point where the only one who had the balls to tell the secrets of Blackmoor was that old librarian. At least this one didn't look at me with disdain or anything. But she worked for the church too. A priest wasn't anything out of the ordinary.

Lucy stood quietly beside me. For that, I was grateful.

After a few minutes, the librarian came back with a full cart.

"This is all we have. Some of it is in Italian, but if you need a translation, I can help you find someone who would be willing to translate for you."

I smiled. "Thank you so much for the help."

She smiled back at me and went behind the desk. I took the little cart and rolled it over to a large study table.

"I wish Doc was here," Lucy whispered.

I pulled out a chair slightly so she could crawl up and sit down.

Then I grabbed the first book.

I sat there for hours reading. It was a shame that I couldn't check out the books to take back to the hotel, but I understood why I. Some of those texts were irreplaceable. Every book was covered in a special plastic cover that I was sure was paper-friendly. A few of the books had been rebound. But I knew the rare books were probably in a vault somewhere and my grubby mitts wouldn't be allowed anywhere near them.

Instead, I took as many notes as I could on the iPad. In a way, scanning would have been better, but I didn't want to mess up the bindings any worse than they already were. There were specific mentions of different rituals and strange items that appeared during exorcisms. Even mention of cases with famous people. It was fascinating. Almost like being in a guarded society for once.

I had to hand it to Lucy. She sat there and kept quiet. Every time I'd look at her out of the corner of my eye, she was simply watching the people that walked by. I could handle that. Maybe the talk yesterday had helped.

Finally, I made it through the last book written in English and popped my back.

"You ready to go?" I whispered.

She nodded.

I loaded the books back on the cart and I wheeled them up to the desk.

"Thanks," I said to the librarian. This was a different one from this morning, younger.

She smiled and took the cart. I led Lucy out of the building and into a little sandwich shop. I hadn't noticed how hungry I was until I walked in.

"Are we going to do that again tomorrow?" Lucy asked.

We were back home in the hotel room. I'd been smart and ordered an extra sandwich so I wouldn't have to go back out. It was currently sitting over the top of a cup with some ice in it to keep it cool.

I stared at her. "No. That was probably a one-time thing."

"Good."

This was the first time I'd seen her react so strongly about a place. Not a good sign.

"What's wrong?" I asked.

She shivered. "I don't know. There's just something I don't like about that place."

"Is where the class is okay?"

She nodded.

"Okay. Well, I'll do my best not to go back to the other place." And since I didn't know what was in the Italian books, there was no way I would miss it. I had enough notes to last me for a while. Worse came to worst, I could always see if the Order had their own library.

She smiled.

Later that night, I jerked awake. I glanced up and there was a long black shadow on the wall. It was deeper than the shadows I had been used to seeing from the window. Every so often, it would move slightly. Herky-jerky, like a stutter. I looked around the room, but there was nothing I saw that could be causing the shadow.

"What the fuck is that?" I asked Lucy.

Lucy stared at the shadow and had her back pressed into her chair. Her being scared was not good at all.

"I told you I didn't like that place." She slowly moved her head and stared at me in the dark. Then she shook her head.

I crept out of bed. The shadow moved toward me. Looming, almost as if it wanted to swallow me. I glared at it for a moment then pointed with my hand—showing that on the inside of my wrist I had the mark. "Go. You have not been invited."

The ripples of magic from my voice stilled the air and the shadow somehow disintegrated.

I exhaled slowly. "Well, that was interesting."

"I think there are entities or whatever you want to call them here. Stuff that is way stronger than back home."

She wasn't kidding. "Sure seems that way."

"Are you doing to tell somebody?" she asked.

I shrugged. "Who? The annoying email monster?"

Lucy giggled.

"That reminds me." I grabbed the iPad and powered it up. After a little, the email notification popped up. I got excited. Maybe something would get done at last.

Mr. Holiday,

We hope that you find Rome a fascinating place. I'm sure that the class is most helpful. Please, feel free to contact me with any problems.

Fr. Joseph Hardy

"You've got to be shitting me!" I almost threw the damn thing across the room. Again, this was proof that the left didn't know what the right was doing and it was bullshit. Then they wondered why people had such high stress levels.

I calmly turned off the tablet and set it on the nightstand and went back to sleep. There was nothing else for me to do.

I goofed off the rest of the week. I knew I shouldn't have, but if they didn't care, why should I? Besides, the one time when I tried to be proactive, I ended up with something in my room—so there.

Lucy and I went a lot of places: the Sistine Chapel, the Leaning Tower of Pisa, a real Italian pizzeria. I tried to make sure that everywhere we went, there was something she could do. I was hoping that would stave off any desire to make more scenes and maybe, she learned her lesson.

We had no more incidences like at the NAC. The more imaginative part of my brain took that as a sign. The problem was, I still didn't know of what.

The tone of the day had been gradually going downhill. I didn't have to ask why—the class was tomorrow. I was not looking forward to it.

Every so often, I'd pull up my email, but there was nothing. I didn't relish sitting for another four hours looking at pictures and not having subtitles. I was going to recommend that either they make an American version of the class, or make sure every marker being sent to learn at the exorcism school have a crash course in Italian.

It was no wonder the people that moved to the US from other countries tried to learn some of the language before they moved. I couldn't imagine much worse than this and I at least knew some Latin.

"You should get Tabby a present," Lucy said out of the blue.

I looked up at her. "What type of gift?"

She shrugged. "Something pretty."

I nodded. "We'll have to go tomorrow. People are in church today."

"Why? Because they are in church? Why can't we shop?" she asked.

"People are more religious here. Restaurants and grocery stores close early on Sundays and open late. Most people go to church here."

"Oh."

"We'll have better luck finding her something after class."

She sighed. "Okay."

"Don't feel bad. I'm getting bored too."

"Those people need to treat you better."

"Who?" I was lost.

"Your bosses."

"The Order?"

She nodded.

"Yeah, I agree. Believe me. Next time I actually get to talk to someone, I'm getting a phone number." And anything else I could get my hands on.

"You'd better or Tabby is going to kill you."

I laughed. Sadly, she was probably right.

The next morning, I dutifully packed my bag and headed off to class, but I didn't like it. There was some small part of me that hoped that I was wrong and that there would be a translator waiting for me. That would be a nice change of pace. But I knew I was pressing my luck.

Lucy followed me through the Regina Ateneo Pontificio Regina Apostolarum to the classroom. This time, I arrived late enough that the door was already open. I chose the chair I had sat in at the last class. I saw no translator, or any teacher for that matter. At least I wasn't late.

I took my Bible and my Roman Ritual out of my bag and laid them on the table along with my iPad. I watched everyone that came in carefully—just in case they could be my translator–but there was no one different.

Finally, someone with some purpose entered into the room and went to the lectern. He wasn't the same guy as last time. Maybe each class was going to have a different teacher. In a way, that was kind of nice...of course, if I could understand them.

He started firing off in rapid-fire Italian. Soon, I lost interest. Lucy was sitting on the floor next to me. She even rolled her eyes and I had to force myself not to doze off.

As the guy in front droned on and on, I felt my attention slip. I didn't care anymore.

I doodled on pieces of paper and made origami animals out of my notebook for Lucy. I even had the animals stage a mock battle on the chair next to me. Granted it was stupid, but it was also kind of fun. Better than staring at the wall anyway.

"And Mr. Pig-bottom had to go away forever and ever," I whispered.

Suddenly, I realized the room had gotten very quiet. I glanced up and the teacher was glaring at me from his lectern at the bottom of the classroom. Then he launched back into class. I shrugged. I couldn't have been that distracting. His voice was damn loud. One of the other students must have complained or something. Oh well.

I stared down at Lucy. She seemed more bored than ever. I felt for her. I did. This trip had sucked donkey dicks and there wasn't a damn thing I could do about it. Since the paper animals were out, I needed to find something else to entertain her. Too bad this wasn't a day when they could dim the lights. I could have done shadow puppets.

"No, after the other disaster, we don't need any more of those," I mumbled.

The teacher continued to drone on and on. It seemed like everyone but me was paying attention. Good for them.

Finally, a light-halo went off in my head. I grabbed the Bible and the Roman Ritual and placed them so that the pages were facing each other roughly six-inches apart. Then, I grabbed some pages and put my thumbs between them in each book. I now had hand puppets. Heh.

Lucy looked up and stared—ready to watch.

I started moving the "mouths" along with Mr. Blowhard at the front of the class. Yeah, technically what I was doing was definitely one hell of a no-no, but I didn't care anymore. Entertaining Lucy was a lot more fun.

The teacher put on a bit of audio that was again some other dude speaking in Italian. I continued with my "puppets." Lucy was trying very hard not to laugh.

And then, her eyes got as wide as dinner plates. I followed her gaze—into the eyes of Mr. Blowhard.

Oh, shit. I'd done it now.

"Cio che nel mondo pensi che stai facendo?"

"What?" I asked.

His face turned red and his eyes seemed like they were going to pop right out of his head.

"Ive!" he pointed with his finger toward the entrance to the classroom. I didn't stall. I didn't even need a translation for that. I showed all my shit into my bag and ran out of the room.

"I am so fucked," I said as I rushed down the hall.

Lucy giggled as we walked from the building. "Good one, Grace."

"Where did you hear that?"

"TV."

I laughed. "Well, seeing that I'm probably kicked out of the Order, want to get some ice cream?"

"Yeah!"

At least that was something both of us could use to put smiles on our faces.

I'll admit it. That ice cream tasted better than anything I'd had in a long time. Maybe it was because I was my own man again? Or it could have been that it was Italian and didn't have the crappy chemicals that get added to everything in the US.

None of that mattered though. Now, I had more problems than I knew what to do with. We went back to the hotel. I started pacing and shit. I wasn't so stupid as to think I'd be given another chance. Old Blowhard would make sure of that. I would be damn lucky if I got to keep my job. The old resume was going to need a brush-up.

My phone rang. It was a number I did not recognize. Maybe it would be a wrong number. It was possible. Especially since this wasn't my regular phone.

"Hello?"

"Mr. Holiday. I don't think I have to tell you how disappointed we are in you." He had the tone of an elementary school principal. It was ridiculous. I'd long since outgrown that, no matter how childish I seemed.

"That's a bit of the pot and the kettle, isn't it?" I couldn't help it. I was tired of holding back.

"I do not understand," he said.

"It doesn't matter. But maybe this wouldn't have happened if I'd been given the translator I'd been promised." It was bullshit and I wasn't going to take flack for that. If he wanted to yell at me about what I'd done in the class, fine, but it wasn't all me either.

He was quiet for a minute. I suspected this was Martin again, but I wasn't totally sure. I'd only heard his voice once, so it wasn't like I was all that familiar with it. It didn't matter who it was, so long as they were from the Order.

"According to my notes, you refused the translator," he said.

"What? I can tell you that's a damn lie. Why would I put

myself through four-hour classes of sitting and twiddling my thumbs for nothing?" They sure knew how to piss me off about right.

He sighed. "It is certainly something to look into. For now, you'll return to America. I will look into this personally."

"Oh, and Martin?" I was pretty damn sure it was him now.

"Yes?"

"I want a phone number where I can reach you. Now. No more of this email bullshit." I wasn't about to let him get away with it this time.

He cleared his throat and rattled off the number. "Yes, with this new development, this is probably best."

"How long do I have before I'm fired?" I figured I might as well ask. It wasn't like being an exorcist offered unemployment.

"I don't know. I honestly don't know," he said.

He hung up then. I finished pacing. I didn't even have the chance to tell Tabby about what had happened. One thing was sure—there was too much to do. My life was, once again, a mess. I was starting to think I liked it that way. Otherwise, I would be quiet and wouldn't cause myself any more undue chaos.

I used the iPad to buy a ridiculously expensive ticket back to the US. Almost three thousand dollars, but it couldn't be helped. At least I'd been smart enough to bring the Order's card along with my own. If I was kicked out of the markers, or at least the organization, the paycheck would be gone and I'd have to jump through some serious hoops. There was no way I was going to ask Tabby to get a job. I was still able to work. She'd go back to school. She needed to finish anyway.

The flight was set to leave at ten in the evening local time. I knew I'd better get out of the hotel before anything else was added to the bill. Lucy and I left the room and I checked out. Then, we went to a restaurant to get something to eat so I wouldn't have to shell out any money on the plane. Besides, plane food kind of sucked.

Once we were seated, I called Tabby.

"Hello?" she asked.

"Hey, can you pick me up at the airport tomorrow?"

"Wait. What?" There was some sort of deepness emanating from her voice I hadn't heard before.

Maybe she had a cold. I sighed. "It's a long story. Can you do it?"

"Sure. What time?"

"I think I should be landing in Charleston about two. I've got a layover in NYC."

"Okay. Keep me posted," she said.

"Will do."

I didn't bother to mention that she had my cell phone, but surely someone or somewhere at JFK would let me send a text. A payphone was probably nonexistent. I hadn't seen one of those in years.

"What are you going to do now?" Lucy asked when I hung up the phone.

"Probably hold my asshole tight. I'll have to find a job if they fire me. It's not like I can sue an organization that isn't supposed to exist. They aren't even part of the Vatican." I set my phone down on the table. It was the truth. Even if I had to take a job at a restaurant or something, that was what I was going to have to do.

"Maybe Doc will be back when we get home," Lucy said.

"I hope so. He's good at ferreting out information." And maybe he could figure out who had sabotaged me in the Order. Fucker.

I ate quickly, and then called a cab. I knew getting through customs was going to take a while. This wasn't like America. Here, they made you open everything. Thank God the only things I'd bought were some stuff for Lucy. Never did get around to buying Tabby something.

Still, it wasn't my fault that I didn't learn anything from the class. Hopefully, Father Martin would be able to find out what had happened and be able to do something about it. Then, at least, I could maybe save my job.

I wasn't denying that I shouldn't have done what I'd done. I'd been stupid. An adult would have sat there quietly and let the class go. I didn't have the attention span for that. I knew I could be out doing something constructive instead of wasting my time. I'd wanted the class originally, but now that I knew it was worthless, I was wondering why the Order didn't have their own class. It was odd.

I'd already performed exorcisms. Granted they weren't exactly successful, but the experienced exorcists couldn't swear theirs would be either. Nobody could.

I hunkered down in the security line to wait. It was going to be a long flight.

As I wandered through the JFK airport, I found myself humming the old Quiet Riot song, *Bang Your Head*. It fit my mood. Though it was probably ironic that an exorcist listened to rock music, but I was so far off the grid at this point it didn't matter.

Hell, I had a witch as a sidekick—though she'd probably kick my ass for calling her that, but oh well. It wouldn't be the first time. In fact, she was kind of sexy when she got angry. I'd been away from her for too long.

Was someone on the inside of the Order working with Big Red or his offspring? What had happened in Rome was too ridiculous. I could see, sure, no translator for the first class. But for someone to mark down that I said I didn't need one? Bullshit.

Especially when I had filled out the form in pen. They had had to make an effort to change it.

There was a stink in the woodpile and I had to figure out what it was.

By the time I landed in Charleston, I was sleeping on my feet. Hell, if it hadn't been for Lucy guiding me where to go, I would have gotten lost for sure. I probably should have tried harder to sleep on the flight, but I couldn't stop thinking about it all. It was way worse than usual.

I spotted Tabby in baggage claim. I ran over and picked her up off her feet. Shit, it was good to see her. Tired or not, I needed to feel her.

She pulled away from me a little. Maybe I'd grabbed her too hard.

"Damn," she said.

I kissed her. "What can I say? I missed you."

Her face stilled, but then she laughed. "Obviously."

I put her down.

"Are you hungry?" she asked. "I could stop somewhere on the way home to get something to eat."

"Nah. All I want is the bed. Food comes later."

Tabby grunted. "I thought you would have missed me more than that."

Kind of odd for her to say that with the way she'd acted a bit ago, but whatever. I laughed. "More than you'll ever know."

She wandered over to the luggage carousel and got my bag. Then we were on our way.

Truth was, I fell asleep in the car. I didn't even make it out of the parking lot. Lucy had been saying something about Doc, and I was out. If I hadn't been so tired, I would have felt bad about it.

It was a bump that woke me up. Tabby was still driving on the interstate.

"Everything okay?" I asked.

"Just a pothole."

She was staring intently at the road. She didn't even turn her head to look at me.

"Ahh," I said.

"You were snoring really loud," Lucy said from the back seat.

I laughed. "Proof as to how tired I was."

"Still sleepy, or do you want food?" Tabby asked.

"Food would be good, but let's wait till we're closer to home." I wanted to get to the point where I didn't have to travel for a while.

"I can do that," she said. "Now, want to explain what's going on?"

I took a deep breath. "I may or may not be fired."

She made a weird noise that was almost the cross between one of Isaac's sounds and a groan. "Okay…I'm confused already. You either are, or you aren't."

"It's complicated." As if nothing wasn't complicated with me, but whatever.

"Obviously."

I sighed. "Apparently, some joker wrote down that I had refused the interpreter, which I didn't. So that's part of it. The puppets were all me."

"The what?" Her eyes grew wide and the corners of her mouth were moving up and down like she was trying not to laugh.

Lucy giggled.

Tabby might as well let it rip. I still thought it was funny.

"These classes were like four hours long," I said. "Think about it. The dude was too far away for the translation thing on the tablet to work, so here's Lucy and me with four hours of droning. Every so often, the teacher would display a picture or play an audio clip, but other than that, it was like watching a foreign film without subtitles."

"Okay. But puppets?" Tabby asked.

I chuckled. "It started out as doodling in my notebook. And, well, you can only do that for so long. Then, I made all these origami animals and was putting on a little play for Lucy when it all got quiet. I kind of got bawled out for being loud. I don't think he could see the animals. Someone had to have ratted me out."

"Oh, Jimmy." She snickered.

"It gets worse."

I watched her roll her eyes.

"How?" she asked.

Lucy laughed.

"Well, when the class got back to normal, I knew I couldn't do animals again, so I pretended my Bible and the Roman Ritual were puppets."

She laughed. Hard. "Oh, Jimmy. You didn't."

"Yep. Soon, Mr. Blowhard had book equivalents. I was totally doing the whole Parkay vs. butter routine. Lucy found it hilarious. I'm not sure how the teacher found out. Could be he noticed something odd from my desk. It wasn't long before he came up there and caught me making my little tableau."

Tabby snorted.

"Needless to say, he kicked me out of class. When I got back to the hotel, I got the phone call that my job was in jeopardy."

"I'm honestly not surprised and neither are you." She laughed again. "So now what?"

I shrugged. "Father Martin is going to see who's been messing with my file. In the meantime, I go home. Don't know anything else yet."

"When will you know?"

I shook my head. "No idea."

FOURTEEN

LIVIN' ON A PRAYER

AS SOON AS we stepped into the house, Isaac leaped into my arms. I was more used to him reacting this way with Tabby, but I guessed he missed me.

I chuckled. "It's good to see you too, buddy."

He meowed, then hopped down. I took a look at the living room. It was brighter with the paler white on the walls. The sofa and my chair had green slipcovers on them. The carpet was still the same old tan.

"You've been busy," I said to Tabby.

She shrugged. "Kind of. Got Lucy's room done, too."

"Really?" Lucy asked.

"Uh-huh," Tabby replied, smiling down at Lucy.

Lucy took off up the stairs. I shook my head.

"Any problem with her while you were gone?" Tabby asked.

I nodded. "Some, but I'll tell you about it later."

Lucy came back downstairs and gave Tabby a huge hug.

"Thank you. Thank you. Thank you!" Lucy buried her head into Tabby's legs.

"I take it she likes it?" I asked.

Tabby laughed. "Now, you don't have to stay all the way down here at night. You can watch TV in your room."

Lucy appeared to hug her harder, and then let go.

Isaac walked over, looked up at Lucy, and meowed at her. She jumped down on the floor and hugged him too.

Then, she jumped up. "Jimmy, come, you gotta see it!"

I laughed. "Okay.

She led me upstairs. The kid wasn't even walking up the stairs in any fashion. She floated above them as quickly as she could. No way could I keep up with her, but it was damn cute.

She led me down the hallway and into her new room. The walls were a pale lavender color. There was a twin bed with a white bedspread and purple flowers on it. A painting of a unicorn was on the wall. In the corner of the room was a TV on a stand.

Lucy was grinning so hard, if she hadn't been a spirit, I would have been afraid that her mouth would split open.

It was so good to be home.

Later that night, after we'd gone to bed, Tabby brought up the thing I'd been trying to avoid again.

"No, seriously. What happened to Lucy?" she asked.

I sighed. I knew this was one of those cases where Tabby wasn't going to let up. No sense in dragging it out further. She needed to know anyway. "This one day after we'd gone to class or the library or something, we were exploring around town. Well, we came upon this little carnival and it had a fun kid's ride. Lucy wanted to ride and when I told her no, she threw a fit."

Tabby shrugged. "Well, a tantrum was bound to happen."

I shook my head. I let my brain wander back to the memory. I still felt chills from it. "Not like this. She screamed so loud that regular people heard it. The screen on this dude's iPhone cracked. Busted part of his face. It was like nothing I'd ever seen, but that wasn't the worst part."

Tabby waited. She seemed like she was trying not to object.

"She couldn't understand what she did was wrong. It took me several times before I got her to understand that she actually hurt someone."

Tabby pursed her lips together. "I'm not sure I'd call that odd."

I shrugged. "You kind of had to be there."

"Guess so."

After that, I arranged my pillow and lay down to get to sleep. I couldn't shake the feeling that something worse was coming and Lucy might or might not be part of it.

The next morning, the house was quiet. I stretched. It felt so good to be in my own bed. Nothing against Italy, but it was too formal. Here, I could run around in fuzzy slippers and most people wouldn't care. There, well, they probably wouldn't care, but I'd get more odd looks.

I got up and went downstairs. Tabby, Lucy, and Isaac were watching TV.

"I take it no phone calls?" I asked.

"Not yet," Tabby said.

"Doc said he'd be back tomorrow," Lucy said suddenly.

I stared at her for a minute. Her eyes were glued to the TV. I guessed spirits had their own sort of communication system or something. She was so focused on the TV that I didn't bother asking her. It wasn't like I had to know right now. Probably best I didn't in this case. It was something a demon could possibly exploit.

"Looks like everything will be mostly back to normal," I mumbled.

I plopped on the couch next to Tabby.

"Did Will call while we were gone?" I asked.

"A couple of times," Tabby said. "I told him what I knew at the time."

I nodded. "Makes sense. Hopefully, the next time he calls, I won't have to lie about why we're back."

Tabby sighed. "I think you worry too much."

"Probably."

Truth was, I was worrying more than she thought. Lucy acting the way she had in Italy had made me uneasy. Then, the fits. Me almost getting fired. Now, Tabby acting a little weird. It was too fucking coincidental. If I had to bet, all of this was coming from the one person I'd pissed off recently and that would be the being known as Leviathan. The fact that he could have a goon in the Order was pretty damn scary.

And then, there was something about me that Big Red wanted. What it was, I didn't know, but it evidently was important enough for the Devil and his children to try to do something to me to get it. And Asmodeus had to have been the first demon to recognize it. Too bad; I'd gotten him in trouble twice. But I did wonder if I was going to have to beat my way through all of the Devil's children. That would royally suck.

The way things stood, I was at a loss. All that was left was for me to wait on Father Martin and hope for the best. If I had any luck at all, it wouldn't be long.

"Jimmy. Lunch," Tabby said from the kitchen.

I got up from the sofa and went into the kitchen.

"Well, you look cheery," she said.

I shrugged. "Just worried."

She handed me a plate. "I know."

"I think the biggest problem is the not knowing." Granted,

that could be for anything, but I wasn't the most patient person in the world.

She pulled out a chair at the kitchen table and made me sit down. "I would tell you not to worry, but I know it's pointless."

I took a bite of my sandwich. "Could be worse, I guess."

"Exactly. It can always be worse."

I finished my grilled cheese in silence. Tabby looked at me every so often. I could tell I was worrying her, but I couldn't stop. I wasn't going to calm down until I knew for sure what I had to do next.

Would it be so bad if I was fired? To me, I would figure out how to muddle through somehow. I very well could be fired by the Order, but not fired by God. That left a lump in my stomach. Could I turn my back on that? I'd be, what, a rogue exorcist? Maybe? I'd still have to have a full-time job. Just the thought of charging for my services made me sick to my stomach.

"Stupid," Tabby said suddenly.

"What?"

"This mooning. There is no need to invite problems."

I sighed. She was right. All the dwelling I'd been doing was wasting my time. "Okay. Distract me. What should we do instead?"

"Kill a llama? How should I know?" She stole my last bite of sandwich and popped it into her mouth.

I laughed. "Come on. Let's go sit outside. Maybe Lucy would like some sun."

"Now that sounds like the best idea you've had all day."

The sun was so bright that I wished I'd brought out my sunglasses, but I was too lazy to go back inside to get them. The patented "hand shield" would have to do.

Lucy and Isaac were playing in the grass. He'd chase a bug

and leap. Lucy would leap behind him and then it would start all over again.

"Who would have thought that a cat and a spirit would play their own version of leapfrog?" I asked.

"What can I say? It's Isaac," Tabby said.

I laughed. "He's special all right."

"What are you going to do when he starts talking?" I heard a deep voice ask.

I jumped and looked behind me. Doc laughed. Lucy ran over and gave Doc a huge hug. I felt the stress leave my shoulders. Even I had to admit I felt more relaxed that he was back.

"How is everything?" he asked.

I exhaled. "Screwed up. Like usual."

He laughed. "Anything I can do to fix it?"

I shook my head. "Not right now. Maybe when we know more."

He nodded, then stared down at Lucy. "I have a feeling you've been busy."

She looked up at him and grinned. "I scared Jimmy."

He stared at her wide-eyed for a moment. "Well, come over here and tell me all about it."

I watched him walk into the shade and sit on the ground. Lucy followed suit.

I wondered if the sunlight depleted his energy or something, but I didn't ask. He had his own activities to do with Lucy. My silly questions could wait.

Tabby took a deep breath. "Why do I have a feeling we're gearing up for something big?"

"Because we usually are and you are usually right."

"I'm going to hold you to that," she said, grinning.

I laughed. "I didn't say all the time."

She snorted.

Isaac walked over and hopped up into her lap. He fidgeted for a minute before settling down.

"Any idea what's coming besides insanity?"

She shrugged. "You were abducted by a demon and kicked out of exorcism school. I don't even want to imagine what the third could be."

"Bad crap does always come in threes. I don't know how you put up with me," I said.

"Because I love you, ya goof."

I checked the iPad throughout the day, but there were no emails. In a way, that was good because it meant that I hadn't been fired —yet. But I would have rather had all of this resolved. My mind kept going back to the possible sabotage and then to Leviathan. Could he really have a minion in the Order? Or was it a simple clerical mistake that had me overreacting? If I learned anything from all of this it was that I had to always expect the worst. And if it came out better, so be it.

"I'm starting to think that you are going to drive yourself into the hospital with all of this," Tabby said.

I was sitting at my desk in front of my computer. My tablet was off to the side, sitting there, calling to me. I sighed. "I'm not trying to drive you crazy too, you know?"

"It isn't me you're driving crazy; it's yourself."

I could have tried to argue about it, but there wasn't any point. I was more nervous than I'd been when I got kicked out of the church. And that was saying something. "Can't you do a spell or something to make this all go faster?"

She laughed. "If I had that type of power, I'd already have my Ph.D. and not be on leave of absence, remember?"

"Oh, yeah." One of these days, I was going to figure out how to increase her power. Somehow.

She patted me on the arm. "One of these days you'll get it. I have faith in you."

"I'm glad somebody does." I sure as hell was starting to doubt myself.

She growled. "Jesus Christ. Stop with all the whining already."

I shut up. She had a point. I'd been so wrapped up in worrying that all I'd done was be a pain in the ass. It was time to get my butt in gear.

"I'm sorry," I said. "I promise to do better."

She grunted. "No sense in making a promise you can't keep. Just get your shit together and go back to being you."

I saluted her. "Yes, ma'am."

FIFTEEN
GONE WITH THE SIN

AT ONE TIME, night was a time of relaxation and quiet. Ever since Sorrow's Point, I kept expecting something to happen as soon as the sun went down. I don't know what you'd call it exactly, PTSD maybe. But I knew it was an irrational fear. Lots of things had happened in the daylight too. Yet not being able to see the horrors somehow made it worse. I liked seeing the monsters I had to fight. It gave me a little bit of knowledge as to what I had to face.

I rolled over and stared at the back of Tabby's head. At least someone was getting some sleep. I gave up and raised myself to a sitting position. The TV was turned to some cooking show. I crawled out of bed and went downstairs. There was no light. Lucy was in her room now, so there was no reason for the downstairs TV to be on, but it felt lonely. I'd gotten used to seeing her whenever I got up when everyone else was asleep.

I flipped on the light, walked over, and started booting up my computer. Then, I started searching for information about Leviathan.

I should have done it sooner, but I'd had my head up my ass. According to the search engine, Leviathan was the demon of envy. I paused to let that sink in. Was I envious of anyone? Not really. Not any more than the average person. So that left another hole. Back to why he would target me.

It wouldn't surprise me if he hadn't been given the task of pestering me. I was going to wind up fighting all of Big Red's offspring before this was finished. Though I figured the seemingly benevolent version of the Devil I'd been shown was gone too. I hadn't fallen for the trap. So that meant a different type of attack.

The problem was I had no idea what type of attack it would be. Be prepared. Check.

And what was going on with Lucy? Intuitively, I'd been afraid that she's kept some of the badness of the being that had possessed her. But now? I didn't know if it was that or what. The Devil, he'd said she'd made a pact with him. If it wasn't for Doc's confirmation, I would have said he'd lied to me. Now, I was worried about whether it was what the pact entailed that he lied about.

Unless Lucy fessed up to something different, I couldn't know that either. Still, she was changing and not for the better.

My life was shit.

The next morning, Doc seemed fidgety. Every time I glanced over at him, he was fiddling with his hands or bouncing his knee. Something was clearly going on.

Finally, it was Tabby who asked. "Okay. I've had enough," she said. "What's going on, Doc?"

He shook his head. "Don't know for sure. I can feel the badness setting in."

"Does it have to do with Blackmoor?" I asked.

"Nah. That place is a burned-out shell."

That was a relief at least. One less thing to have nightmares about.

"Where'd you get the number for Lucy's dad?" Tabby asked.

Doc laughed. "Real estate office. There was a file on his desk, so...well...you know."

Lucy spun around from the TV to look at us. "How is Daddy?"

"Last time I talked to him, he was okay. Kind of sad, but he's all right," Tabby said.

Lucy nodded, then turned back to the TV.

Her not liking the telephone much was kind of interesting. The only person she'd asked to speak to had been Tabby. She'd barely spoken to her father for five minutes on it.

Doc was scowling. That wasn't a good sign. Every so often, he'd look at Lucy and shake his head.

I motioned for him to follow me and I went outside. I closed the door behind Doc and walked under the tree in the backyard so we could have a little privacy.

"What you want me out here for?" Doc asked.

"Lucy. What the hell is wrong with her?"

He stared at the ground and shook his head. "I don't think there's anything wrong with her per se. She didn't live long enough to be human."

I raised my eyebrow. "What?"

"Do you know how long she was possessed?" he asked.

I exhaled slowly. "Months. Not sure exactly, but I know she was sick for a long time."

"And her age at the time of the exorcism?"

"Six." It didn't escape me that part of her problem was that she was going to be like that little vampire girl in those Anne Rice books. Forever a child, but the brain of someone much older. There were only a certain number of years before it would really hit home.

"To a child, a few days can seem like forever. Her last tie to her old life went away when it died," Doc said.

I blinked. "So she's what? Evil?"

"Nope. Didn't say that. Just she has no idea of right and

wrong really, and with the stuff she'd been exposed to, it's more extreme."

"Her body dying made that much of a difference?"

Doc coughed. "I think she used to go to it when you were asleep. Not visit it in person, but let her mind drift. Could have been imagination of sorts. Now that her body is dead, her last bit of hope of going home is gone."

That made some sense. "She's like the grumpy old man who's been kicked out of his house by a big corporation?"

Doc shrugged. "She's angry. All she wants to be is a little girl and she can't be that anymore."

"So what do I do?"

"What you been doing. Keep teaching her when she does something you don't like. Don't be afraid to get mad right back."

I nodded. "I take it she told you everything about Italy."

"I'm guessing. Even then, she was surprised I didn't find what she did right. I'm thinking that maybe she'll believe me better because I'm almost like her."

"We'd best figure out a way for you to charge up here, or for you to take her with you."

He chuckled. "Only one way to do that, Jimmy. Next time, you'll have to come along."

"I had a feeling you were going to say that. Let's hope I still have a job and can afford the trip."

Doc crossed his fingers and smiled.

Being a parent wasn't going to be as easy as I thought it would be. I never would have imagined that Lucy wouldn't be human anymore. I'd heard, too, that angels weren't human at all—not in appearance and not in the way they were emotionally. And yet they were considered benevolent beings. Maybe that was something I could teach her.

As long as Doc made sure to watch Lucy like a hawk, everything should be okay. I was going to have to step up to the plate, too. It wouldn't be fair to make him do all the hard work. Besides, Lucy was my charge.

My cell phone rang. I grabbed it out of my pocket. The number was one I recognized. This was it. I took a deep breath and swiped my phone screen.

"Father Martin?" I asked.

"Mr. Holiday."

I swallowed. "I'm assuming you have some news for me."

I almost didn't want to hear. The waiting sucked, but now that I was getting an answer, I wanted to go back to ignorant bliss.

He cleared his throat. "It is most strange. I have your paperwork that you submitted in my hands, and, of course, nowhere do you state that you do not want a translator."

"Yeah." At least he'd found the proof. That was score one in my favor.

I heard some rustling. "For that, I am quite sorry," he said. "Though even more strange is the fact that there was no one logged into the servers at the time the network states that the refusal was posted."

I rocked back on my heels. This was something new. "Wow."

Maybe someone inside the Order hadn't tried to screw me after all. Maybe Big Red was involved.

"Because the powers of the supernatural are involved, you are not dismissed, but suffice it to say that the senior members are not happy with you."

Yeah, stuffed shirts wouldn't be. "That makes sense," I said. "I freely admit that I was an idiot."

He laughed. "I must say it is nice that you admit it." I heard some more papers rustling in the background. "You are not welcome back to the school. This means that you will receive no more training in regards to exorcism." He chuckled again. "Not that the standard way seems to be your forte. In any event, you either sink or swim. God will decide what to do with you."

Since that was kind of what I wanted in the first place, I wasn't all that unhappy about it. I would have been better off working with a mentor, teaching me the ropes. Evidently, it wasn't in the cards. "That seems fair."

"You may be able to find some…." He cleared his throat. "… willing partner in terms of mentors. I am going to make sure you have access to the Order's marker list."

Something useful at last. It was close enough that I was starting to think he could read my mind. "I appreciate that."

"I will make sure it is sent to you sometime soon. But I'm not sure you'll thank me after this," he said.

Here it was. The catch. "What?"

"The seniors feel that you should be punished for your antics. So you are to be given the case that no one wants."

I laughed. "I thought that was every case."

"You do have a point. Also, this one isn't so far from you. It is in Kitzmiller."

I'd never even heard of it. "Where's that?"

"Close to Maryland. I'll be sending word so that they will be expecting you."

"No more information?" They were hanging me out to dry.

"I think it's best to hear from those who have witnessed the phenomenon. It isn't something we've heard before and I'd like a fresh mind on the matter."

That wasn't as bad as I thought, but still not great. "So I'll be able to call you during this case?"

"From now on, I hope you will keep in touch rather frequently. Certain avenues cannot be trusted."

This might be a man I could actually work with. "Okay, then. I'll leave tomorrow."

"Tell your witch friend good luck."

I choked and he hung up.

What the fuck did he mean by that? No sense in worrying

about it now. I had to pack. Unless I royally screwed this up, my job was safe. I finally relaxed.

I headed into the living room.

"Well?" Tabby asked.

She probably had heard me talking.

"I'm not fired," I said.

She blinked. "That's good."

I nodded. "And we have a case."

"Where this time?" she asked.

"Kitzmiller."

Her face fell. "Oh, shit."

"What do you mean by that?" Apparently, she'd been there. Her reaction wasn't good.

She shook her head. "It's better for you to see it for yourself."

"Why do I have a feeling that this is going to be the trend with this case?"

She laughed. "Guess we need to pack, right?"

"You guessed correctly, madam."

Packing was the easy part. Well, sort of. Isaac kept lying down inside the suitcase. Silly shit. Granted, he was going too, but I planned for him to have a better ride than that. No way would I ever do that to an animal. A demon, however...they could ride in my dirty gym sock.

"Listen, you. We're taking you along. Now, get out of there," I said to him.

He meowed at me, got up, stretched, then farted.

"Oh, Jesus Christ. Thanks, Isaac." I fanned the air in front of my face. That cat had worse gas than any other creature I'd smelled in my life.

He trotted nonchalantly out of the room.

"I take it you pissed him off," Tabby said.

I ran into the bathroom and sprayed down the room with Lysol. "I swear. That cat's ass gets worse and worse."

Tabby giggled. "I could almost swear that he had a special compartment for these occasions."

"You may be onto something. Shame we can't market it."

"Now that would be the end of the world."

I laughed. "Probably."

The next morning, we all piled in the car early. Isaac was in his pet carrier in the backseat with Lucy and Doc. I'd been smart enough to call in advance and find a hotel. It was a plain old Best Western. They made me add on a pet deposit, but at this point, I didn't care. As long as no one tried to break into the room, like in Arizona, we'd be in good shape.

Tabby had made sure to bring plenty of warding materials, so I knew what her first task was going to be.

"I can't believe we are going to Kitzmiller," Tabby said.

"Why the hate?" I asked.

"Because there's nothing there. It's just grass and trees and rocks and a general store."

I rolled my eyes. "There's got to be more than that."

"If you say so."

Doc snorted from the back.

"Hey, no comments from the peanut gallery," I said, looking in the rearview mirror.

He chuckled.

"I think there's something weird about this...Kitz-...place," Lucy said.

"Do you have a bad feeling?" I wanted to ask what else she had a bad feeling about, but I was probably pushing my luck.

"Maybe. I'm not sure. It's just weird." She crossed her arms.

"Okay. I'll keep my eyes open."

Lucy stared out the window.

"Did the Order give you any indication as to what this case is about?" Tabby asked.

"You know what they told me. I guess whoever we need to

meet will get in touch with us. Martin said he'd let them know we're coming."

'That's ever so comforting," Tabby said.

'Tell me about it. I'm already having flashbacks of Arizona."

"Ever notice how we always refer to the last case we dealt with?" Tabby asked.

"What do you mean?"

"Well, in Arizona, everything was like Sorrow's Point. Now, everything is like Arizona."

I laughed. "God help us if next time everything is like Kitzmiller."

"I have a feeling that, if that's the case, we'll have done nothing wrong."

"Or something fantastic." Hey. Might as well be positive.

"That too."

"How much longer do we have to do this?" Lucy asked.

"What, drive?" I asked.

"Yeah."

"Still a few hours left," I said.

"I've decided I don't like car rides," Lucy said.

I laughed. The classic kid mantra.

"Why not?" Tabby asked.

"Because they're long."

I chuckled. She was killing me today. "Well, want to play a game?"

"Like what?"

"A color game. My dad used to play it with us when I was a kid." One of the few happy memories from my childhood I had, but I wasn't about to lay that on her.

"Okay. How does it work?"

Woot. I had her attention. "It can be the color of something in the car that we all can see. Then, once you've chosen the thing, you say, 'Willy, Willy, I, Dee, Dee. I see something you don't see and the color is—whatever the color of your thing is. Then, we all have to guess."

"Okay!" Lucy said.

At least she wasn't bored anymore.

We decided to stop in Morgantown for lunch. At least they had lots of places to go. It was still springtime, so I didn't have to worry about leaving Isaac in a hot car.

"Any suggestions?" I asked as I pulled into town.

"Well, the Indian restaurant went downhill when I was here last." She drummed her fingers on the dashboard. "Want Italian?"

"Fine with me. Where?"

"Go to the town center. There's one up there," Tabby said.

"You're cleansing us," I said. I remembered that when she'd come to Sorrow's Point, she'd smelled like garlic. Tricky witch.

She shrugged. "Sort of. It's not like I meant for it to happen exactly."

I nodded. "I'm not mad. I find it interesting that you do it even without thinking about it."

"Guess I'm used to it."

"It was easy in Arizona with Vespa's love of pizza." I'd never eaten so much damn pizza in my life.

Tabby laughed. "That it was."

"Anything else we can be doing?"

She smirked. "Nothing legal."

Doc snorted.

"I don't think I'm even going to ask," I said.

"That's probably a good idea," Tabby said, then got an evil glint in her eye.

After lunch, we headed to Oakland, Maryland. That was the closest town to Kitzmiller. The scenery was already changing. There were a lot more trees. The green leaves were still that lighter green they were after they first budded.

Checking in happened without a glitch. As I was unloading the car at the hotel, my phone rang. I almost dropped my suitcase.

I fumbled with my pocket and finally retrieved my phone.

"Hello?" I asked after I swiped the screen and put the phone to my ear.

"You the marker?" he asked.

His voice was gruff and countrified. Okay. One, I wasn't used to people calling me that. Two, I wanted to know their ulterior motive.

"Who's calling?" I asked.

"Name's Sam Moore. Got your number through your boss."

Well, that part checked out.

"How'd you know I was here?" It wasn't like I had a special GPS tracker or anything. Or, at least, I knew the Order hadn't given him one. They might be accessing my phone. At this point, I didn't put anything past them.

"What are you talking about?" he asked.

Maybe I was getting way too paranoid. "Never mind. We just got here."

"All right. Call me back when you're ready to meet."

"Okay. Sounds good."

"Yup."

Then he hung up. I was starting to wonder what happened to normal telephone etiquette.

I hauled the suitcase and Tabby's large witchy bag up to the hotel room, then knocked on the door.

She opened it soon after. "What took you so long?"

I hauled the luggage inside and set it on the bed. "Our contact got in touch already."

"Damn. That's fast."

Glad it wasn't only me that felt it was odd. "Tell me about it. Makes me feel kind of weird."

Isaac meowed from his carrier.

Tabby rushed over and let him out. He leaped free and darted under the table Doc had settled at.

'That doesn't look good," I said.

"Do we have time for me to ward the room?" Tabby asked.

"Looks to me like we'd better make time." I wasn't going to take any unnecessary risks.

Tabby grabbed her witchy stuff. I snatched the remote from the nightstand and turned the TV on for Lucy. No sense in her being without it when she didn't have to be.

"Thanks, Jimmy," she said.

"No problem, kid."

I sat on the bed and watched Tabby go through her routine. She used sage and a few other herbs, wound together in a stick and lit one end. Then, she went to all the heating vents, windows, and doors to the room and drew symbols with holy water. Each symbol glowed green like it usually did.

Tabby's magic always looked green to me. I wasn't sure why. Maybe it had something to do with the type of magic she did. Since I had no one to ask, I shrugged it off and put it on the "to be answered" list. That list was getting pretty damn long.

I'd seen other colors come out of her magic before, but the predominant color was green. It reminded me of nature. That was probably a good thing.

It didn't take her long. Maybe twenty minutes and then she extinguished the herb bundle. The smell was pungent, but not horrible. Just herby and burnt.

"That should do it," she said.

"I love watching you work."

She paused, then blushed. "You're crazy."

"Nope. Really. It's cool watching you do what you do." Hell, I wished I could do it.

She shook her head. "Well, thanks, I guess."

"Should I call the guy?" I asked.

"Might as well." She sat on the bed beside me.

I pulled my cell phone free and dialed the number.

"Mr. Holiday?" the guy asked.

"Yup. Where do you want to meet?" I was hoping it was going to be a decent place and not some hole in the wall.

"Where are you staying?"

"The Best Western in Oakland."

Tabby was making odd faces at me.

I rolled my eyes. She could be such a dork.

He paused for a minute. "There's a diner down the road. I forget the name, but it's only a couple of places from the hotel. How 'bout I meet you there in a half-hour?"

"Works for me. My assistant and I will see you there." I wasn't ready to eat again, but whatever.

"All right." And the guy hung up again.

"Must be a cultural thing," I mumbled to myself.

"What?" Tabby asked.

"Never mind. We're to meet at a diner nearby in a half an hour."

"Guess we're officially involved then."

"Guess so."

"Do we have to go?" Lucy asked.

"No. You and Doc are staying here I think." There wasn't a reason at all for them to come along. "If someone breaks in, do what you did in Italy."

She grinned at me. "Okay."

What was I getting myself into?

SIXTEEN
POSSESSION

TABBY and I headed down to the lobby. I stopped at the front desk. After a minute, a young girl with long brown hair came over.

"Can I help you, sir?" she asked.

"How do we get to the local diner?" I asked her. It was much easier than checking online. Besides, Sam hadn't even told us the name of the place.

"Turn right at the parking lot. It's a couple of places down. Look for the sign that says, 'Mabel's.'"

"Okay. Thanks." If I'd been wearing a hat, I would have tipped it to her. Maybe Doc was rubbing off on me.

When we got to the car, Tabby paused. "Are you ready for this?"

I shrugged. "It's not like that part matters, does it? I have to do this, or you and I are going to have to get very creative about our finances."

Tabby got into the car and I crawled into the driver's seat. What I wanted to do was spend the rest of the day hiding in the hotel room, but that wasn't going to happen.

"I'm thinking we'd better start saving more anyway," Tabby said as I pulled out of the parking lot.

"For what?"

"So you aren't beholden to the Order forever."

I didn't answer. In a way, she was probably right, but this wasn't the time for that conversation. I had to stay focused. Demon time was upon us.

I spied the Mabel's sign about two seconds later and had to slam on the brakes not to miss it. It was an older, smallish sign with "Mabel's" spelled out in cursive writing.

"Jesus Christ," Tabby said.

"Sorry. The oaf can't handle doing more than one thing at a time." I pulled into a parking spot.

Tabby waited until we were about going into the restaurant. "You are not an oaf."

She stepped past me and entered the restaurant.

I had to smile. I got that goofy feeling in my gut. My girl loved me.

It was an old-timey-looking place with chintz curtains. I stepped over to the "Please Wait to Be Seated" sign, but then Tabby poked me on the arm. I stared at her. She was pointing at a guy dressed in a plaid shirt that was unbuttoned. He was waving us over.

I followed Tabby's lead.

The guy stood up from the table and held his hand out to me. I noticed he had sidestepped Tabby. That, I wasn't too crazy about. Countrified or not, being a dick wasn't going to get you on my good side.

I took it and shook.

"Mr. Holiday. I'm glad you could make it," he said.

I nodded and sat down. Tabby sat beside me.

I pointed to her. "This is Tabby. My assistant."

"Sam Moore. Nice to meet ya, ma'am."

She smiled. "Nice to meet you, too."

She was good at hiding her real feelings. I had to give her that. I knew, in a different situation, she would have kicked his ass.

Sam turned back to me. His eyebrows were bushy. I was tempted to get out a weed whacker to trim them.

"I thought we'd get somethin' to eat while I explain this mess."

The food made sense. These were country people. If you didn't share a meal with them, they figured you couldn't be trusted. "Sounds good to me."

In general, food was a good way to make a connection with people. Granted, it had only been a few hours since we ate, but a little discomfort was a small price to pay for creating a sense of ease. Maybe we'd get some solid information.

A waitress came over and took our drink orders. When she stepped away, Sam leaned forward. "I don't think I have to tell you that there are some weird things going on here."

"Weird seems to be the norm with this type of thing," I said. I glanced at Tabby. "Tabby and I have seen a lot."

Sam nodded. "Might as well get it all over with. It all started with Mikey Fisher's funeral."

I nodded.

The waitress came back with our drinks, then took our food order. I got a hamburger. Tabby got a club sandwich.

As soon as she left, Sam continued, "The thing you have to understand about Mikey is that he never did anything. I mean nothing. His mother was his slave."

He picked up his soda and took a drink. "You can imagine what his health was like. Every so often, you'd see them come into town, but Mikey couldn't walk very fast. If he did, he'd get out of breath so bad you'd think he was going to drop dead in the street. 'Long about three weeks ago, he up and died."

Tabby exhaled slowly. I had to admit, I was interested too. But I still had no idea how this had anything to do with exorcism. Hell, if that was the case, I could solve the obesity problem systematically.

"They had to cut a hole in the side of the house to get his body out."

"That's so sad," Tabby said.

Sam nodded. "He did it himself, but still don't change how horrible it was. Anyway, they had to use a stretcher that would be used for a large wild animal. His mother was hysterical of course."

He took another drink of his soda. "We all went to the funeral. Not many of us left in town, so we kind of stick together. It was awful. Not so much because it was a funeral home, but because of the stink."

"What stink?" I knew morticians washed bodies and stuff, so there shouldn't have been any smell.

"Mikey's family are kind of backwoods believers. They don't believe in having a body formaldehyded or whatever you call it. Even had an autopsy refused in the will. Cited religious reasons, I think. So it's spring. And around Mikey's funeral, we had a warm spell. The smell wasn't pleasant and here we all were hoping the minister would get on with it."

"If they aren't Catholic, how did we get involved?" Tabby asked.

Sam chuckled. "Impatient, aren't you? I'll be getting to that in a minute."

The waitress came with our food and set it all down in front of us. We were all quiet for a few minutes while we ate. Kind of said something about what we had gotten used to. Talking about a funeral stink hadn't affected our appetites. Sam's either. It was almost as if Sam couldn't stop himself.

He wiped his mouth with a napkin. "So we were all there, listening to this fire-and-brimstone preacher, when old Mikey sat right up in his coffin. We all freaked out. Women screamed. He turned his head, looked at us all, and laughed. I don't have to tell you, I hauled ass outta there."

He shoved a French fry into his mouth. At least he chewed with his mouth closed.

"Were they sure he was dead?" I asked.

Sam nodded and swallowed. "By the time I had the funeral, his body was all bloated like a fish. Even green and black in places. He was right dead."

"I have to say, that's different." I scratched my head. I hadn't ever heard anything like it.

"But that ain't all," he said. "Ol' Mikey went back home. I shit you not. He was totally different though. First thing he did was fix the hole in the wall of the house. In days, his mama's house was a hell of a lot better than it ever had been. He was still discolored in spots, but it was like all that excess fat melted away."

I froze. I *had* heard of that before. "That almost sounds like an old episode of *The Twilight Zone*."

Sam laughed. "Believe me, I wish that was the case." He pushed his plate away. "Every day, Mikey changes more. He don't even smell anymore."

Now, I had to admit, that was weird. "How did we get notified?"

"I guess the church got people who look for stuff like this. Our local newspaper published an article about it. A few priests tried to talk to ol' Mikey, but he run them off with a shotgun."

"He looks normal now?" Tabby asked.

"Yep. Fit as a fiddle. Nothing like what he was in life. Only thing is his eyes."

"What about his eyes?" I asked.

"Milky-white dead. Ugly they is, but nothing to help that."

"Yuck," Tabby said.

I rolled my eyes at her. "Guess that's why I was put on this."

"What do you mean?" Sam asked.

I stared at him. "I tend to get the weird cases. Weirder than usual, I mean. This is the first time I've heard of a dead body being possessed."

"Might be the first time you've heard about it, but the Jews have a legend about it," Tabby said.

I stared at her. This was news to me. "Really?"

She nodded. "It was in this movie I saw a few years ago. Let me think about it and I'll try to see what I can find out."

"Sounds good to me." I turned to Simon. "Looks like we have some research to do."

He nodded. "I feel better knowing you all are gonna try to make this right."

"We'll do our best," Tabby said.

"We'll give you a call when we're ready to meet Mikey," I said.

"Fair enough," Sam replied.

"I gotta say I didn't expect that," I said when I got in the car.

Tabby slapped her hand on the dashboard. "I remember what it's called now. A dybbuk."

I started the car. "And those entities can possess dead bodies?"

"According to the movies they could."

"It's a starting point at least." I had a feeling that I needed to start reading more books dealing with the occult when we got home. There was too much I didn't know and watching movies didn't cut it. Too much stuff was changed to be more dramatic.

"Yes, it is." As soon as we got back to the hotel room, I pulled out the iPad from the suitcase.

"I take it you got a hell of a case," Doc said.

"Know anything about dybbuks?" I asked him.

"Duh—what?" He raised his eyebrow.

"Never mind." Maybe they were called by other things by different cultures.

Isaac hopped up on the bed beside me and watched me fiddle with the tablet. That cat was something else. One day, I was going to wake up and find him searching for kitty porn or something.

Lucy got up from the floor, came over, and sat on Doc's knee.

"I don't like this," she said.

"I know if you feel bad about it, it's going to be bad, but I have to try."

She nodded. "I still don't like it."

"Duly noted."

Tabby sat on the bed beside me and started flipping channels. One of us might as well relax.

I typed "dybbuk" into a search engine and got a bunch of hits.

"Aha!" Tabby said suddenly. She was on a movie channel. Some scary movie was playing.

"What?" I asked.

"This is it. It's called *The Unborn*."

I set the iPad down on the bed. Not exactly the best way to research, but hell, maybe it was better than nothing. Better than general descriptions I was finding online anyway. I needed to start creating my own occult library. This was getting to be ridiculous.

Was the movie any help? Not really. I'd dealt enough with demons to recognize when someone could be faking. I already knew that there was some truth to it or the Order of Markers wouldn't have brought me in. I wasn't going to make the same mistake as last time, either. I would still do all the tests. Whether alive or dead, this was a possession. I didn't know by what. Whether that mattered remained to be seen.

Even odder was that I felt more at home in this hotel room than I did in my own house. Maybe because home was now soiled by what happened to Lucy. When I got home, I needed to fix that. I hadn't felt it so much before Italy, but after, the house felt almost suffocating.

I knew Tabby wanted to save money, but I thought the proper thing to do was get rid of that fucking carpet and pad. At least then all vestiges of what the fleshing rod had done to Lucy would be gone. If nothing else, it would make me feel better.

"You think too much," Doc said from his spot at the table.

I laughed. "I'm that bad, eh?"

If Doc noticed it, I needed to reassess what the hell I was doing when I wasn't working on stuff. Shit.

"Yup," he said. "Gotta let all that go. You need to focus on the task at hand."

He was right. As usual. "What would you suggest?"

"Does it really matter what this thing acts like? You fight demons with a mish-mash of witchcraft and discombobulated Christianity."

"Yeah."

"Point is—why concentrate on the type of thing it is? I can see the little gears in your head rolling round and round— mostly getting stuck on the religious aspect of the thing. That part doesn't matter in the way you think it does. Do what works for you."

"You know, you are really wise sometimes."

Doc laughed. "You know better than that."

"Okay. Okay. I'll stop."

I stared at Tabby asleep beside me in the bed. It was her words that had kept me going. Her attitude, too. Doc was right.

"I promise," I said. "I'll listen to you more often."

He laughed. "Don't make promises you can't keep, boy."

"So again, what do I do now?"

"Tomorrow, I'd call your boss, see if they gathered any evidence about the case, and if the men sent here ran away like little chickenshits."

I snorted. "Okay. That's a good a place to start as any."

"Whatever answer he gives you, you'll know what you have to do."

I exhaled. "This is going to be a weird one."

Doc shrugged. "Just when you think you've seen it all, something worse comes in to take its place."

"Ain't that the truth," I said.

SEVENTEEN
I'LL FOLLOW YOU

I TOSSED and turned all night. My brain wouldn't stop working. I knew, because of the last time, that whether they had investigated or not, the best thing to do would be for me to investigate myself. Other information might give me extra stuff to look for, but it wasn't a replacement for me seeing it with my own eyes.

I got up about five, went down to the hotel's conference room, and grabbed some pastries and coffee. Then, I carted it all back to the room.

Tabby sat up as soon as I walked inside and closed the door.

"What are you doing?" she asked, rubbing her eyes.

"Couldn't sleep, so I come bearing coffee and breakfast."

She forced herself into a sitting position. Then she grabbed her cell phone off the nightstand and stared at the screen.

"Do you know how early it is?"

I laughed. "Sadly, yes."

I handed her a cup of coffee and set the plate of pastries on the bed. Then I went to my side of the bed and sat.

"Figure out what we're doing?" she asked.

"I'm going to call Father Martin. Find out what the other

priests knew, if anything. After that, I'll call Sam and see about going to see our subject."

She nodded. "And Doc and Lucy?"

"They can come along and stay in the car. I'd rather Mikey not see them if he is possessed. They would be close enough if we need their help. All I plan on is a meeting. Maybe do an investigation. Nothing more."

"You do realize that your plan is destined to fail," Doc said after he popped into his chair.

I looked at him. "Why?"

Lucy got up from the floor in front of the TV and walked over to me. "Because your plans never work."

I laughed. "What is this, Gang Up on Jimmy Day?"

Tabby snickered. "No, I think we all know enough by now to expect all hell to break loose."

"Okay, fine. But if I don't plan, I'll never get anything done."

Tabby patted me on the shoulder. "Do your best. So when are you going to call?"

I took a sip of my coffee and grimaced. It tasted like black tar. "Probably at least eight. I hope I can catch him before Mass."

"All right."

I tried to call, but all I got was voicemail. As usual, the others were right. Still, it didn't prevent me from moving on with my day. I could do my own thing. So I called Sam.

"Hello," he said.

"Yeah. This is Jimmy. I wanted to know if you could set it up for me to meet Mikey."

"Don't know about that. One, he doesn't have a phone. And two, don't know how I feel about just going over there."

That was a bunch of help. No wonder this case was such a

clusterfuck. "Well, if I'm going to do anything about this, I have to meet him sometime."

"I wish there was some way to let him know we don't mean him no harm."

I sighed. I was starting to get irritated. "That's the problem. We do mean it harm. That spirit needs to go back from where it came from."

Sam tsked into the phone. "It ain't gonna like that."

I started laughing. "You know, you are something."

"How?"

"You are all hell-bent on telling me about this guy, but the minute I choose to do something, you turn chickenshit and run." I knew I was adopting Doc's term, but shit. It fit. If I was willing to risk my rosy-red ass, he could too.

"Hey, nobody said anything about me having to get involved more than I already am."

"Fine." I rolled my eyes. "What's his address?"

"1473 Turnbill Road, Kitzmiller, WV. You need the zip?"

"Nope. Got GPS."

"All right then." And he hung up.

"Sonofabitch!"

"What?" Tabby asked.

"Old Sammy boy is too much of a pussy to even show us where the home is." No wonder this was the case no one else wanted. Jesus Christ.

"Seriously?"

"Yep. I'm not kidding." I wished I were.

"All right. I'll go get my shower. We might as well try to go out there."

I nodded. "My thought exactly."

As soon as I got off the phone, Tabby and I packed up our tools and got ready to leave. One problem: Isaac was standing near the door.

"Where do you think you're going?" Tabby asked.

Isaac meowed at her and stared at her with wide eyes.

She crouched down. "I know you are my familiar, and while I don't exactly know what all it is that you can do, I'm not about to put you directly in the path of danger. Stay here and protect the room."

Isaac huffed and stomped off into the bathroom. I made sure his water bowl was full and shut him inside where he couldn't cause too much damage. At least I knew for sure where he was. Worrying about Lucy was enough. I didn't need to add another thing to my list.

We left the hotel and went downstairs. We all piled into the car as fast as we could. No sense in holding back now. I got the car started and set up the GPS.

"How far is it from here?" Tabby asked.

I glanced at the GPS. "Says about five miles."

All we saw were lots of trees and old homes that probably needed to be torn down. Every once in a while, we'd spy a decent looking house. I kind of worried about that nice house next to all the desolation.

"Does everyone around here have fourteen dogs?" Tabby asked.

I knew she was exaggerating, but almost any house we passed had a bunch of them. "Probably crime."

"It's a shame. This was an old mining town. You can tell from the row houses."

"What are row houses?" Lucy asked from the back seat.

"Back in the old days," I said. "Each coal mine would build housing for the miners. They paid a certain amount of rent to the mine company out of their paycheck."

"Wow. That's weird," she said.

I nodded. "The mine companies controlled everything for the miners. They even gave them their own type of money so the miners could only shop at the company store."

"That's so wrong."

"They don't do it anymore. Laws were written against it," Tabby said. She turned in her seat. "Were the gold miners out West the same way?"

Doc shook his head. "Gold miners were mostly independent. If a seam of gold was found, the miners worked until it was gone. There wasn't enough to support something like that."

"That makes sense," Tabby said. "If there'd been that much gold, nobody in this country would have to work."

I laughed. "Nah. One lucky bastard would have it all and the rest of us would still be scrimping and saving."

"My, aren't you a ray of sunshine today," Tabby said.

Doc laughed. "Ain't he always?"

Lucy giggled.

At least someone found this funny.

Mikey's house was bad. There were tatters of plastic hanging in between the support beams of the porch. The wooden siding was gray from years of weather beating away at it. The porch seemed like it would break off the house if someone stepped onto it.

I didn't even make it to the porch. A man barreled out of the house holding a shotgun. "Whatcha want?" he asked, harshly.

I held my hands palm up. "To talk. Am I speaking to Mikey?"

He spat a wad of tobacco juice at my feet. "Mebbe."

His coal-black hair was flying around his head in the wind, but it was clean. His skin was pale and his eyes were blue. If this was Mikey, either Sam had been lying or the transformation was complete.

"I heard about what happened from Sam. I'm here to investigate."

His eyes narrowed. "Investigate what?"

"Your possession." I figured there was no sense in lying.

He started laughing hard. "All right. You and your lady friend can come in, but don't touch nuthin'."

I motioned for Tabby to get out of the car. She followed me up the steps.

As soon as I got close to Mikey, I smelled it. There was still a faint scent of death. It wasn't enough to make me gag, but it was there. Sam hadn't been lying.

"Thanks for talking to us," I said to him.

He chuckled. "You're the first one that's shown up here with some sense."

"How did the others act?" Tabby asked.

He guided us into the house. In the front room, there was a sofa, a rocking chair, and a recliner. An elderly woman sat in the recliner.

"Ma," Mikey said. "We got company."

She turned her head up to look at us. "What are you nice folks doing here?"

"We came to talk to you and your son," Tabby said.

Tabby and I sat on the couch. It smelled strongly of body odor, but I forced myself not to make a face. I seriously doubted the old woman could manage to even buy a new couch, so there was no sense in making her feel bad.

Mikey leaned the shotgun against the wall and sat in the rocking chair.

Mikey's mom turned to us. "Would you folks care for something to drink?"

There it was–the country test again. If we refused something when it was offered to us, it made us out to be untrustworthy. Tabby didn't miss a beat.

"That would be great," she said.

The old woman smiled. "I have water and I can make coffee if you don't mind sitting a spell."

"No need to trouble yourself with us," I said. "Water is fine."

"You sure?" she asked.

I nodded. "Thank you."

Mikey spit another wad of juice into a cup. "Momma don't get a lot of visitors no more."

"That's a shame," Tabby said.

Mikey nodded. "Ain't her fault I come back from the dead. Not like it's catching or anything."

"In general, people are idiots," I said. I was thinking of old chickenshit Sam.

Mikey laughed. "Ain't that the truth. Them priests they sent before, didn't take much to scare 'em."

Mikey's mom came back with the drinks and handed each of us one. The glasses had painted yellow flowers on them and they were clean.

"Thank you," I said.

She settled herself back down in her recliner with a grunt.

"How long have you lived here?" Tabby asked.

"Lived in Kitzmiller my whole life. Don't imagine I'll live long enough to go anywhere else," Ma said.

Mikey spat in the jar again. "Don't say that, Ma. If I got anything to do with it, you ain't leavin' this Earth anytime soon."

"I don't want you messin' with that book again. Look what it got you."

"What book?" I asked. I had visions of the book from those demon movies with Bruce Campbell.

"Found it in the woods out behind the house," Mikey said. "Went back there 'cause I heard something, but I wasn't fast, so I missed whatever left it."

He reached into his overalls and pulled out a stained volume. It had a wine leather cover. "I did a spell in it and it kept me from bein' dead for good."

"Wow. Must be an amazing book," Tabby said. "May I see it?"

He spit more chaw into the jar. "You promise to give it back?"

"I promise."

He handed it to her.

I leaned over and started looking. It was written in Latin. No way was I going to be insulting and mention how odd it was he could read Latin. Besides, at this point, I wasn't all that great at reading it myself. Kudos for him.

Tabby flipped through the pages. Periodically, there would be a passage I could kind of understand. Hell, it was a good thing I'd boned up on it when I was in Italy, but I was far from fluent. From what I could read, there were a lot of animal sacrifices.

Tabby closed the book gently and handed it back to him. "It must be very old."

"Guess so," he said. "Don't find a lot of books in Latin no more."

I wasn't sure if that could account for knowing a language a person shouldn't know, since it happened before he died. I'd be more inclined to say Mikey was a smart kid. Shame he'd been stuck here.

"Where did you learn Latin?" Tabby asked.

Inwardly, I cringed.

"My poppa. He was always reading something. Was even educated at college." He watched Tabby carefully, but she didn't give any expression at all. That, in and of itself, was weird.

Ma started to laugh. "Then he fell for me, and since I wouldn't leave the holler, he dealt with it. Been gone fifteen years this December."

"Sorry to hear that," I said.

Ma nodded. "Why are you really here?"

It was time to come clean. No sense in lying. They'd know anyway. "I'm an exorcist. I'm here to see if I can help Mikey."

"Help me with what?" He glared at me.

"Help you be in the place you are supposed to be. That is, if you are possessed," I said.

He laughed. "They send you all the way out here for that?"

I shrugged. "Well, you did scare those priests."

His eyes flashed yellow so fast, I wasn't sure if it happened or not. "Now, that was something to see."

His voice was different. Darker. It almost sounded like more than one person had spoken. I knew his real soul was gone, but this...this was doing a hell of a good job hiding. I needed to remember that.

He stopped and glared at me. "You're a priest too."

"Sort of. I was defrocked by the church."

He laughed then. "So they sent the outcast to deal with little-ole-me. I love it."

Ma cleared her throat. "See. He ain't my little boy no more. Roses die when he touches 'em. I had rose bushes all around the outside of the house until he came back from the dead."

I glanced at her. She was about the only sane person I'd met in investigating this mess. Well, normal, anyway. "What is it that you want?"

She shook her head slowly. "If it weren't for that damn book...I don't tarry with things that are unnatural."

"Oh, not this again," Mikey said in the demonic voice.

I didn't think there was any doubt about him being what everyone said he was, but I still needed more proof.

"It's true. Somethin' here ain't right. It's against the Lord."

He gnashed his teeth and angled his head toward the wall.

I stared at Ma. "You want him back to the ground?"

"It's only what's right."

I looked at Tabby, then back at Ma. "We need to look some things up, but we'll be back."

Mikey snarled. "I don't like it, but I can't go against Ma."

I didn't know what that was about, but I wasn't going to question why he deferred to her either—not if it got us back in the house. His choices were his own and I wasn't about to say a word about it.

"We will be back after we figure out a few things," Tabby said to her.

I nodded at Mikey and we left.

We got in the car almost as fast as we could. Just because Mikey was listening to his mother didn't mean that he couldn't do something to us out of her sight. Besides, now that I was pretty damn sure a demon or something was involved, I didn't want Doc or Lucy anywhere near the place again.

"I'm guessing it didn't go too well," Doc said.

"Oh, I wouldn't say that. We just have to find out where the courthouse is," I replied.

"What for?" Lucy asked.

"I want to look at Mikey's death certificate," I said. It would be nice to know what he died of. And if he'd been declared dead. He could have had the smell because he rubbed a dead squirrel on himself. I wasn't about to believe anything.

"Who's Mikey?" Lucy asked.

"Our case. I want to look at his death certificate."

"Oh," Lucy said. "To find out if he really was dead?"

"Uh-huh. Gotta look at everything." I steered the car back onto the main road.

Now, where the court house was, I had no idea. Best thing to do was go back to the hotel and use the holy iPad. Then, if we could find out in time, maybe it wouldn't be such a big deal. And if I couldn't get a copy. I would have Doc use some of his swarthy talents and get a copy that way.

"I think I'd like to get some lunch first," Tabby said.

I glanced at the clock on the dash. It was just after eleven thirty.

"All right, madam. Where would you like to eat?"

"Anywhere, kind sir, just as long as the food is warm and the drinks are cold."

Lucy giggled. "You guys are silly."

Tabby and I smiled at each other.

As a team, we worked pretty damn well together.

EIGHTEEN
BODIES

WE GOT to the hotel room around twelve thirty. Part of me wanted to lay down on the bed and grab some sleep. The other part knew that I didn't have that luxury. I'd have time to sleep when I was dead. I picked up the tablet and started looking at rules about death certificates in West Virginia.

"Shit."

"What?" Tabby asked.

"I can't get a copy of the death certificate." Again, I found myself wanting to swat whoever abandoned this case. It was the biggest pain in the ass I'd encountered in a while. I almost preferred sitting in that class in Italy. Almost.

She wrung her hands together for a minute. "I was afraid of that."

I stared up at Doc. "Looks like I'll need you to do your magic."

He laughed. "Gotta wait until tonight. Won't be good for people to see a piece of paper traveling through an office on its own."

I laughed. "A big part of me would love to see that, though."

Tabby cuffed me on the arm lightly. "You are so bad."

"Jimmy isn't bad," Lucy said.

I laughed and patted the bed beside me. She walked over and hopped up.

"Since we can't do anything else today, what would you like to do?" I asked her.

"Can we take Isaac for a walk?" Lucy asked.

I glanced at Tabby, and then back at Lucy. "I think we can do that. That is, if Isaac will put on his leash."

"I'll take care of it," Lucy said.

Tabby and I looked at each other again and watched as Lucy crawled onto the floor. Isaac trotted over to her. She crouched down and whispered something in his ear. He licked his lips and sat up on his haunches as if someone had asked him to look pretty, but there had been nothing.

"Isaac says, 'okay,'" Lucy said.

Tabby laughed. "Okay."

I wouldn't have believed it if I hadn't watched it. Usually, when Tabby pulled out the leash, Isaac would have a fit. Thus, the whole reason we use the pet carrier in the first place. This time, when Tabby pulled out the leash, he just sat there. She attached the harness to him and then clasped the leash to it. He didn't bat a paw. Leave it to Lucy to be the ghostly animal whisperer.

So that's how we were outside when my phone rang. I looked at the caller ID. It was Father Martin.

"Hello," I said.

"Mr. Holiday. How can I help you?"

At least he sounded jovial for once, and I had to be happy he was finally returning my call. It seemed like ages ago. Too much had happened in the meantime. "I was wondering if the other priests had managed to investigate Mikey at all."

The father cleared his throat. "Unfortunately, they did not get close enough to perform an honest investigation."

I laughed. I couldn't help it. They must have sent eighteen-year-old novices. Jesus Christ. "Did they get to look at the death certificate?"

I heard him typing on a keyboard. After a minute, the typing stopped. "It appears that they simply abandoned the project."

"Okay, at least I know where I stand." Right where I started. In a way, that was better.

"I take it he did not scare you off?" Martin asked.

"No." I cleared my throat. "There's something weird going on between him and his mother. He seems to not to want to do anything she objects to—except things to do with spellwork."

"That does seem odd. Be careful."

"I will."

Then he hung up.

"Well?" Tabby asked.

"Nothing. The other guys were too wimpy." And, honestly, that made me scratch my head. Being a priest, you had to deal with some stuff that wasn't pretty. The Last Rites for one. I couldn't reconcile these guys running away from Mikey, then being put out into the world to perform all of the rituals priests needed to do. If this was what the priesthood was becoming, the Catholic church was in a sorry state.

"I thought exorcists were supposed to be brave?" Tabby stared at me.

I shrugged. "No one said that they were exorcists, just that they were priests sent to investigate. But still, damn."

"Hmm. That may make a difference."

"At least you know you're doing the right thing," Doc said.

"I hope so," I replied.

I had to get my head screwed on straight. Okay. The other priests had done jack and shit. The only thing that meant was that I had to start at the beginning, which wasn't a bad thing. Doc could get me a copy of the death certificate as soon as he could.

For the rest of it, I needed to go back to the old rules of exorcism. I needed Mikey to speak in a language he could not know, tell me the location of a lost or hidden object, and display powers of some sort that were not of this world. All of these things were not easy to get. The demons liked to hide their power. If they were blatant with it, they would be easier to discover, and thus, easier to expel.

I had a feeling witnessing all of these things was going to be tricky. I guessed his voice sounding the way it had when Tabby and I were there would loosely be considered an out-of-this-world power, but I was looking for something more.

Then there was this weird say his mother held over him. I'd never even heard of a demon not doing something because its last wish can't go against his mommy. It didn't make any sense. The only thing that made sense to me was if the old woman was a practitioner not unlike Tabby, but I'd seen no evidence of that. It was strange.

We'd gone back to the room after the walk with Isaac. I felt tired all of a sudden. "I think we'll find out where the nearest delivery place is and order some pizza for tonight."

"Yay," Lucy said.

I laughed. Kids and pizza.

"Fine with me," Tabby said. "I wanted to look at what the town has to offer anyway."

I raised an eyebrow. "Are you looking at the same town I am? Granted, yes, there are some pretty farms, but there is nothing here."

She laughed. "I was talking about the guide here in the hotel room to try to find a pizza place."

I blushed. "Oh."

Tabby walked over to the dresser, started ruffling through papers, and looking in binders. "Aha!"

"I take it you found it?"

"Yup." She walked over to the bed and sat down.

I picked up the iPad and checked my email. Nothing. It was kind of interesting that, ever since I had gotten a phone number for Father Martin, it was no longer as important that I had an email address. Of course, my stuff wasn't being passed to the general clerics anymore either. And with the results I'd had with them, I was kind of glad. Still no list of Markers, but there was time. It wasn't like I needed it for this case or anything.

Lucy was staring at the TV again. We were going to have to do something about that. Spirit form or not, she needed to learn something not from TV. I shook my head. When all of this calmed down, maybe Tabby could try to homeschool her somehow. I wouldn't even know where to start beyond handing her books she didn't know how to read.

Doc cleared his throat. "I'll be off for a while now. Can't say when I'll be back. Though I'm hoping this won't take long."

I nodded. "Good luck. If it proves too hard or puts you in danger, just forget it."

He tipped his hat at me and disappeared.

"This whole thing seems somehow more complicated, doesn't it?" Tabby asked.

"Yeah. And I'm not sure I like it either."

Hours ticked by. As each one passed, the more nervous I got. It wasn't like the local courthouse should be hard to find. That meant that Doc had encountered something that made his task difficult. I was starting to think it was a bad idea to send him out. Granted, he got results, but I didn't think I could live with myself if he somehow got hurt.

With so many weird things going on, I wouldn't be surprised if someone hadn't created a ghost catcher. But if they had, how would they have targeted Doc?

What made more sense was the possibility that Mikey could see Lucy and Doc. I would be surprised at this point if he couldn't. It was possible, with that infernal book, he could have done a spell on anything connected to him—not that I knew enough about magic to know how that would work. But anything was possible.

The person I could ask was asleep. She'd passed out about ten. I didn't want to wake her up because I got another shiny new idea. And, well, Doc being gone left me uneasy.

"What's taking so long?" Lucy asked me.

I shrugged. "I don't know, honey. I'm hoping it's as simple as a computer problem."

I didn't say that I didn't think that was it.

She nodded slowly. "If he doesn't come back?"

'That's simple. I'll go look for him."

That seemed to calm her down. But she went and sat in his chair instead of plopping in front of the TV like usual. Isaac snored at Tabby's feet.

'Long about twelve-thirty, Doc popped in. He was slightly less opaque than before, but seemed no worse for wear. He dropped a piece of paper on the table.

"What happened?" I asked.

Doc shook his head. "Nothing interesting. Some kid they hired to clean pissed around more than anyone I'd ever seen. I thought he was never going to finish. Finally, he moved onto a different floor and I was able to get your paper.

"Thanks. I late that it was so much trouble," I said.

He shooed Lucy out of his chair. She giggled, then sat in the other chair.

He took his seat and sighed. "If it was too much longer, I was going to forget it, but dammit, I didn't want to fail because of some stupid pipsqueak."

I got off the bed and picked the death certificate up from the table. Yep. Mikey Frazier, age thirty-four, died on April nineteenth. There it was in black and white.

"Thanks again, Doc," I said.

"If it helps ya, I don't mind doing it."

In a way, it would be nice to have a coroner's report, but I didn't think it was all that necessary. Sam hadn't lied about Mikey's death, so why would he lie about how he died? It didn't make sense. And if it didn't make sense, it wasn't true.

"Well, guess tomorrow it begins," I said.

"Can I come?" Lucy asked.

I shook my head. "After the way I felt in there, I think you and Doc better keep Isaac company. Anyway, the only thing I plan on doing is investigating for the exorcism. I'm going through the whole thing this time."

"Like you did with me?" Lucy asked.

I nodded. "I am assuming nothing. That's what got me into trouble last time."

I wouldn't admit it to her, but I wondered if I would have ended up meeting the Devil anyway if I hadn't been so damn dumb. There was a chance he wouldn't have been involved because I would have backed out. The deep part of my brain knew that it probably wouldn't have mattered, but I still felt guilty for the fleshing of Lucy. And if I had anything to do with it, I was going to make it up to her—somehow.

NINETEEN
PRIVATE EYES

THE NEXT MORNING, I had a notebook, a pen, and a vial of holy water sitting together on the table next to Doc. An aversion to religious objects was also a sign of possession, but I didn't want to use it if I didn't have to. It tended to piss the demons off.

"Are we going to get breakfast first, or are we heading out?" Tabby asked.

"Better to go ahead. I think fasting would be the right thing, don't you?"

She shrugged. "The exorcism, for sure, but I don't think we fasted before you did any of these tests. At Blackmoor, Tor was always cooking something."

I paused for a minute. She was right. Every time you turned around, Tor was cooking things. So that meant I couldn't have fasted. Especially when I did the investigation thinking I would not be the one to do the exorcism. It made me sad to think that she was gone from this world.

"So breakfast?" I asked.

"Where do you want to go?"

I shrugged. "I guess back to the diner. It's closer."

"All right."

I didn't talk much while we were eating. I think between

what had happened in Italy and the thing with Lucy, I was getting burned out. If I survived this latest round, I was going on a vacation whether they liked it or not.

I was dealing with the case no one else wanted, punishment be damned. If I resolved the fucking thing, I deserved a treat.

"Boy, you are in a mood this morning," Tabby said.

"Why?" I asked.

She threw her napkin down on her plate. "You won't look at me. You griped about even having breakfast. Frankly, Jimmy, you're being a dick."

I stared at her for a minute. "Shit. I didn't realize. I guess I want to get all of this over so bad that everything else has been pushed off to the side."

She sighed. "I understand that. I do. But us going in there half-cocked is not only sloppy, but stupid."

I nodded. "You're right. Okay. So how do you want to handle this?"

"It would make the most sense to decide what test you're doing today."

I blinked. "It doesn't necessarily work like that. Sometimes, you can get proof of a few things at once."

She shook her head. "Well, that's fine, but you still need to know how you want to start."

"The first things to come up are usually the language thing and the shying away from holy objects, but I'd rather not do that one." Mikey did have that shotgun. He didn't need to pull anything supernatural to hurt me.

Tabby nodded. "Yeah. Let's not piss off Mikey until we have some protection."

She paused. "We could go ahead and hide something of yours."

I nodded. "That will work. What do you want to use?"

Tabby laughed. "Never you mind. It is a test after all."

"Okay, ole wise one. I'll defer to your grandiose knowledge."

"Smartass."

We got on the road about ten. At least we shouldn't run the risk of disturbing Mikey's mother at that hour. She'd seemed so little and frail that I was half afraid that she couldn't take the stress of her son's exorcism. Of course, him coming back from the dead hadn't helped either.

The road was as twisty-turvy as it had been the day before. It was warm enough to drive with the windows down. Forsythia bloomed along the roadway. All that yellow hid the ugliness of the place. It was pretty until you ran across a run-down old house.

I pulled into the driveway at Mikey's place. Mikey stood on the front porch—watching. At least he wasn't holding his gun this time.

I got out of the car.

"You couldn't get information?" he asked.

I laughed. "Guess not. Mind if Tabby and I come in?"

"Suit yourself."

He turned around and walked into the house without giving us another look.

I stared at Tabby. She shrugged. Then I walked to the house and opened the door. Ma was seated in her chair, fiddling with some yarn.

"Come on in, folks. I'm mighty interested in hearin' what you have to say," she said.

Tabby closed the screen door softly behind her. We walked over and sat back on the couch.

"How are you doing today, Mrs. Frazier?" Tabby asked.

She waved her hand at Tabby. "Don't be calling me by no formal names. Ma's just fine."

Tabby smiled. "Okay. How are you feeling today, Ma?"

She smiled back. "Been better. Been worse. Just another day."

Mikey walked into the room and sat in the rocking chair. "Might as well do them things you want to do to me."

I blinked. It wasn't proof enough, though. He could have been operating off what he knew about possession. I didn't see a TV, but that didn't mean he'd never seen a movie about it or anything. We hadn't exactly seen the entire house.

It wasn't that I didn't believe he was possessed, but I wanted to see if his demon operated on the same rules. If it didn't, I wasn't sure what I was going to do.

"What's in my bag that belongs to Jimmy?" Tabby asked suddenly.

I stared at her. I hadn't quite been ready to leap into that, but whatever. I knew, at least, that this would be the real thing. Tabby wouldn't fake something like this.

He stared at Tabby for a minute, then smiled. "Dunno if I be wanting to do parlor tricks all day."

Tabby smiled back. "Just a few. Your case interests us."

He nodded then. "His wallet is in your bag."

Wait a minute. I felt around to my back pocket. Holy shit. She'd pickpocketed me. I wrote it down in my notebook. Add that to yet another thing Tabby could do.

He chuckled and leaned forward toward Tabby. "He's pretty easy, ain't he?"

Tabby laughed. "Yep."

"Hey, um, sitting here, ya know," I said. Granted, she was creating a rapport with the guy, but I didn't feel like having my ego trampled either.

Ma started cackling so hard I thought she was going to keel over at any second. "You people are so funny. Just a laugh riot."

I liked Ma. It wasn't her fault her son was such a fuckup. I was kind of glad I was entertaining to her. She needed to laugh.

"What the hell else ya need?" Mikey asked me.

I shrugged. "Do you have any special talents?"

"Like what?"

I sighed. He was making this as difficult as possible. "Moving objects with your mind, being able to fly, do something that's supposed to be impossible?"

He leaned back in the rocking chair, then looked at Ma. "I don't know. Can I do anything like that?"

She shook her head. "I'd say coming back from the dead is pretty impossible."

Mike turned to me. "There ya go."

Now things were going to get ugly. I could feel it. "See, the thing is, I gotta witness it."

The room grew so silent you could have heard a pin drop. "Don't know what to tell ya 'cept I ain't leavin' this body."

I figured this was where it was going to go. "Ever ask what Ma wants?"

It was a whim, yeah, but it was worth a try. With that weird co-dependency that was going on, I might as well exploit it if it helped me out.

"Don't go rilin' him up none, ya hear? Last time took three days for them eyes to stop a-glowin'," Ma said.

While interesting, it was not what I needed, so I dropped the testing for the moment.

"Do you have any pictures of Mikey from before?" I asked.

Ma stared at Mikey. "Bring out the album."

"Yes, Ma."

Again, I was flummoxed. I'd never seen a possessed person defer to the living before. There was something I was missing. But I didn't know what.

Mikey left the room for a minute and came back with an old photo album. He quickly handed it to me.

"Thanks," I said.

He grunted and sat back in his chair.

Tabby and I started at the beginning. There was Ma's wedding day. Pictures of her looking carefree amongst a passel of dogs, and then there was Mikey.

As a baby, he was like any other critter, but as he got older, he got bigger and bigger. By the time we were looking at the end of the album, Mikey had to have been seven hundred pounds or more. From the photos, it looked like he lived on the couch we were sitting on. I was honestly surprised it was still holding together. His father had to have reinforced it with extra wood or something. Damn.

I stared at him, then back to the last photo in the book. The likeness was there, right around the eyes. Unless there had been two boys, this was definitely Mikey.

"How quickly did he lose the weight?" Tabby asked.

"You mean after the funeral?" Ma asked.

"Uh-huh," Tabby said.

"Right about two weeks, give or take. Skin was loose for a while, but it all seemed to go back where it oughta."

"How did you do it?" I asked Mikey.

He grinned evilly. "Magic." Then he winked.

Not wanting to stir stuff up more than I had, I figured we'd overstayed our welcome for the day. We'd gotten some answers anyway.

"How about we come back tomorrow? Give things time to calm down," I said.

"That there might be a good idea," Ma said. "Maybe Mikey won't be as cantankerous tomorrow."

I stood up and Tabby got up beside me.

"See you tomorrow," Mikey said. Then he began to laugh.

I nodded to him and Tabby and I left.

"I'm not sure if I like this," Tabby said after we were out of sight of the house.

"You aren't the only one. He's like a regular demon, but not. There haven't been any of the theatrics presented by Lucy, or, hell, even Vespa."

"Maybe he's trying to lull you into a false sense of security?" Tabby asked.

I shook my head. "I don't know."

"Was it just me, or did Ma seem a little weaker than yester- day?" Tabby asked.

"I don't know. She has white hair and a face with a road map of wrinkles. I'm not sure how much weaker she can get."

Tabby tapped her fingers on her leg. "She still seemed more frail to me."

"I'll take your word for it, then."

"What do we do now?"

I sighed. "I'd better ask Father Martin if he knows a thing about dybbuks."

"Fun stuff."

"Yeah."

By the time we got back to the hotel, Tabby and I were more quiet than we had been that morning. There wasn't much more to say. We had gotten physical proof of one item. The photos, while real-looking, could have been doctored, but it was beyond me how they could afford something like that. With the house falling in, I couldn't imagine there being a computer in that house. Hell, they didn't even have a phone. These were moun- tain people.

Tabby opened the door to the hotel room and Isaac jumped into her arms.

"Whoa," I said.

I closed the door behind me and stepped into the room. Everything was fine. But I remembered putting Isaac inside the bathroom. Maybe Lucy learned more tricks.

"What's going on?" Tabby asked Lucy.

"Almost the whole time you were gone, we could hear something scratching at the window, but Doc and I couldn't see anything," Lucy said.

I stared at Tabby. "Looks like Mikey isn't as beholden to his mother as we thought."

Tabby set Isaac down on the floor. "I'm glad the wards held."

"Me too." I did walk through the room in case I smelled something foul or strong, but there was nothing.

"How powerful would you say he is?" I asked Doc.

He scratched at his chin for a minute. "Outwardly, not all that strong, but he's hiding something."

I nodded. "And the hidden part is what has me worried."

"Why not ask Levi?" Lucy asked.

I blinked. "Who's Levi?"

"My friend. He's really nice. Too bad he doesn't like you very much though."

I froze. A normal little kid having an imaginary friend was one thing, but this? This was scary on a whole other level. My asshole grew tight and I hoped this wasn't going the way I thought it was.

"How long have you known Levi?" Tabby asked.

"Before we went to Italy."

I glanced at Doc. "Do you know who she's talking about?"

He shook his head slowly. "But I'll keep an eye out."

"Thanks."

TWENTY
WITHIN YOU, WITHOUT YOU

IT HAD BEEN a long time since I felt this freaked out. Little things, like how Lucy knew to contact the Devil to clean the carpet and what she'd done in Italy, now made a whole lot of sense. I had my suspicions about who Levi was, but I wasn't about to jump to any conclusions. I'd thought it before, but I needed proof before I jumped in with it. Mostly because, if they weren't the same entity, I could leave myself open for some bad shit.

Something demonic was influencing Lucy and it was something hugely powerful.

I wasn't so obtuse that the name Levi didn't automatically make me think of Leviathan. It was so easy. I now wanted to know how he got past Tabby's wards. That is, unless he was careful not to even want to cause us direct harm. It was something to ask about for sure.

"Hey, Tabby," I said.

"Yes?"

"When you ward the house or this room, do you tell it to protect us from any harm?" Granted, I had been in here when she did it, but I tended to pay attention to the magic I could see more than the words coming out of her mouth.

"Yeah, pretty much. Why?" Tabby asked.

"What if there's a loophole?"

She blinked. "Explain."

"Okay. If the spell is being interpreted as direct harm, then isn't it possible that someone could, say, have someone cause us harm and yet still enter because they themselves did not mean us harm?"

"What?"

"I mean, like, if some creature-thing hired a hit man or something."

She stared at me like I'd turned into a giant platypus. "This is why spellwork is so damn tricky. Shit."

"Believe me, I wish I could think of this shit a hell of a lot sooner too," I said.

She got up and started digging through her witchy stuff bag. "So they want to play hardball, do they?"

I scooted back on the bed. This was a witch on a mission and I was staying out of her way.

'Those fucking bastards," she mumbled under her breath. "If they think they can enter *my* house."

She frantically began drawing symbols in the air. This time, the color of her magic was red—and only red.

From someone who usually glowed green, this was not good. I had no idea what it meant, but I hoped it was just her being mad.

After about twenty minutes, she collapsed in a heap at the foot of the bed.

"There."

"Are you okay?" I asked.

"As okay as I'm going to be. Now, anyway. No one or no thing can enter this room without your or my permission. So right now, that is Isaac, Doc, Lucy, and you and me, of course."

"I take it, when we get home, you'll do that to the house?"

"You betcha."

As soon as it grew dark, the scratching on the window began again. I got close enough to see that there wasn't any person or thing close by to be causing the phenomenon. Compared to the stuff Lucy had pulled, a little scratching was nothing. Though the little voice inside my mind reminded me that this was how it started with Lucy, too. All Mikey needed to do was get a little stronger.

I forced myself to stop dwelling on it.

I texted Father Martin and asked him if the Order had any books on dybbuks I could use. His reply was a simple "no." I was on my own with this thing. It wasn't all that different than usual, but I didn't like it. Not with that book I couldn't read. There was too much that was unknown involved.

"If there was something you could change about all of this, what would it be?" Doc asked.

I stared at him. "I'd get hold of Mikey's book and, after finding out everything it said, I would destroy it."

"Do you know where he keeps the book?" Doc asked.

"No. Don't you dare," Tabby said. "If you do this, Doc Holliday, I'll never speak to you again."

He laughed. "Yes, you would and you know it."

He glanced over at me. "One book coming up."

"No," I yelled. But it was too late. He was gone. "Shit."

Lucy stared at me, her eyes brimming with tears. "Why does he keep going away?"

I crouched down to her level. "Because he wants to help, no matter what it costs him."

My phone interrupted the moment. I looked at the caller ID. It was Will. I hit speaker.

"Hello, Will. How are you holding up?" I asked.

A gnarled voice answered. "Will won't be talking any time soon."

"No!" Lucy cried.

"See you tomorrow, Jimmy boy."

Then the line went dead.

I took a deep breath. Lucy was nearly hyperventilating.

"Tabby, do me a favor and call Will using your phone," I said. While I hadn't seen this type of thing before, I'd heard about it.

Tabby took my phone and typed Will's number into hers, then called.

"Will? Oh, Thank God. We had a scare."

She paused. "No, Lucy is fine. Just a case we're working on has…some new tricks…Yes, of course."

She cropped the phone down to her side. "Lucy, honey, do you want to speak to your daddy?"

"Uh-huh."

The little ghost drifted over and Tabby held her phone so that she and Will could talk.

"It's either the speaker phone or just my phone," I said quietly.

"I'd say it was speaker. My phone has been in that house as long and as many times as yours."

"At least we got Lucy calmed down."

Tabby nodded. "And now we know how tricky he can be."

"That too."

"What do you want to do for dinner?" I asked.

"Well, I'm not feeling pizza again," Tabby said.

"I say we find a place besides the diner and Lucy can come into the restaurant with us." Kid needed something fun. And, well, this was the only thing we'd discovered that made her excited.

"That works," Tabby said.

We all climbed into the car and I plugged the place into the

GPS on Tabby's phone. We left and started following the directions. Suddenly, I realized, it was not taking us to the restaurant
at all. We were heading in the direction of Mikey's house. I
stopped and turned around in the driveway of a construction
business. Interesting that Mikey's prowess was connected to
technology.

Tabby turned her phone off completely.

"I'll admit it. We should have just stayed there. That was
stupid." I wanted to kick myself. We knew better than to leave
the protected area when a demonic attack was going on. Hell, I
was starting to wonder if Mikey was affecting our brains too.

Tabby sighed. "It is almost like someone or something is
messing with our minds."

"You know who it is, don't you?" Lucy asked.

"Who?"

"The one. The light bringer. It's he who wants it."

"Well, he's not gonna get it. Hear that?!" I belted out. "You
can't get me that way."

Then time stopped. Tabby was frozen beside me. Lucy was
still in the back seat. The Devil, back in his business suit, sat on
the other side of Lucy. I was getting tired of him invading my
space.

"What is it with you and cars?" I asked.

He laughed. "Every day, someone always dies in a car
accident."

"That's sick."

"I am. Isn't it marvelous?"

"What is it you want?" I knew he wasn't here for bizarre
chitchat.

"Your soul, of course," he said.

"Oh, there's more to it than that. This isn't your usual thing."

He grinned. "That is what I love about you, Jimmy Holiday.
You are so astute. It is ever so refreshing." He leaned against the
seat. "Think of this as a job opportunity of sorts."

"Why me?"

"Because, don't you know, you're the most powerful one he has. That's why your paperwork was altered. That's why you never get any help. They are all jealous."

"Wait. Isn't envy a sin?" I *knew* it was Leviathan's expertise, but the Devil was master of them all.

When he laughed this time, ripples of power shook the car. "I want you, Jimmy Holiday."

It dawned on me then, not the part about me being most powerful or not. This was the Devil, after all. He could well be lying about that. But it did make more sense regarding the paperwork. I didn't think a human had any part in that. It was all a part of his grand design. Suddenly, I realized what it was.

"You want your own marker," I said.

He dropped his smile. "Of course I do. No reason for him to always have the upper hand."

"Well, I'll beg to differ, but you figured that."

"Which is precisely why it must be you. You are not afraid. Think about it."

And he disappeared. I sat there staring out the window. Of all the job offers I've ever gotten, that one I wasn't going to accept.

"Are we ever going to go, Jimmy?" Tabby asked.

"After I get my bearings straight," I said.

She paused. "He came again, didn't he?"

I nodded. "He wants me to be his marker."

I put the car in gear.

"Fuck."

"Yeah."

"What are you going to do?"

I swallowed. Hard. "I'll do what I always do. I'll prod on."

On the way back to the hotel, we stopped by a mini-mart and grabbed some cereal, candy, and chips. It wasn't healthy, but it was food. I had no plans to go out after dark at all until this case was resolved.

The only good thing was that I knew not everything that had happened had to do with Mikey and that took a bit of a weight off my shoulders. I wasn't going to underestimate him, though. He was still dangerous, but it was like comparing a rattlesnake to a black mamba.

Isaac meowed when we got back into the room.

"I know," I said to him. "Next time, speak up."

He ignored me and started licking his balls.

"Are you going to help me with this?" I heard Tabby ask.

I spun around. Tabby had all of the bags from the mini-mart.

"Shit. I'm sorry." I grabbed some of the bags and set them on the table.

"Doc's not back," Lucy said.

I sighed. "No, he isn't, but remember last time. He wasn't back for hours."

"Yeah." She settled down in front of the TV.

I ripped open a bag of chips with my teeth. "Find us something to watch, Lucy."

"Okay."

Tabby fell asleep around ten like usual. I stayed up with Lucy to wait for Doc. I sure as hell hoped he made it back. If he didn't, I knew Lucy would never forgive me.

I wasn't planning on doing the exorcism the next day, but it felt like I was going to. With every hour that passed, I suspected more and more I was going to have to rescue Doc. I didn't like that at all.

'Round about four, I was putting together a kit to prepare for battle when Doc popped in. He was holding the infernal book.

"Here," he said. "Put it in with your Bible. That should prevent him from knowing where it is."

I did as I was told. After the visit from the Devil, reading the book could wait.

"Are you okay?" Lucy asked.

"Was close there," Doc said. "I had to hide and make sure he didn't see me. Eventually, he went to sleep."

"Won't he know the book is gone?" I asked.

"I replaced the inside. The book he's holding is a collection of Donne's poems."

"All right. That works." I tapped my finger on my leg.

"Don't tell no one. Keep it completely to yourself. You don't know what he was digging out of someone's head."

I nodded. "Like last time, you and Lucy are staying here. I don't want to have to worry about you."

Doc returned my nod. "I think we all can work with that."

I grabbed items to do an exorcism. No sense in putting it off. This was coming. In my pack I put in the hotel's Gideon Bible. My Bible stayed where it was next to the evil book.

"I might as well write my ritual," I said.

"If you did it on that thing, you wouldn't have to write it every time," Lucy said, pointing at the iPad.

I laughed. "One of these days, I'll do that. For now, though, I think I'd feel safer with my own paper and pen."

Tabby cracked open an eye at first light. "What are you doing?"

I looked up. I was sitting in Doc's chair staring at the sunrise. He and Lucy were on the floor watching some TV show. I didn't know what it was. I hadn't been paying attention.

"Getting ready to do an exorcism," I said.

"This soon?" She sat up in bed.

"After the night we had, it's time to end this." I meant it too. I wasn't willing to have each day amp up more and more until Mikey gained enough power to truly fuck with us.

She nodded slowly. "Would you like to confess your sins?"

"I'm glad I don't have to worry about marking this one. His soul is already gone where it was supposed to go. I hate secrets. I don't like keeping stuff from you, but sometimes it can't be helped. And I'm horny, but that doesn't seem appropriate on the morning of an exorcism."

Tabby snorted. "If that doesn't take care of it, nothing will. So we're fasting?"

I nodded. "After this is over, I'm going to buy the biggest steak I can find and eat the whole damn thing."

Tabby chuckled. "I'll go grab a bath."

"Take your time. We actually do have all day." It was six-thirty in the morning. We had nine hours until nightfall.

TWENTY-ONE
SUSPENDED IN DUSK

NO WAY in hell was I going to do this exorcism at night. I hoped I would be home by then, too. It would be stupid—somewhat like going to stake a vampire right before he's ready to have dinner.

Doc and Lucy were leaving me alone. It was probably better that way. My eyes kept drifting over to the giant-size bag of Hershey's Kisses one of us had bought last night during the junk food run.

Maybe it was me who got grumpy being forced to not have chocolate instead of Tabby. It was something to ponder.

"Jimmy?" Tabby asked from the bathroom doorway.

I glanced up. "Yeah?"

"Have you put any thought into how we are going to create a safe place for the exorcism?"

I stopped. Shit. That place was full of objects that could be used as weapons. Around the outside, there were numerous old rusty cars, flat tires, and tons of various metal junk. Inside the house, well, it was full of old stinky furniture, Ma's knickknacks, and whatever the fuck Mikey had in his bedroom.

"Can you do an exorcism in a bathroom?" I asked.

Tabby choked. "It would be a little small, wouldn't it?"

I blew air through my mouth and wiggled my lips. "This sucks."

"Tell me about it."

I glanced around. Technically, the hotel room was exactly what we needed, but no way was I doing that either. Too many potential witnesses.

"Do you have to do the exorcism today?" Tabby asked.

I nodded. "I mean, it isn't like someone is holding a gun to my head or anything, but I feel like this is it. I can't explain it."

"If that's the case, then we don't have a choice," she said. "Let's prepare for battle."

I laughed. "I guess we'll see if there is a room we can clean out and hope for the best."

"If he even lets us do that."

"That's the other thing."

I almost expected some magnetic source to keep us driving in circles, but that didn't happen. The Devil would have thought that was funny. Perhaps there was something to this case that he wanted taken care of as well. I had a funny feeling that God and the Devil were using me. Otherwise, my exorcisms would be a hell of a lot more by the book.

Tabby had her witchy bag in the back seat. I had my holy water in my pocket and the Roman Ritual, the Gideon Bible, and my scribbles on the seat behind me.

The closer we got to Mikey's, the more nervous I became. I'd now seen a bit more of what he was capable of last night, and I didn't like it.

"What are we going to do with Ma?" Tabby asked.

I shrugged. "She'll go into the protective circle with us. I don't think she has anywhere else to go."

Tabby sighed. "Let's hope she doesn't bean you over the head or something."

I shook my head. "That would suck."

We made it to Mikey's around eight. It was easy and I almost expected them all to be asleep, but as soon as I parked, Ma shuffled out of the house.

"You come to make things right," she said.

I held my hand up to shield the sunlight from my eyes. "I'm going to try."

She nodded. "That's all I ask. He's in his room."

She shuffled back inside the house and Tabby and I followed behind her after we grabbed our stuff from the car.

"Is there a place where it would be best to do this, Ma?" Tabby asked.

"Basement's where he does all that foolishness," she said.

My asshole grew tight. I didn't even know this place had a basement. Shit. Note to self: start getting a tour of the house before getting involved in the exorcism process. The tours had happened organically the last two times. I needed to stop assuming shit.

Ma shuffled through the house and led us down the steps. They were rickety and moved with every step you took. The basement itself had a dirt floor. On one side, there were shelves and shelves of canned goods. On the other, there was a bunch of old rusty tools. Just ducky.

"Mikey's stuff is in there." She pointed to a wooden door that had a new padlock on it. Of course it was locked.

"How are we going to get in there?" Tabby asked.

Ma cackled, shuffled over to the workbench, and came up with an old crowbar. "Step aside, children."

She jammed that crowbar up under the hasp and in no time at all, the padlock was pried loose from the door. The nails Mikey used to attach it were bent off to the side.

"Wow," I said.

Ma smiled. "I know. I'm stronger than I look."

"I'll say," I said. Her being as frail as she was, well, that show of strength was odd. Since Ma had never threatened us, I had no reason to believe she would now. But maybe the hold she had over Mikey was somehow connected to the magic. I still didn't know how.

She pushed open the door and Tabby and I stepped inside. The smell was foul—like rotten goat's milk. All over the walls, symbols were painted in what seemed suspiciously like blood.

"Did Mikey do any of this before he died?" I asked.

Ma chuckled. "Hell, before he died, he couldn't even get off that couch upstairs."

The light bulb went off in my head. That old stinky couch was the true heart of the home. This room was a decoy.

"I think it would be best if we go back upstairs," I said.

Tabby stared at me strangely.

Ma shrugged.

"It's better to take everything from where it started," I said.

Ma's eyes twinkled. "Living room it is, then."

We all shuffled back up the stairs and through the kitchen. Right before we entered the living room, Mikey stepped into the doorway.

"Help you with something?" he asked.

His eyes were dark. I could almost feel the hate radiate off him.

"Your mother was giving us the grand tour," Tabby said.

Ma swatted at Mikey. "Get yourself somewhere useful, boy."

He stepped away. Again, I'd never seen anything like that. I almost wondered if it shouldn't be her that performed the exorcism.

Mikey loomed, but he did not touch us.

"Go on and sit down," Ma said to Mikey. He complied and sat in his rocking chair.

I glanced at Tabby. "I guess we wing it."

"I guess so," she said.

Tabby set her bag on the floor and started rifling through it.

Soon she had a piece of chalk in her hand as well as a few other items.

"Just go ahead and relax, Ma," I said. "We'll do this with your chair inside."

Ma laughed, then sat down. Mikey was giving us all the stinkeye.

I forced myself not to stick my tongue out at him, but was I tempted.

Tabby drew a lopsided circle around Ma's chair. Unfortunately, there was nothing to tie Mikey down with, and since he wasn't going to be cooperative, he'd have to run loose. Well, sort of.

Tabby left a part of the circle open, went around the house with ribbons, and tied them to the windows and doors. That little trick was coming in handy. Mikey watched her closely, but did not say a word.

Then she stepped back into the circle and closed it with her piece of chalk.

"Hail to the guardians of North, South, East, and West— Earth, air, fire, and water. Hear my call. Aid us in our struggle. Keep us safe from harm within this circle. So mote it be."

When she touched the edges of the circle with her finger, the whole thing grew up into a faint green-colored bubble. I was kind of relieved to see the color of her magic go back to normal.

Tabby stood up and whispered into my ear, "He's bound to the living room, kitchen, and hallway. I put a ribbon on every door."

"Good girl."

I stared at Mikey. "Now, I know you've fought long and hard to become part of this world, but you do not belong here. It is time for you to go back home."

Mikey laughed. It seemed to echo around the house.

"You didn't think it would be that easy, did you?" He gnashed his teeth together. His eyes turned back to sickly white and his skin took on a lovely greenish purple hue. This was his true face.

The ceiling over my head cracked and plaster floated down onto my head.

I took a deep breath. "Evil being from a distant place, you have no purpose here. Be gone from this place."

Mikey, well, it laughed again. "If you tell me where my book is, I might let you in on a little secret."

Ah. So he'd discovered the ruse after all. I kind of figured that it wouldn't take all that much time for him to figure it out.

"Be good and get gone," Ma said.

Whoa. Okay. Note to self: parents as part of exorcism aren't necessarily a good idea. I got my focus back.

He was smiling. Suddenly, the wall separating the kitchen from the living room buckled. The house groaned.

"Who gave you that book?" I asked him, operating on a hunch. I had to keep focused. If the house collapsed around us, so be it. I didn't know what else to do.

He narrowed his eyes. "I found it in the woods, like I said."

"No way." I held myself ramrod straight. "You couldn't get up off that couch."

He stopped smiling.

"Now, tell me the name of the person who gave you that book. Or rather, tell me your name." I said it with that special voice. The power rippled through the air, outside of the bubble, and into him.

The body convulsed. He angled those milky-white eyes on me and snarled.

"Sit in your place, heathen." I pointed to the couch. "That is where it began."

It laughed. "You know, I find it hilarious that you are giving me orders from behind a protective circle. Hilarious."

I blinked. I knew it was only trying to bait me, but damn it was annoying. "What is your name?"

"Can't you think of anything else to say?"

I closed my eyes and prayed to God. "Please, Heavenly Father. Help me return this body to the earth. Help Ma get some peace in her last days. And help this thing go back to Hell."

I opened my eyes. "Tell me your name."

That time, I felt something extra. I couldn't explain it exactly, but it felt strong.

Mikey's body flopped out of the rocking chair and onto the floor. A pool of green liquid seeped onto the floor.

"Levi," he said in a grunt.

I glowered at him. "Your full name."

His eyes glowed yellow. "Leviathan."

Now, knowing what I knew about this stuff, a demon might be the actual demon or an emissary. This was not Leviathan. I knew better. Nothing about this dude had the power of a Prince of Hell.

"Give me *your* name."

It choked and sputtered. "Grandier."

Tabby gasped.

I whipped around and stared at her. "What?"

"That's the name of the priest who made a pact with several demons to possess nuns in Loudin, France."

I blinked. "Okay. Be quiet."

Jesus Christ. We were all acting like amateurs.

I stepped forward to the edge of the circle. "Grandier, I command you to take your rightful place in Hell. Leave this world and give back this body to the earth."

His body convulsed once more, then settled. There was a smell. A rotten smell. The skin on the body burst open and turned black.

"Thank you, dear ones," Ma said. Then she literally slumped over dead.

"Motherfuck!"

I smudged my foot against the circle and stepped out to look at the room. Sunlight shone dimly through the window, which was odd since it was noon. It should have been brighter. Something was not right.

I heard deep laughter. I peered at Tabby. She was grinning and her eyes were glowing yellow. "You never answered me whether you wanted to know the secret."

I backed up against the wall. I was staring at my worst nightmare. Her face had become almost reptilian, complete with scales. "Shit."

"Like my new look?" She licked her lips seductively.

All I wanted to do was puke. How in the hell did Tabby become possessed?

She floated out of the circle and grabbed me around the throat. She wasn't squeezing. Not yet.

"I do not bargain with demons," I choked.

It laughed. Tabby's skin began to crack around her mouth and the skin was turning a bit purplish. It was almost as if the deadness was coming to her.

I had to pull myself together and fast. "Stop it!"

The Tabby-thing threw me against the opposite wall. I landed on Mikey's corpse. The rotten mess smashed underneath me and I got some of it in my mouth. I coughed and heaved, but nothing, not even saliva, came out of my mouth. The taste was like breathing in the ashes from a charnel house.

"You see. We are much stronger than you are. Give in. Join your queen."

I ogled the creature I was in love with. The travesty that she'd become. "In the name of God and all that guard the Watchtowers, I command you to stop!"

She backed away, sidestepped Mikey's corpse, and sat on the sofa. It was so nonchalant, I almost forgot I was dealing with a demon.

"Tricky witchy got bit by the great big bug," it said. It chuckled and pulled a chunk of hair from her head. There was some blood.

Jesus. I wasn't sure how much longer I could deal with this. "You can tell Asmodeus to go fuck himself for me."

It grinned. "I'd be glad to, but he is indisposed."

So Big Red had stepped in. Good to know, but that did not help me here at all. And if Big Red was my "friend," then why would my fiancée be sitting in front of me all possessed? Screw this shit.

"What is it you want?"

It blinked. "Your soul, amongst other items."

"I don't think he is going to let that happen when he wants it for himself." Then I paused. It all began to make sense to me now. "All of this for a book?"

It chuckled.

"That's what you are concerned about, isn't it?"

It got quiet. "The book is very important to me."

I closed my eyes. None of this had gone like the other times. I started thinking back to Tabby's magic going red. Her seeming less sure of herself. The house feeling off. He'd been strong enough to hide very, very well.

"You aren't the same demon, are you?"

It cackled and clapped its hands. "You are ever so smart."

"How long have you been with her?" I asked.

"You were in Italy, I believe. Poor Tabby was all alone."

It was coming together now. The time frame. The look. Lucy's sudden new friend. Her pact with the Devil.

"You're Levi," I said.

It nodded.

"Or, shall I say, we meet again, Leviathan."

He sidestepped out of Tabby. Literally. Her body fell to the floor beside Mikey's.

"You didn't kill her, did you?" I ran over and felt for a pulse. It was weak, but it was there.

He slowly shook his head. "She'll come to after a few of my playthings have their way with her."

"You sonofabitch!" I darted over to Tabby's bag and started digging.

He kept watching me, as if amused.

Suddenly, my hand fell upon something I could not believe. It wasn't in its protective case either.

"If I give you your book, will you bring Tabby back?" I kept staring at the bag, trying not to let on what I was doing.

"That would be ever so nice, but if that's the way you want it, I can oblige."

I took a deep breath and launched myself at him. This was it. My only shot.

He stared at me as if I'd turned myself into a flying squirrel. But it worked. I whipped up my hand and held the fleshing rod to his head.

He howled and sunk to the ground. Flesh began growing on him.

I dropped the rod and watched the magic work. Right before his body was fully formed, I licked my finger and made the sign of the cross on his forehead.

"You belong to God now," I said.

There was an electric jolt. It was flung across the room into the wall.

"No!" he screamed.

The flesh melted off him in a great puddle. Even what was left was sinking into the floor.

"What is that smell?" I heard Tabby ask.

I crawled over to her and held her head in my hands. "Are you okay?"

"Now I am." She glanced around the room. "What did you do?"

I shrugged my shoulders. "Caused havoc. Got my point across. You know. The usual."

She shook her head. "What am I going to do with you?"

"Love me."

"I already do."

"How do we take care of all of this?" Tabby motioned around the room.

I laughed. "I think it's time to give old Sam a call, don't you?"

I waited until Tabby had the fleshing rod hidden back in the car. I wasn't going to risk anyone's hands getting on it. But I had to admit, if it hadn't been there, I would have been sunk. Maybe I was going to become the Devil's boogeyman. He sure liked having me correct his children.

"Did you remember putting it in the bag?" I asked.

She shook her head then she walked back into the house. "I remember most of what happened after he was in me. He wasn't there all the time like with Lucy. I honestly thought I was just getting depressed."

I nodded. "So if you didn't put it there and Lucy or Doc didn't, that means this is another one of those things."

TWENTY-TWO

PAINT IT BLACK

"ALL RIGHT. YOU HAVE MY ATTENTION," the sheriff said. Sam had told me he was calling him in. Tabby and I were at the police station. It was so small it was just a little set of offices behind the jail.

Tabby was in another room.

"I am an exorcist and I was called in to help with the Michael Fisher situation."

The sheriff was this older guy. Kind of reminded me of this old actor, Wilford Brimley. He was balding and overweight with short white hair, and he sported a mustache.

"How'd this all happen?" he asked.

I took a deep breath. "We made sure Ma was behind us. Mikey was sitting in the rocking chair. There must have been some odd connection between the two of them because when the dyubbuk, spirit, whatever-it-was left, Ma died."

The sheriff shook his head. "Hopefully, she won't sit up in her coffin."

I sighed. "Believe me. I hope she doesn't either. I just want to go home and relax."

He nodded. "Is it as bad as they say?"

"What?"

"Performing an exorcism."

"The best I can tell you is that the movies don't give it justice."

He sat in his chair. "If we ever have something like this come up again, can we call you?"

I shrugged. "Why not? It isn't like there are all that many people around who can do my line of work."

"This was so messed up," Tabby said.

I was driving home. Or rather, driving back to the hotel room. It was too late to head back for the day. Not if we wanted to drive in daylight.

"When we get back to the hotel, do one of those cleansing baths."

"You know those wards on the hotel room and the house are worthless right?"

I shrugged. "You can redo them. It's going to be okay."

She slumped in her seat. She still hadn't told me what part of Hell she'd seen, but she had plenty of time. I wasn't going anywhere.

Doc and Lucy jumped up when we walked in. Isaac meowed at us. It felt good.

"Get it taken care of?" Doc asked.

"Yup. Tabby's going to get a bath and then I'm going to find a place to get a big steak."

Tabby laughed. "Men and their steaks."

"Hey, meat is good."

She walked into the bathroom.

I wandered over to the dresser and grabbed one of the drinking glasses. I unwrapped it and threw the wrapper in the trash. Then, I grabbed that bag of Hershey Kisses, unwrapped a bunch of them and put them into the water glass. I upended it into my mouth. It was heaven.

My cheeks were stretched out like a chipmunk's.

Tabby walked back in and froze. "I thought we were getting steak?"

I grinned around the chocolate. "Appetizer."

Thank you for reading! Did you enjoy? Please add your review because nothing helps an author more and encourages readers to take a chance on a book than a review.

And don't miss the next book of the *The Marker Chronicles*, SORROW'S LIE, available now. Turn the page for a sneak peek!

You can also sign up for the City Owl Press newsletter to receive notice of all book releases!

SNEAK PEEK OF SORROW'S LIE
END OF THE BEGINNING

SOMETIMES, YOUR DAY just sucked. It all started before light, when someone or something startled Isaac, the amazing cat, and he pissed on my head. I couldn't figure out what had happened at first. Then, I discovered the sewer system had backed up.

"Tabby?" I still couldn't believe I was doing what I was doing, but every now and then you have to get in the thick of it.

"What?" she called from upstairs.

I'd saved her the horror.

"Are you bringing me the plunger or not?" I tried not to gag from the smell.

"If you'd hold your horses, maybe I could get down to you and not break my neck." Her feet clunked on the wooden basement steps.

I shut up. She was getting close to chopping my head off. Right now, she was still trying to help me.

When she got within reach, her face screwed up and she whipped her hand over her nose. "Here."

I took the plunger from her and attacked the drain again. It burped. Then, I felt something bump into my boot. I screamed.

"What is wrong with you?" Tabby asked.

My face reddened. And I was embarrassed as hell that I squealed all because of this. Guess it was a good thing she liked me. "Something touched my foot."

"Since I doubt there are unholy shit demons, I recommend you suck it up."

I laughed and swallowed my injured pride. "Call the utility board. I give up."

"Like I told you an hour ago?"

I sighed. "Love you."

She didn't say a word and headed back upstairs. I stared at the mess and wanted to cry.

***

After I discarded all the crappy water clothes, pulled myself together, and got a shower, I went downstairs to find Lucy watching yet another scary movie. Isaac sat beside her, ignoring me. They were watching some gore fest, but I was silently thankful it wasn't another exorcism flick.

"Do you ever get tired of these?" I asked her.

She glanced up at me. Her white dress flowed in stark contrast with my mustard yellow carpet. "Not really. They're more interesting than anything else."

I rocked back on my heels. "Don't you like other stuff?"

She shrugged. "SpongeBob is okay."

I laughed. Once again, worrying over nothing. I needed to get a grip. "Okay. Go back to your movie. Where's Doc, anyway?"

"Looking into something."

"Got it." I left the living room and went into the kitchen long enough to grab a soda out of my awesome green fridge. Then, I passed back through and headed outside. Tabby sat on the front stoop, waiting on the city services folks. Her red hair sparkled in the early morning sunlight. She looked like a goddess in jeans and a white shirt. I was too lucky.

"They say when they would be coming?" I asked.

She shook her head. "Soon. I don't know."

I plopped down next to her and put my arm around her shoulders. Spring had been slow to come to Virginia, but it was finally warm enough to be outside without a coat. I was thankful. I needed to feel more normal again, not closed in. "If they don't get here in time, go ahead to see the wedding planner. I'll deal with the shit brigade."

Tabby snorted. "As if you don't want to get out of it anyway."

"It's not like Doc can handle it. Never mind that he isn't here now." I scratched my arm and peered down the street. Nothing but birds.

"No, but Mom will be here in about a half-hour."

I took my arm back, put my elbows on my knees, and buried my head in my hands. "Just when I thought the day couldn't get any worse."

She swatted me on the arm.

***

Tabby's mother arrived about twenty minutes later. Her little blue Toyota pulled into my driveway next to the SUV. Her bleached blond hair was arranged in a bouffant cloud around her head. More than once, I wondered how Tabby came from this woman. She must take after her dad.

"At least the drive wasn't bad," Tabby's mom said.

"Hello, Betty." I waved at her.

She glared at me. "Hello."

Tabby hopped up. "Thanks for coming, Mama. We really appreciate it."

"And that cat of yours is secured?"

"I put him in the bedroom. He won't bother you."

I could hear Isaac meowing from upstairs. I didn't relish us letting him out later. He was pissed.

I watched Lucy creep upstairs. I knew she couldn't let Isaac out, so that wasn't even a thought. I was more concerned that Tabby's mom would notice that a TV was on upstairs. Lucy, undoubtedly, was going to her room.

Tabby led her into the house. I glanced down the street, begging for the utility company to arrive. But they didn't, and I was stuck going along. I sighed and went into the house to grab my wallet and keys. Luckily, I didn't encounter Tabby and her mom. Wandering outside again, I climbed into the driver's side of the SUV. Tabby came out a few minutes later and hugged her mom on the stoop, then headed toward the car. Things had gone so easily, I couldn't help but wonder if Tabby hadn't performed a little witch-a-roo to make things go so smoothly.

"Okay, are you ready?" Tabby asked as she hopped into the car.

"I feel more like I'm going to the gallows."

She swatted me again. "Stop."

"Yes, ma'am."

I sighed as I put the car in gear. She peered over at me and regarded me carefully. I think she was afraid I was going to go rogue and drive us to Mexico or something.

"Jimmy, seriously, it isn't going to be that bad. If we don't like her, we can interview someone else."

I sighed again. "Guess I don't understand why we even need a wedding planner."

She glanced at me out of the corner of her eye. "If you get a case, we aren't going to have time to deal with flowers, setting up the church, where the reception will be, and the cake. The idea is to let the wedding planner know our budget, what we like, and let her take care of the rest. That way, if all hell breaks loose, the wedding can still go on as planned.

"What happened to the 'simple wedding'?" I know my folks got married in a church. My mom's parents showed up. My dad's didn't. They had pieces of cake in the church basement. That was it. I didn't have any idea why in the world we needed something bigger than that, but I had a feeling if I said much more, I was going to get my ass kicked.

"These days, this is a simple wedding."

"God, help me." It slipped. But instead of getting my ass kicked, Tabby stared out the window. I had dodged a bullet.

***

The first thing I saw when we arrived at the wedding planner's office was the flowers. Now, don't get me wrong, I don't mind flowers as much as the next guy, but this—this was over the top. There were so many of them; they seemed to burst forth from the walls, the floors, and even the desk. They weren't any one color either. And they were artificial, otherwise that much pollen would have sent me into a bizarre allergy fit. Luckily, the chairs were open and free.

"I'm so sorry," the older woman said. Her hair was dyed black, and I could still see the crow's feet at the corners of her eyes underneath all the make-up. "I had to pick up flowers for a client."

Part of me was impressed by her dedication, but the other side was inwardly cringing as to why she dumped all the flowers in her office when she knew she had an appointment with new clients.

Tabby grinned. "Nice of you to go out of your way."

The woman smiled tiredly. "I try to do everything I can." She held out her hand toward Tabby. "Eliza Donahue."

Tabby took the offering. "Tabby Settle, and this is my fiancé," she pointed at me, "Jimmy Holiday."

"Nice to meet you," I said. I was hoping this would be over with as fast as possible, but it wasn't looking like luck was going to be on my side today.

"Please sit," she said and started opening drawers in her desk and pulling free colorful brochures.

Tabby and I sat in the chairs on the other side of her desk.

Every so often, Eliza would hand over a pamphlet. I let Tabby take them. This was her dog and pony show.

"We want a simple wedding," Tabby started.

Eliza leaned back and stopped pulling things from her files and closed up the drawer in her desk. "Then what do you need me for?"

I forced myself not to roll my eyes, but it was hard. I didn't like the attitude she was copping. "We have jobs that take us away from town a lot. That makes it hard. We need someone to do as much as possible."

She stared down her nose at me. "And what is it you do?"

I grinned. "I'm an exorcist."

***

"Really, Jimmy. Did you have to?"

We were walking to the car and I had to rush to keep up with her. I hadn't seen her this upset in a while, but I was willing to take the hit. I couldn't stand it anymore. It wasn't my fault the woman freaked. Granted, I could have probably put it in a better way, but I was done with her attitude.

"You do know she's the best in these parts?" Tabby threw open the car door and shut it hard after she climbed in.

I got back in on the driver's side. Whether she was the best or not, I didn't care. She was more about the money. That pissed me off. "I didn't like her attitude."

"Obviously."

I shifted in my seat to look at her. I didn't care that she was annoyed at me. I wasn't kissing that wedding planner's ass. "Listen, why don't we go to the justice of the peace?"

Tabby paused, and then sighed. "Because there is no point in me getting married unless it feels like it means something. A judge feels so sterile."

I would love to know where women come up with this stuff. My head was starting to pound. "Can you say you are comfortable with a minister either?"

"Like you'd be willing to have a handfasting." She seemed to curl in on herself.

"Why not?" Not that I knew what that was, but wedding stuff was not my forte.

She turned toward me. "You'd do that for me?"

Obviously, she didn't figure in that I was willing to die for her, but I'd forgive her for it. I'm not exactly vocal. "I want you to be happy. We don't need any wedding planners. We'll take our time. Make sure everything is taken care of. Then do this...whatever it is."

She swatted me on the arm.

"Besides, this way, Doc and Lucy will be able to participate."
She beamed. "I love you, ya goof."
"I love you too."

Don't stop now. Keep reading with your copy of SORROW'S
LIE.

And sign up for Danielle's newsletter to get all the news,
giveaways, excerpts, and more!

Don't miss book four in the *The Marker Chronicles*, SORROW'S LIE, available now, and find more from Danielle DeVor at www.danielledevor.com

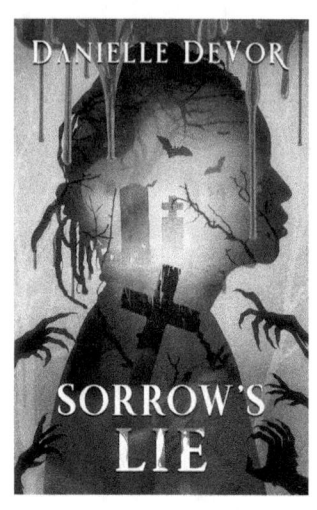

A defrocked priest turned exorcists faces his greatest challenge —a baby—in this horror novel from the author of Sorrow's Turn.

Jimmy Holiday, exorcist extraordinaire, is about to embark on his most unusual case yet—a baby that may be possessed by the demonic...or worse, a true demon spawn. The Order wants him to make sure it is a true case and not some hoax...or so they say.

Once Jimmy arrives, the situation changes into a living nightmare. The Order is not what he thought at all. And now, they demand he commit an unspeakable act. But Jimmy has enough scars of his own.

When the full truth of the corruption within the Order comes to light, Jimmy must act. With a voudou woman who lives down the lane as an ally, Jimmy must fight for the life of this supernatural child, but at what cost?

All reviews are **welcome** and **appreciated**. Please consider leaving one on your favorite social media and book buying sites.

Escape Your World. Get Lost in Ours! City Owl Press at www.cityowlpress.com

ACKNOWLEDGMENTS

There are so many people I would like to thank, but I will likely miss a few. In no particular order: Joshua Devor, Julia Long, Maer Wilson, Charles and Linda DeVor, Tina Moss, Em Shotwell and all the other wonderful folks at City Owl Press, and finally, Darwin. Thanks for being there.

ABOUT THE AUTHOR

Danielle DeVor is the author of many spooky things including, The Marker Chronicles: *Exorcisms or bust. Half price offer. The exorcisms, not the book. Jimmy will exorcise you for a fee. Just call him;* Maw: *Space Vampires, woo;* and other ramblings. She's won awards, yay, *Examiner's list of Women in Horror: 93 Horror Authors You Need to Read Right Now.* Her pet iguana, Sam,  has since passed into the ether, living with vampires in a big house where they feed him treats everyday. She wears a lot of black and listens to some pretty out there music, talking your ear off about Motionless in White and Type O Negative. *Beware.* And she loves anything horror or monster-y. *No, that isn't a word. But it's more fun than saying monstrous. Bite her.*

www.danielledevor.com

facebook.com/danielle.devor
x.com/sammyig
instagram.com/danielledevor76

ABOUT THE PUBLISHER

City Owl Press is a cutting edge indie publishing company,
bringing the world of romance and speculative fiction to
discerning readers.

Escape Your World. Get Lost in Ours!

www.cityowlpress.com

facebook.com/CityOwlPress

x.com/cityowlpress

instagram.com/cityowlbooks

pinterest.com/cityowlpress

tiktok.com/@cityowlpress

www.ingramcontent.com/pod-product-compliance
Lightning Source LLC
Chambersburg PA
CBHW071254250626
47159CB00004B/1182